# The EX Dilemma

## Also by Elle Wright

### The Wellspring series

*Touched by You*
*Enticed by You*
*Pleasured by You*

### The Pure Talent series

*The Way You Tempt Me*
*The Way You Hold Me*
*The Way You Love Me*

# The EX Dilemma

## Elle Wright

**KENSINGTON**
PUBLISHING CORP.
kensingtonbooks.com

KENSINGTON BOOKS are published by

Kensington Publishing Corp.
900 Third Avenue
New York, NY 10022

All Kensington titles, imprints, and distributed lines are available at special quantity discounts for bulk purchases for sales promotion, premiums, fundraising, educational, or institutional use.

Special book excerpts or customized printings can also be created to fit specific needs. For details, write or phone the office of the Kensington Sales Manager: Kensington Publishing Corp., 900 Third Avenue, New York, NY 10022. Attn. Sales Department. Phone: 1-800-221-2647.

Kensington and the K logo Reg. U.S. Pat. & TM Off.

ISBN: 978-1-4967-5231-4 (ebook)
ISBN: 978-1-4967-5230-7

First Kensington Trade Paperback Printing: February 2026

10 9 8 7 6 5 4 3 2 1

Printed in the United States of America

The authorized representative in the EU for product safety and compliance
is eucomply OU, Parnu mnt 139b-14, Apt 123
Tallinn, Berlin 11317, hello@eucompliancepartner.com

To the strong women who have left a situation
that wasn't serving them and are now soaring
because they dropped the dead weight. I see you.
And to the fellas who fuck everything up
but work hard to make it better.

# Prologue

## *Wesley*

*Sixteen years ago*

Days like this were rare. Especially after the year I'd had. Beautiful blue skies, a balmy breeze, my carefree existence, and her lying beneath me at our spot . . . Everything was perfect. When I woke up this morning, I knew two things to be true.

My family was fucked up.

Albany Keyes was everything.

I should've known euphoria wouldn't last. I had been lulled into a state of ignorance I never really had an option to embrace before. In a few minutes, I would have to pay the price for trying to forget about what was wrong with my life. Before sunrise, I would drown in the heartbreak of my reality. But not right now . . .

Albany cuddled into my side. "You made everything so special."

I raised a questioning brow. "Are you sure? Because I—"

She cut me off with a soft kiss. "You were amazing."

We were young, sixteen years old, but I knew that being

with her like this was a gift. One that she'd given me freely, without reservation. We'd talked about sex many times, but I never expected it to happen tonight. And even though I knew what was coming, I couldn't walk away.

She was right, though. It was amazing. Beautiful. The way our bodies moved together, the smell of her skin. Every moment, every kiss, every touch . . . The memory would console and haunt me for the rest of my life.

I pressed my lips to hers, brushed her nose with mine. "You're so beautiful."

Albany never knew how to handle compliments. Her first reaction was always to hide, so I wasn't surprised when she buried her face in my chest. "Wes," she whispered.

"You're perfect. I wish I could stay here forever," I confessed. She giggled. "Stop."

Her soft laughter wrapped around me. I wanted to record the sound of it so that I could remember how she always made me feel, how much she trusted me, how much she loved me. Because tomorrow she would hate me.

Leaning back, I tipped her head up. "I mean it, Bug." To others, her nickname might have sounded like an insult. But only she knew what it really meant to me. It was mine—and mine only. "Always remember that."

She searched my eyes, her brow furrowing with confusion. "What's wrong?" We'd spent enough time together for her to sense the shift in my mood, no matter how much I wanted to spare her. "Who was that on the phone?"

I glared at my cell phone, fighting the urge to crush it with the wooden bat in the corner of the room. A few minutes ago, I'd taken the call that had cast a dark shadow over a pure moment of bliss.

"Wes?" she called softly.

Earlier, she'd confessed her love for me. Albany had always been more brave, more secure than I was. Fearless. Strong in her beliefs. Even when the world was against her. While I didn't voice my thoughts at the time, my love for her was real. And I wanted her to know before I walked away from her.

When I met her gaze again, instead of answering her question, I kissed her. "I love you," I murmured against her mouth, swallowing up her gasp with another kiss.

With our mouths fused together, I reached for a condom. Seconds later, I slipped it on and inched inside her. Slowly. She was so tight. So warm. The first time—for both of us—was quick. Lasted about a minute. I'd tried to make it last, but my inexperience wouldn't let me. *This* time, I moved slowly, trying to extend my release while praying that she would come with me. I didn't expect my body to run ahead without her again, but it did. Just like before, I shook as an orgasm rumbled through me, stealing all my energy.

Collapsing on her, I struggled to catch my breath. "I'm sorry," I murmured, sucking her nipple. "I'm so sorry."

Her fingers raked through my hair. "It's okay, baby. We're okay."

I sighed heavily, glanced at her. "I had high hopes."

Albany laughed and my heart cracked open a little bit more. "We have time to get this right."

Shame rolled through me like choppy waves. Our time had run out. Squeezing my eyes shut, I sat up. "Albany, I—"

I felt her mouth on my back, her hands on my skin. "Wes, are you sure you're okay?"

In the past, I would've told her everything. The stakes were too high, though, and I'd been sworn to secrecy. "I'm fine," I lied. "I just wanted to do better for our first time."

That part was true. I realized a while ago that fucking around with every girl in school wasn't what I wanted, especially since Albany was the prize. I'd loved her for so long, it was a small sacrifice to wait until she was ready.

Albany rested her forehead against my shoulder. "You were gentle, kind, loving . . . perfect for me."

Her words were like a salve over the chapped parts of my

soul. From the time she'd tossed my Game Boy in a puddle because I hurt her feelings, she'd been a constant in my life, my biggest cheerleader, my best friend. And I would miss her. I kissed her brow. "My mom wants me to come home."

She peered up at me. "Now?"

I nodded. "I promised that I'd bring dinner home." The lies kept coming. Just like my father. He'd told many tall tales and ended up dead. *Am I next?* My mother had existed on saltine crackers and tea for the last several weeks. She wouldn't eat, barely slept. "She's still pretty sad."

"That's understandable," she said. "I can't imagine losing a husband."

My father's death had devastated our family. But the turmoil he'd left behind would have lasting impacts on all our lives. Mom had been stressed, saying cryptic things. Strange people called at all times of the day. I had to sneak out this morning because we were forbidden to leave the house. The freedom that I'd once taken for granted had vanished the moment Mom received that dreaded call. "Yeah."

"You should go then."

"I'll walk you to the door."

She shook her head. "No, I'm fine. Just a few steps to my front door."

Brushing my lips over hers again, I asked, "Are you sure?"

"Very." She cupped my face in her tiny palms and kissed my eyelids, my nose, then my mouth. "Call me when you get home."

Several minutes later, after another make-out session, I walked to the door of the carriage house, situated on the far end of her grandmother's estate. We'd spent many days holed up there, doing homework, sharing our dreams, talking about everything good and bad in our lives. Turning back to her, I took her in. Her brown skin, her ruffled hair, her sincere eyes . . . She held a small fleece blanket against her naked skin as she watched me, a smile on her lips.

THE EX DILEMMA / 5

A heaviness settled in my gut, my chest, my limbs. I had only ever felt this way one time—when my mother told me my father died. Just like death, I couldn't see how we would come back from this. At the same time, I couldn't bring myself to tell her the truth. We weren't going to have a tomorrow. Tonight was it. A perfect memory.

My vision blurred as I swallowed against the hard lump in my throat. "Albany, I—" I dropped my head, unable to walk away. I wanted more time with her. Damn the consequences. My mother would be angry, but I didn't care. "Can you stay here?" I asked.

She frowned, confusion lining her features. "You want me to wait for you? What about your mom?"

"I'll go home, take care of her. Then, I'll bring food here for us."

Her face lit up. "Sure." She picked up the book she'd brought with her and held it up. "I can read while you're gone."

I nodded. "Good." Finally, I unlatched the lock and opened the door. "I'll be back."

# Chapter 1

## *Wesley*

I'd always tried—and failed—to forget. Enough whiskey to make me numb, a beautiful woman in my bed, and a warm place to lay my head hadn't helped dull the ache in my gut or my heart when I opened my eyes that morning. The anniversary of my father's death.

May 30th.

Somehow, the other dates never mattered. Not my birthday or the anniversary of my parents' marriage or the day the man I'd once thought was invincible was indicted on corporate fraud charges and set to spend years in a federal prison.

The memory of that morning had never really seemed to fade away with the passage of time. I still remembered the smell of my mother's perfume when she'd awakened me with the news. An accident. A fishing trip gone wrong. My father had fallen into the Detroit River. Its turbulent waters had been too much for him. The current was too strong, too swift. The details were a blur but the feelings . . . Despair and loss mixed with vulnerability and fear. *Abandoned.* Because that was the day my life had changed, and not for the better. That was the day I'd ceased being Good Little Wesley Batchelor. The Wes that had survived that day and the days after was not the same boy who believed good outweighed bad, that love conquered all. No, the Wes that lived was a man that had done everything I could to achieve my goals, even if that meant I had to hurt people to get where I needed to be.

*But today . . .*

Even the raging hangover I woke up with had only served as a small distraction, a nuisance really. One that would inevitably go away once I either took another shot or gulped a gallon of water and ate a piece of dry toast. I wasn't sure which route I'd take but the bottle of Johnnie Walker Blue sitting conveniently on the nightstand next to my bed was winning the war. Because I had shit to do, meetings that couldn't be pushed back, things that couldn't wait until tomorrow.

Decision made, I poured myself a healthy taste of whiskey and gulped it down. Sighing, I glanced back at the woman sleeping peacefully next to me. *Mia . . . No, Alicia . . . Hm, Brynn?* At this point, it didn't even matter what her name was because I would never see her again. She was nice enough, had even offered me scintillating conversation about politics and sports. But I had rules—no promises, no forever.

I stood, stretched, and turned to her. Bending down, I nudged her arm gently. One beautiful brown eye popped open, then she sat up, holding a sheet over her naked body.

She blinked. "I'm sorry," she grumbled. "I . . ." She scrambled off the bed and dressed quickly. "Thanks for—" She blew her wild hair out of her face. "It was nice. I would tell you to call me, but yeah . . . no."

The woman buzzed past me, darting around my room looking for her belongings. I couldn't help but smile, pleasantly surprised that her demeanor this morning matched the façade I'd originally thought she might be putting on last night once I'd told her my stance on relationships. Long story short . . . *I'm not interested.* If only I could remember her name.

She bent down and zipped up one boot. After she did the same with the other one, she stood and grabbed her leather jacket. "It really was a fun time," she assured me in her haste to leave. "I hope you have a good day, despite everything."

Apparently, the whiskey had done its job a little too good last night. I froze, struggling to remember the conversation from the night before. It wasn't my style to divulge anything personal, but had I said too much? "Despite what?" I asked.

Fully dressed now, she turned to me and offered a not-so-shy smile. "You mentioned an anniversary of somebody's death. Honestly, I can't remember." She shrugged. "Sorry."

Relieved, I said, "No apologies necessary. Can I call you an Uber?"

She waved a dismissive hand my way. "No, thanks. I can take care of that myself." She zoomed toward the front door but stopped short of opening it. "I'm not sure who Albany is, but maybe she's the one you should've been with last night?"

I managed to keep my face devoid of emotion, but inside I was cursing myself out for talking too much. Not only did I mention the significance of the day, but I'd tossed out that name in what . . . Some fantasy gone wrong? *What the hell is wrong with me?*

The worst part? I'd been caught so completely off guard, which signaled I needed to tighten shit up again. I opened my mouth to speak, but . . . *I got nothing.* Swallowing, I stared at her and waited for her to finally walk out.

With a heavy sigh, the woman swung the door open. "By the way, my name is Amber. Next time, maybe do a better job remembering who you stick your dick in?" She shrugged. "Just sayin'."

Unable to help myself, I laughed. The fact that she'd had the nerve to call me on my bullshit almost made me want a repeat. Almost. But *Amber* was funny.

Surprisingly, she laughed too. "Anyway, bye."

Chuckling, I rubbed the stubble on my jaw. "Bye, Amber."

Then, she was gone.

While I could've spent several more minutes dissecting our interaction, racking my brain on the specifics of the evening, I knew I didn't have time. Duty called.

There was a bouquet of roses at the grave site, in front of the headstone. *Cedric Wesley Batchelor.* Even though Mom was now happily married to her second husband and living on the other side of the state, she still sent flowers to the cemetery every Memorial Day. For the life of me, I could never understand why.

The dark shadow my father had cast over our entire family should have destroyed any love she felt for him, but it hadn't changed anything. Although my mother would always hold a special place in her heart for her first love, it made me sick to think about the turmoil my father had taken her through—in life and in death.

I glanced at the words engraved on the tombstone. *Loving son, husband, and father.* Every year, I forced himself to visit the cemetery on this exact day. Every year, I read the engraving over and over again. Every year, I thought about the lies my father had told. Every year, I wondered if Cedric—*because even now I can't bring myself to call him Dad*—even knew what love was. And every year, I walked away resolute in the plans I'd made for my own life. Taking one last look at my father's resting place, I whispered, "I'll never be like you. I'm better. I'm smarter. I'll succeed. And I'll do it without you."

The buzz of my cell phone drew my attention away from the tombstone. I glanced down at my phone.

**Hendrix: Heads up. Ms. Tea strikes again.**

Closing my eyes, I typed out a response, letting my cousin know that I would handle it. I jogged back to the car and slid into the driver's seat. It only took a few seconds to find the latest social media post from the woman who'd made me a trending subject.

After months of posting random celebrity and local news, the anonymous influencer, Ms. Tea, had zeroed in on me. My life had become fodder for this mysterious content creator, and she'd devoted countless minutes and too many short videos on my exploits. I clicked on the latest post and listened as the robotic voice babbled on about my penchant for no-name flings and meaningless hookups while still photos and videos of me played in the background.

The TikTok had already generated hundreds of thousands of likes. And the comments . . . People who didn't even know me had taken an interest in my life. Some mused about the size of my dick. Others accused me of *being* a dick. Then there were those who'd diagnosed me as a narcissistic asshole, speculated on my religion and labeled me a heathen. No doubt this one reel would spawn dozens of other videos analyzing my body language or adding fake context to everything as if they'd been in the room. Not to mention there would be that one person who claimed they were a family friend who'd seen my downfall from middle school. It was a muthafuckin' mess.

The topic veered to my activities yesterday, accompanied by images of me at the club. Before I'd taken Amber back to my place, it had been a typical night. I'd entered the venue late, had several drinks with random women, picked one, then left. Nothing too out of the ordinary for a single man. Tame. Almost boring. Until . . .

"Shit," I grumbled when a pic of me cuddled up next to the daughter of a potential business partner appeared. Because Amber wasn't the *only* woman I'd attempted to sleep with yesterday. She was actually my second choice. *Maybe I am a narcissistic asshole?*

Real talk, though. I loved a challenge. An off-limits woman

was like catnip, something I could never really resist. And there was always a small part of me that wanted to fuck my life up. "Damn it."

After a few minutes, I gave up. I didn't bother listening to the rest of the video because the damage had already been done with that photo. It was all bad. And my grandmother would be livid. *Shit, I might even get fired.*

Joyce Batchelor had spent years growing the media company that she and my grandfather had founded together back in 1969. The infamous scandal surrounding my father's countless crimes and his subsequent death had threatened the company's existence as well as our family's wealth. After that, she'd made it a point to have a hand in every single division of the company. As long as Granny was alive, her word was final. She'd made that very clear when she'd given me a job in the company, when she'd promoted me to my current position as Director of Commercial Strategy and Business Development, and when she'd asked me to work with her on the deal to absorb the cash-strapped Garland Production Company.

Granny had warned me to stay far away from temptation. Which meant, stay the hell away from Bishop Edward Garland's daughter. The megachurch pastor had a very public platform where he preached "family values" to his many followers. He was very protective of his baby girl and was known for his fiery sermons from the pulpit about the seven deadly sins. His daughter, Candice, had supposedly followed in his footsteps, building her individual brand as a "tradwife" influencer. She espoused traditional gender roles, wore a purity ring, encouraged women to prioritize being wives, and talked about motherhood being the ultimate goal.

Except . . . she didn't practice what she preached. Behind closed doors and against her father's wishes, she had a very robust sex life. She'd made that very clear when she squeezed my dick under the conference table during our first business meeting.

Any perceived impropriety would not only jeopardize the deal we'd been working on for two months, but my own job. Because the blame would undoubtedly fall on me, the wicked son of a criminal as opposed to the preacher's innocent angel. After all, I'd willingly committed the deadly sin of lust on a regular basis. And the sun had indeed set on my wrath every night. Then, the other sins . . . *Shit*. There was only one course of action—keep Granny from seeing the latest post from her favorite influencer, Ms. Tea Spills It.

The twenty-minute drive to the Batchelor Corporation offices in Downtown Detroit was uneventful. No traffic, no road rage incidents, no flooding in the streets, and no tires ruined due to potholes. Confident that I could mitigate the damage when I entered the building, I greeted the lobby receptionist and grabbed a coffee.

Unfortunately, my morning turned even more sour when I entered my tenth-floor office and found my uncle lounging in my chair as if he owned it. Frowning, I asked, "What the hell are you doing here?"

It was no secret that I couldn't stand my father's brother, John. The older man had taken pleasure from making my life a living hell. The vendetta between the Batchelor sons had been well-known in the family's circle. They'd barely tolerated each other. And my father's death had done nothing to dampen the ire that had been evident since they were little boys.

My uncle crossed a leg over his knee. "Running late this morning?"

"What the hell are you doing in my office, John?" I repeated.

I learned a long time ago that nothing was guaranteed. Time. Money. Status. Trust. Family loyalty. Everything was subject to approval by the person giving it. Anyone expecting to receive those things was often left empty, lacking. John was a bottom-feeder, an opportunist, the worst kind of man. He had no problem trouncing over his competitors to turn a profit or gain an advantage. No one had to tell me that he was full of shit. My instincts had warned me early on, maybe when I was around twelve. I refused to call him "uncle" because the man had never acted like anyone other than an adversary.

"It's the anniversary of my brother's death."

"I know what day it is," I growled. "I'm surprised you care, considering you probably danced on his grave after his funeral."

It was no secret that I had struggled with my father's life and legacy. I'd spent years running from the past, from my family, from my mistakes. The rage dwelling deep inside made me want to destroy everything around me, especially myself. My sole identity was wrapped up in my father's failures. No direction. No job. Just liquor, women, and mayhem. Until Granny offered me a second chance and ordered me to get my shit together.

John shrugged. "Call me curious, I thought I'd stop by to make sure you were managing better than in years past."

I snorted. "You'd like that, huh? To finally be rid of the daily reminder that my mom chose him over you?"

The bitter sibling rivalry was amplified when my father stole John's girlfriend and married her. The fact that I was a product of that union rankled my uncle in ways that had affected me negatively throughout my life.

John let out a humorless, sinister chuckle. "Actually, no. Watching you fuck up your life has been pure joy, proof that Harriett picked the wrong Batchelor."

"All that bitterness," I mused. "I would think being a father of three and preparing for your third divorce would give you more to worry about than which Batchelor my mother chose over thirty years ago. Maybe it's time you move on? She has, and so has everyone else."

"It's only a matter of time before my mother realizes that you're full of shit just like Cedric was," John continued. "When she does, I'll make it my mission to destroy you."

I clenched my fists, took several slow breaths. *Three. Two.*

*One.* The urge to pummel him wasn't a new emotion for me. I'd followed through once, too, which landed me in the county jail. Since then, I vowed to never lose my composure again. Instead, I forced a smile. "Have a good day." Opening a file my assistant had left on my desk, I scanned the front document and waited for John to leave. When the older man made no move to get up, I met his waiting gaze. "What?"

John finally stood. "My mother made a mistake when she brought you into this company, mentoring you, handing you Garland on a silver platter."

"Too bad I don't care what you think."

"Maybe you should," John sneered. "The only person standing between you and me is her, and when she dies, I'll make sure your unworthy ass has nothing."

I folded my arms over my chest. "I hope that day doesn't come anytime soon because I actually love *her*, and not her money. I'll play along for your sake, though. On that unfortunate day, John, you'll realize that I don't give a shit about you or your kids. I have never needed you before and I will not need you then. Fuck you. Get the hell out of *my* office."

We stood there for several seconds, eyes locked. The dare was there. *Do something.* John should've been thankful Granny was still alive because she was the only person stopping me from beating his old ass.

John turned away and took a deep breath before he walked out without another word. It took a few minutes, but I managed to regain my focus on the matter at hand. I called Granny's office.

Granny's assistant answered the phone. "Hey, you. You saved me a call."

I massaged my temples and prayed I wasn't too late. "You're looking for me?" I asked.

"Yes, your grandmother would like to see you."

I swallowed hard. "When?"

"Now," she chirped. "The others have already been notified."

*The others?* "What is this, Jeanette?"

"I wish I could tell you," she said, "but she told me to keep my mouth shut."

Letting out a heavy sigh, I told Jeanette I'd be there right away. After I hung up, I texted Hendrix: **What the hell is this meeting about?**

**Hendrix: Hell if I know. Could be anything.**

I stared at the wall, my mind racing with wild scenarios. It wasn't uncommon for my grandmother to summon us to her office on a whim, but I'd learned the hard way that Granny never wasted time on meaningless things. She definitely had a plan of action, she never held her tongue, and she always got her way.

Five minutes later, I entered the conference room. I half expected to find my uncle sitting next to Granny, vying for attention, but John wasn't in the room. Only me, my sister, and all the cousins minus one. I took the empty seat next to Erica on the other end of the room, far away from my grandmother.

"What's up," I grumbled.

Erica leaned in. "You fucked up, brother," she tossed back with a wicked gleam in her eyes and a smirk on her lips. "I caught that Ms. Tea post this morning."

"Shut up," I murmured through clenched teeth. "Any idea what we're doing here?"

Hendrix walked into the room and sat next to me. "Interesting," he whispered. "No Uncle Fathead, no mom? It might be a trap."

Erica snickered. "Maybe she found out about your affair with Jeanette?" she mused quietly. I choked on the water I'd just gulped down, and Erica patted my back. "You okay, Wes?"

Wiping my tie with a napkin, I assured her, "I'm good."

Hendrix glared at her. "What part of mind your own damn business don't you understand?"

Erica shrugged. "I might need to call in a favor later. So I pay attention."

"Who are you? The bone collector?" Hen argued.

I often wondered the same thing. I loved my sister, but she spent a lot of time collecting dirt on everyone in the family. I'd once assumed it was a defense mechanism. After our father died, we lost almost everything and were forced to move out of Detroit due to the stigma—and the threats. On top of that, John ensured much of the extended family treated us like peasants. For a long time, the only contact we had in the family was . . . the woman staring at me right now.

I elbowed Hen to get his attention, but my cousin was too busy whisper-yelling at my little sister.

"Or you could always just ask for what you need," Hendrix said. "No need for blackmail."

"Where's Cyn?" Erica said, changing the subject.

I cleared my throat again. "Heads up."

They both knew what that meant, and all conversation ceased instantly. Granny met my gaze again before she scanned the room.

"I'm surprised you called us here today, Granny," Jackson said in his usual constipated tone. Jackson was just like his father, John. Arrogant. Hypocritical. Liked to hear himself talk.

"I'm surprised you called us here today, Granny," Erica mocked, under her breath.

Hendrix shook his head. "Fucking clown."

My cousin and my sister gave each other a fist bump, previous conflict forgotten.

Granny eyed me, her light brown eyes assessing me thoughtfully. *Shit, she knows.*

As if my sister had read my mind, she whispered, "Oh shit, Wes. You're in trouble."

"Big trouble," Hendrix cosigned.

Granny stood, setting her glasses down on the table and smoothing a hand over her salt-and-pepper hair. Although she would be considered petite to an average observer, to me she seemed larger than life, taller than her five-foot-four frame. I had never seen her frazzled or nervous. She exuded confidence in everything. No hair out of place, no sign of a wrinkle in her clothes, no visible flaw in her appearance. The years had been good to her. Dressed in a fitted navy pantsuit and white blouse, she looked closer to fifty-five than seventy-five with flawless mocha skin and a sassy short haircut. I knew it had a lot to do with how she lived her life, always active. Judging by her choice of shoes—a pair of blue Nike Air Max sneakers—she was planning a workout of some sort. When she wasn't on the golf course, she was walking in the park, doing yoga with her friends, and riding her Peloton in her home or office gym. Granny ate clean, never ate fried food, and stayed away from liquor.

"Where's Cyn?" one of my cousins asked. I didn't bother looking to see which one had spoken because I didn't care.

"She's out of town," Hendrix replied. "I'll fill her in."

"No need," Granny said. "I'll speak with Cynthia myself." She cleared her throat. "This won't take too long. I need everyone's attention."

The room descended into silence. It felt like five minutes, but it was more like two minutes of tense, uncomfortable quiet while we waited on Granny to say anything.

Jackson cleared his throat. "Do you need water, Granny?"

Granny shot him a sidelong glance. "If I needed water, I would have water." She sighed. "I've made some decisions about your future that I felt you should be aware of." Once again, Jackson opened his mouth to speak, but Granny shushed him. She glanced at each of us again, but her gaze lingered on mine a little longer than the rest. "I'm not getting any younger. I thought I raised my children to revere the sanctity of marriage, love, and family. Yet, my only living son thinks it's acceptable to have side chicks in multiple area codes. And my daughters . . . One is content sleeping with the boy toy of the month and the other doesn't have any children."

"What does this have to do with us?" Jackson's sister, Amelia, asked.

Granny shot her a glare. "Do you have somewhere to be?" she challenged.

Amelia sunk low in her chair and shook her head. "No, ma'am."

"That's what I thought." Granny rounded the table and stopped behind me. She reached out and massaged my shoulders. Hard. "Since they couldn't be what I want, I decided it's up to you. I want all of you to settle down and get married." She dug her thumb into the back of my neck. "I thought about making it a contingency upon my death, but I decided to make it a contingency while I'm alive." Granny gripped my chin and turned my attention to her. "I hope you've had all your fun," she whispered.

"Granny," I mumbled, "I—"

But she walked away before I could get anything out. Once she made it back to her seat, she planted both hands on the table. "It's simple. If I don't see you walking down that aisle, you won't be walking away with any of my money."

The room erupted then, cousins talking over one another, all vying for the opportunity to be heard. I just sat there, staring at Granny.

"I'm not ready to get married," Erica said, panic in her voice.

Granny sliced a hand through the air, effectively signaling to everyone to shut the hell up. "This isn't up for a discussion. I said what I said. You're dismissed."

As my cousins scrambled to exit the room, I let out a sigh of relief. There was no way Granny would've dismissed me if she'd seen the post. So I grabbed my shit and practically sprinted out of the office, only to nearly collide with someone in the lobby.

"Sorry," I grumbled. But when I glanced up, I was face-to-face with the one person I hadn't expected to see. Albany Keyes. I stared into beautiful eyes that I'd seen in my dreams more times than I'd ever dare to admit. She was stunning, from her long, boho braids to her black oxford flats. Every part of her was perfect—her smooth brown skin, full hips, long legs. . . . It had been years, but she still had the same effect she'd always had on me. With my heart beating out of control, I struggled to find words, to bring myself out of our shared past and into our distant present, but I couldn't speak.

Albany spoke for me, though, when she averted her gaze and walked past me without a word.

Behind me, I heard Erica's high-pitched, "Albany!" and nearly tripped over a chair that I swore wasn't there a minute ago, in my haste to get the hell out of there.

Granny's voice stopped me in my tracks. "One more thing . . ."

*Shit.* I sucked in a deep breath and turned to meet Granny's hard glare.

She approached me slowly. "Fix it or find another job."

# Chapter 2

## *Wesley*

Choosing to move in silence and being rendered speechless were two very different things. I had barely escaped the family-slash-business meeting with my job, which was bad enough.

Yesterday, I would've left that meeting with an idea.

Yesterday, I would've formulated a plan to win Granny's trust back before I'd even entered the elevator.

Yesterday, there would've already been meetings on the calendar, irons in the fire. Something to mitigate the crisis that *I'd* caused.

But today . . .

So many thoughts were running through my head, too many questions that needed answers. None of them had anything to do with Batchelor Corp. None of them had anything to do with Granny or her approval. All of them had *everything* to do with Albany.

*Who asked her to come?* That answer was obvious. Granny. Because once Albany greeted everyone except me, she'd disappeared into my grandmother's office.

*What did Granny want with her?* No one showed up on

that floor without an invitation. And Joyce Batchelor had never wasted time on meaningless meetings.

"This is some freakin' bullshit." Erica slammed my door, kicked off her shoes, stomped over to the love seat in the corner of my office, and slumped down onto the cushion. "Who the hell makes their grandkids get married?" she shouted, frustration rolling off her in waves. "This isn't *Bridgerton*. I'm not walking around here in floor-length dresses, short-ass bangs, and long gloves up to my elbows. I'm not some chaste maiden waiting to get deflowered and knocked up by an ugly-as-fuck man with a title. This is toxic behavior."

Staring at my sister, I grumbled, "Stop panicking. You're not getting auctioned off to the highest bidder."

Erica ranted about marriage, men, and unrealistic expectations for several minutes, while my mind drifted back to Albany.

*When did she get here?* Not that she would've called me when she crossed state lines, but it was common knowledge that Albany hated Michigan. Once she graduated, she'd hightailed it out of Dodge and rarely looked back. Detroit wasn't a small city by any means, but we'd traveled in the same circles for years and I had never run into her. Not at an event. Not at the gym. Not at a restaurant. And definitely not at work.

*Where is her husband?* The fact that Albany married some useless muthafucka still irritated me. I didn't need to know where that guy was, and I didn't really care. *Is she still married, though?*

*Why do I even care?* Because I just did. I always cared about Albany. More than I would ever admit.

Erica clapped her hands, drawing my gaze back to her. "You didn't see the email?"

*How fucked up am I?* No comment. Another obvious answer. Fed up with myself and the questions in my head, I sighed and refocused my attention back to my little sister, who'd jumped up and paced the office. "Email?"

Muttering a curse, Erica gestured toward my laptop. "Where are you, brother? Granny sent us a summary. Of the meeting?"

Frowning, I scrolled through my unread messages. Other than the typical mailbox fodder, there was nothing out of the ordinary. "What are you talking about?"

"Obviously, I've been talking to your wall. Check your personal email."

I opened my private account and spotted the message in question. I scanned the text quickly, then met my sister's waiting gaze. "Shit."

She planted a hand on her hip. "Still think I'm panicking?"

As I reread the email, I wondered what my grandmother was really going through. I thought back to the meeting, to Granny's demeanor. Other than her obvious irritation with *me*, nothing signaled there was anything wrong. But this . . . The message was brief, but clear.

> *You are required to go on a date with someone of my choosing. Over the next few weeks, I'll meet with each of you individually to discuss. I expect your full cooperation.*

"Can you talk to her?" Erica asked.

I frowned. "Who?"

Erica let out a dramatic sigh. "Granny! Damn!"

The door swung open, and Hendrix entered the office. "You know this is fucked up, right? First, she tells us we need to get married before she dies. Now, she wants to play matchmaker?"

"See! We're the Black Bridgertons." Erica opened my small refrigerator and pulled out a bottle of water. "I'm not getting married for a check."

Hen glanced at Erica. "How much is it, though?"

My sister rolled her eyes. "It doesn't matter," she snapped. "I'm not doing it."

"Enough," I ordered. I needed time to process everything

that had happened today. As much as I loved my sister, Erica's tendency to overreact made me tired as hell. "Let me think."

"This is your fault, Wes," Hen announced.

"That part," Erica agreed. "Granny was on the warpath because your ass can't keep your dick in your pants."

I glared at her. "Do you really think Granny pulled this wedding shit out of her ass because of some TikTokker?"

"You have a point," Hen conceded. "She had to have come up with this months ago." He crossed his leg over his knee. "Business deal?"

While Granny was ruthless in the boardroom, there was no doubt she loved my grandfather. She'd devoted her life to him and had never even considered remarrying after his untimely death. It seemed unlikely she'd use us as a bargaining chip for some sort of financial payoff.

I shook my head. "Nah. I don't see it."

Erica raked a hand through her hair. "It feels so unexpected. A provision in Grandad's will that we don't know about?" Erica suggested.

"I doubt it," Hen said. "This is all her."

I had no memories of John Batchelor Sr., only the stories told to me by my grandmother and my father. From everything I'd heard, my grandfather valued his family above all else and he was known just as much for his kind nature as his business acumen. And since he'd passed away before there were any grandchildren, I doubted Granddad had concocted a marriage plan for us.

"Wes!"

The sound of both shouting my name grabbed my attention again. "What?"

Erica arched a questioning brow. "Do you even care?"

"I actually don't care." I ducked when an ink pen whizzed past my head. Chuckling, I said, "You're a little over the top with this, sis." I eyed my cousin. "You, too. Our grandfather has nothing to do with this. Like Hen said, it's all Granny."

Erica glanced at Hen, then back at me. She nibbled on her thumbnail, something she always did when she was nervous or scared or sad. "What if she's sick?"

The thought of life without Granny was too much to consider, especially today. "She's not," I assured them. *And myself.*

"You don't know that," Erica argued. "Would she even tell us?"

"Probably not," Hen muttered.

"Even healthy people die." Erica swallowed. "You know that. Look at Dad."

I closed my eyes. My sister had a rose-colored view of Cedric. She believed our father hung the moon and the stars. And I'd never had the heart to ruin that image for her. Because my role as big brother had always been to protect her.

"It's already hard enough," Erica continued, tears filling her brown eyes. "Today is—"

"I can't do this right now," I interrupted. "Granny is fine. Give it a few months and she'll turn her attention to something else."

Hen shot me a skeptical look. "You don't even believe that. Even *you* have to admit this is weird."

*Of course, I don't believe that shit.* Which was a problem because if I'd learned anything from my father it was the importance of believing my own lies. Especially if I wanted someone else to buy in. Shrugging, I said, "It *is* weird," I confessed. "But it doesn't mean Granny is dying or even deathly ill."

"She is getting older," Hen argued. "We all know how tragedy can strike with little warning."

It had only been three years since Hen's sister passed away suddenly. The entire family had been devastated because Halle had been a shining star, the only cousin that got along with everyone. *Including* John. Her death had thrown us all for a loop.

Erica's expression softened. "I miss her too, cuzin."

Hen sucked in a deep breath. "I'm just sayin'. We didn't expect my sister to die either. But she did. We don't know what Granny is hiding."

"True," I agreed. "Let's think about what we *do* know then. Granny can think all of us under the table—and outrun most of us on our best day. She hasn't shown any indication that she's slowing down or even thinking about retiring. She's still kicking ass—at work and at home."

Erica shook her head. "Wes, she basically told us we had to get married before she dies to access any of our inheritance. It feels like a dying wish." She smacked Hen on his shoulder. "Tell him."

Hen hunched a shoulder. "It definitely sounds like a last request."

"Don't y'all have work to do?" I asked, opening my laptop. I didn't have the bandwidth to commiserate with them over the whole marriage thing. I'd already wasted too much time thinking about Albany, drowning in the memories of her.

"I can't believe you're not worried about this." Erica gasped. "Oh."

My eyes flashed to hers. "What?"

She shrugged. "Of course, you're not worried. The woman you wanted to marry just breezed back into your life."

"Ah." Hen smirked. "That's right. Albany is back in town. Coincidence?"

"And she's meeting with Granny as we speak," Erica chimed in. "Wonder what that's about?"

Glaring at my sister, I grumbled, "That's their business. It has nothing to do with me."

"Granny said *all* of us had to get married, brother." Erica crossed her legs and leaned in. "That means you, too."

The thought of marrying Albany had never crossed my mind. At least, not since we were younger. And not until my damn sister just mentioned it. While Granny was convincing, Albany was resolute. She hated me. *It's my fault.* She was also never one to follow orders blindly—even if it involved money. "Albany is not here for me."

"You don't know that."

"I know Albany." I reviewed the spreadsheet and jotted down a note on a pad of paper. "I'm done with this conversation."

Erica folded her arms. "Sure about that?"

"Very," I confirmed. "I don't have time to worry about the future when my present situation is fucked up. Shifting *my* focus back to *my* shit. I have deadlines to meet and a job to keep. If that means I have to let Granny send me on a date with a random woman, whatever."

Hendrix stood. "Yeah, nah. I'm not agreeing to that." He gave me a dap. "See you at the gym later."

"You heard what she said," Erica pressed.

"I did." I pulled up the report my assistant had sent earlier. "And I meant what *I* said. Talking about this all day isn't going to change Granny's mind. Or mine."

Erica grumbled a curse. "Men have it so much easier."

Hen scoffed. "How you figure? I've watched my mother emasculate my father for thirty years, talking to him like he's a piece of shit daily, putting her hands on him, blatantly cheating on him every chance she gets. And he takes it because he's accustomed to the Batchelor lifestyle."

The Batchelor name made us seem larger than life to the community. The only thing that made our family different than any other, though, was money and status. Dysfunction was universal. Growing up, we'd witnessed the ongoing conflict between my father and his siblings. Family functions typically devolved into chaos. Several members suffered from various types of addiction, from drugs and alcohol to sex to gambling. The first time I'd ever seen a fistfight in my life wasn't on the playground, but at a birthday party. Hendrix's mother attacked a distant cousin who'd dared to call her on her bullshit. It was also the first time I'd seen Aunt Nina get arrested.

Erica's gaze softened. "I guess I don't know what to say to that."

"It wouldn't change anything if you did." Hen shrugged. "That's life. None of us are married—or want to be married—for a reason. Because, aside from *your* mother, all of our parents are weak-ass, fucked-up individuals. Granny called it herself today. And I may be an asshole on a good day, but I'm in no hurry to bring another person into this dysfunctional family. Let alone an innocent child." He glanced at me. "I'll catch you later, bruh." He kissed Erica's cheek and left.

Seconds later, Erica grabbed her stuff. "Fine. I'll figure it out. I always do." She hugged me. "See you later, big head."

"Later, baby sis." I grabbed her hand, squeezing it gently. "It's going to be okay."

Nodding, she whispered, "Hope so." She walked out of the office and closed the door behind her.

Hendrix had a point. Money and status made everything sparkle. The truth always dulled the shine, though. From the outside looking in, we had everything. But inside . . . our house of cards was on the verge of collapsing under the weight of secrets and lies. And I absolutely planned to expose the cracks. That was the only way to preserve the legacy my grandparents built.

## *Albany*

Establish boundaries.
Stay focused.
Ask questions.
Practice self-care.
Say no.

I repeated my *"Keep it cool"* list in my mind several times. Therapy had been integral to my survival—especially in my line of work, definitely with my ex, and absolutely when I was around my family. After many sessions, angry tears, crushing despair, I'd finally gotten to a point where I felt confident walking into any room. I'd transitioned from uncertain, unhappy, unfulfilled Albany back to capable, strong, badass Albany.

*Yet . . .*

My current situation? Sitting across from Joyce Batchelor, the woman who'd known me before I knew myself, the woman who'd been at every important event in my life. And even though I knew I could trust "Granny," I couldn't bring myself to spout off the sixth and most important item on my list.

*Accept the challenge.*

Why? Because I simply didn't want to.

"I assume you're thinking about my proposal." Joyce stared at me. Actually, she stared *through* me, dared me to decline the offer with her all-knowing eyes. It was the older woman's gift and the reason she was still on top of her game. It was also the reason Batchelor Corporation continued to grow and expand when so many corporations had floundered.

Clearing my throat, I opened my mouth to speak. But nothing came out. Instead, I nodded. Because the desire to work, to be able support myself again was strong. But my need to protect my peace was strong, too. A few minutes ago, I'd been elated, so grateful for the opportunity to work for Joyce as her personal private investigator. And I'd wanted to accept—until I received my first assignment.

"It's a great opportunity for you to grow your business," Joyce said.

I sucked in a deep breath and counted to ten before I met Joyce's waiting gaze again. "Thank you for thinking of me, but no."

Joyce shifted in her chair, but never broke eye contact. "Can I ask why?"

"I have to prioritize myself," I explained. "Inserting myself in the middle of your family drama when I actively avoid my own wouldn't be good for me."

Leaning forward, Joyce rested her elbows on her desk. "How can I assure you?"

I shrugged. "You can't." I swallowed past a hard lump in my throat. "I've been through a lot since I've been away. I've crawled my way to a healthy place. As much as I want to help you, I can't do it." The job was so desperately needed, but the cost would far outweigh the benefits. "I know several local PIs that could assist. I can put you in touch."

"I understand," Joyce said finally. "I don't want to put you in a position where you would question your spiritual, physical, and mental health. I consider you family. Your grandmother is my best friend, my *only* friend. And if you can't do this, I'll accept that."

A sigh a relief escaped my lips. "Thank you for understanding."

Joyce swiveled in her seat and peered out at the skyline. "I want Wesley to succeed. But I worry he's too angry, too distracted with his own endgame—and his vices—to be effective. This latest thing, the TikTokker, is intent on ruining him."

It had been years since I had seen Wesley, but time had done nothing to qualm the pang of hurt that had shot through me at the mere sight of him this morning. When Joyce had requested my services to find an anonymous blogger, Ms. Tea, it was the sort of thing I would've jumped at the chance to do.

Yesterday.

For someone else.

Someone who had nothing to do with Wesley Batchelor.

"I may have to fire him," Joyce admitted softly.

My chest tightened. *Damn it.* Even after all these years, the notion that Wesley could suffer in any capacity still affected me, made me want to protect him. To help him. "I'm sorry."

With her back to me, Joyce continued, "I would still like you to work for me. Like I mentioned earlier, I need someone I can trust on my team."

Granny was never one to beat around the bush. She'd always

been forthcoming, direct. Even if the sting of her words left a scar. I sensed she was holding back, though. It wasn't uncommon for a business to need the services of a private investigator, especially one as large as Batchelor Corp. Yet, her words made me think she knew that something was amiss at her company, that *someone* in her circle was untrustworthy.

"I'm not sure it's a good idea." My conflicting emotions only confirmed that I wasn't ready, no matter how appealing the offer. "Not right now."

Finally turning to me, the older woman smiled. "I won't push you, but I truly believe that you are perfectly equipped to handle the job." I opened my mouth to speak, but Joyce rushed on. "And my grandson. Sometimes the past is just a vehicle to drive you into your future. Nothing more. Nothing less."

I turned over Joyce's words in my head. She'd given me something to consider. It didn't have to be a big deal. An investigation *involving* Wesley didn't necessarily translate to being involved *with* Wesley. Of course, I would have to talk to him. *Maybe.* Even that was avoidable. And it was just *one* investigation, a small part of the job.

"Sweetie?" Joyce called, pulling me from my thoughts.

Nodding, I asked, "Can I think about it?"

I couldn't get out of Joyce's office fast enough. As soon as we'd agreed to table the discussion for next week, I'd fled and made a beeline straight for the elevator. Stepping inside, I jabbed my finger on the "L." Once the door closed, I closed my eyes and leaned against the cool metal wall. *What the hell am I thinking?*

When the car stopped, I glanced up and noticed it'd stopped at the tenth floor. My stomach fell when the door opened, because of course Wesley would be standing right there. Shifting to one side, I waited for him to enter. He pressed the "L" button again and stood next to me.

Impatient, I jabbed at the button as if that would somehow transport the elevator down to the lobby in an instant. The damn door still didn't close. I pushed it again. And again. *Close, damn it!* Finally, we were on our way down to the lobby. But the silence made the short ride feel like forever.

Wes scooted closer. Too close.

*And he smells so good.* "Don't," I warned, stepping forward, away from the heat emanating from his body.

"Why are you here?" he whispered, his voice low.

I gripped the strap of my purse and willed my body not to react to the feel of his breath against the nape of my neck. Because, apparently, he still made me wet and horny. "Can you move?"

"Are you going to answer the question?" he murmured.

I felt his nose brush against my shoulder, heard him taking in my scent. The elevator stopped. *Thank God.* When the door opened, I blew out a slow, steady breath. Five. Four. Three. Two. One. Now in control of my emotions and my body, I glanced at him over my shoulder and asked, "What do you think?" Then, I walked away from him as fast as I could without looking like a bitch in heat. It wasn't until I'd sunk into the driver's seat of my car that I allowed myself to acknowledge the truth. *There is no way I can do this.*

# Chapter 3

## *Albany*

*I should've known better.*

The writing was on the wall from the moment my ex-husband insisted I use his studio name on the wedding invitations. Not his real name, Darrell Washington Steele. But . . . Grim. In hindsight, it was foreboding. Because his rap persona showed up at the church that day. High as a kite, but charming as fuck. *Grim.* Just like my entire marriage.

The signs were there all along, though. At the engagement party when Darrell's own father, a sitting United States senator, offered to drive the getaway car. That was after his mother passed me a note that read, *I love my son, but I don't love him for you.* During the bridal shower when his Aunt Ethel whispered—loudly—that it wasn't too late to cancel everything. On the bachelorette trip when his sister begged me to leave her brother alone. In the limo when my friends threatened to kidnap me and whisk me off to an undisclosed location.

Still, I persisted for one reason. Darrell was the man of my father's dreams. On paper, he was perfect—articulate, wealthy, and from a well-respected family. At the youthful age of nineteen, Dad's approval had meant the world to me because I'd never really felt it. And for the first time in my life, I was Daddy's Little Girl. He smiled when I entered the room and bragged about me to his colleagues. He was proud of me.

Before the wedding, though, my doubts intensified. When I finally expressed my reservations to my father, Dad claimed I was overreacting, that things weren't as bad as I thought, that Darrell had potential. And he did. He had the potential to steal from me, to destroy my credit, to cheat on me, to lie every damn day of our marriage, and to destroy my faith in love and commitment.

*Lazy, conniving, philandering muthafucka.*

Scanning the divorce decree, I silently cursed Darrell for making everything difficult. Although the marriage was technically over now, my legal trouble had just begun. I'd already received several certified letters from his bankruptcy attorney and letters from creditors threatening to sue me because, in his latest attempt to screw me over, he'd filed for chapter 7 protection. Which would effectively leave me to pay all our joint debts. Not that I had the money to pay it because I was flat broke. The only way out of this was to follow suit and declare bankruptcy myself or hit the Mega Millions. Since I didn't play the lottery, I was down to one option. All my savings had been wasted hiring an attorney to dissolve my ill-fated marriage.

Sighing, I tossed the latest letter into the pile with the rest. Clearly, my morning had gone from promising to shit after my meeting with Joyce Batchelor earlier. Now I was home—*correction*, at my best friend's house because I no longer had a home of my own—with a bunch of mounting bills, cheap wine, and questions about my once certain future. I closed my eyes and prayed that my life would even out, that I would at least be able to regain some peace in the midst of this terrible storm.

I heard my bestie, Brianna, behind me before I felt a comforting hand against my back. "Are you okay?" she asked softly, setting a plate of two loaded tacos in front of me. "You need food with your wine."

I breathed through the tears threatening to fall. I'd already shed too many. Nodding, I wiped my nose with the tattered tissue I had in my palm. Staring outside the window, I fixed my gaze on a family of four playing with their puppy in the courtyard outside of Brianna's condo. The pang of hurt in my heart intensified as I wondered if I would ever be as happy as the woman smiling lovingly at her husband and kids.

"Just more proof that I fucked up," I admitted. "That's all."

"No, he's the fuck-up. You did what you thought you were supposed to do. Love and support him. You're not the first woman to give her all to a man, to work on her marriage. None of that makes you less of a person and it doesn't make you weak."

I let out a humorless chuckle. "Why do I feel this way then?"

"Because you're a control freak, not used to needing help. But we all need it at some point. And it's okay."

I poured myself another glass of Merlot. I didn't bother to glance at my watch. I knew it wasn't five o'clock and I didn't care that I was on my third glass of wine. "At least, it's over." I pivoted to another topic I had mentioned every day since I'd shown up on her doorstep. "I can't thank you enough for letting me move in with all my baggage." I was grateful that my best friend had offered me a place to stay, but I hated feeling like a freeloader. No matter what was going on in life, I always paid my way. To not have the resources to do that made me grouchy and a little depressed. "I promise I'll pay my rent as soon as possible." I pulled out a hundred-dollar bill. "Here's something on the groceries."

Brianna waved a dismissive hand my way. "Sis, stop. You know that's not what we do. Put that money back in your purse and use it to set up your post office box. I'm not hurting for money. I just want you to be okay. Take the time you need to build your business and find work."

Keyes Investigations was still in its infant stage, started because I had been laid off from my position with the FBI months
ago. Initially, I'd relished the chance to realize a dream I'd had
since I was a teenager, but the reality of launching a new business, losing my home, leaving my husband, and then relocating
to a different state had made everything bad. I'd spent years
building a life away from here. I wasn't proud of the fact that I
had to return home with *nothing*. No home. No job. No money.
No marriage.

I swallowed against a lump in my throat. "Fine."

"Don't *fine* me. You've been there for me at some of my
lowest points. Do I have to remind you of that drama with
Hendrix?"

Shaking my head, I said, "No. Let's not go there."

She raised her hands in the air dramatically. "Exactly! Anyway, it's time for you to let me be there for you. And it's also
time for you to call your family."

My stomach churned at the thought of my father and his
wife finding out I was in town. I didn't know it in the beginning, but my parents had leveraged *my* relationship for their
own personal and political gain. Once it became clear that I
was a means to an end for them, and not a cherished part of
their family, I limited contact.

We'd barely spoken in years, and although I'd recently
turned thirty-two, I had no doubt that my stepmonster—er,
step*mother*—would jump at the chance to have me under her
thumb again. When I was younger, she'd dictated what I wore,
what I ate, who I spent time with . . . Everything.

While I'd been in Detroit for weeks, I'd purposely avoided
certain places in the city so that I wouldn't run into her. Involving her in anything, especially my struggle, would only make
things worse.

Bri's soft touch pulled me from my thoughts. "I'm not talking about Allisifer, sis," she assured me. The nickname my bes-

tie had given my stepmother was fitting—a cross between her name and Lucifer—because she was as charming as she was evil. "I understand why you wouldn't want to tell her anything."

I closed my eyes and took a deep breath. "I'm glad I don't have to explain that to you."

"But your—"

"I'm not calling my father either," I interrupted.

Gregory Keyes was married to Allison when he got my biological mother pregnant. Unfortunately for them, a tragic accident claimed the life of my mother when I was a toddler. I was forced to move in with a man more concerned with his next mistress and a woman who resented me for existing. As a result, I'd always believed they both considered me *his* biggest mistake, despite their assurances to the contrary.

"Why would I call him now anyway?" I asked. "He's been a distant observer since I was born except when he needed Darrell's family to get a government contract. All my life, he tossed out checks to make himself feel good while simultaneously making me feel like shit for surviving the car accident and making him accountable for his failure as a husband. There's always something more important than me for him. His wife, his cars, his side pieces . . . I'd rather slice my hand with a piece of paper than ask them for anything."

"What about Grandma Liv, though?" she said.

"I don't want her to know about the mess I made of my life." Especially since Grandma Liv had cautioned me against marrying Darrell. In fact, she was so against the union that she almost didn't show up to the wedding. "Besides, she's been sick. I don't want to add more stress to her."

Getting away from Darrell was partly why I made the move back to Michigan, and being around for Grandma was also a factor. We talked every week, and I'd visited as often as possible, but I knew my grandmother had recently had a hip replacement. And that wasn't her only health concern. High blood pressure, diabetes, unreliable family, and years of working had taken a toll. I wanted to be close, to help in any way, and spend as much time with Grandma as I could.

Grandma had fought to be an integral part of my life, often inserting herself into disagreements between me and my parents. She was my saving grace, even bringing me to live with her when Allison convinced my father to send me to a boarding school in Colorado. I would do anything for the woman who'd never hesitated to be there for me.

Brianna squeezed my hand. "Don't shut Grandma Liv out. I have a feeling she'd be angrier if you kept this from her."

*No doubt about that.* Still... "I love Grandma, but she's getting older. She could slip and say something to my father, and then he'd tell *her*, and all hell will break lose. And I don't want them to know."

At one point, it felt like Allison had made it her life's mission to ruin mine. When I excelled at anything, she'd ride in on her broom, under the guise of being a concerned mother, and burn my dreams to the ground. Initially, I fell for it because I wanted—no, I needed—the connection. But my willful ignorance only lasted until third grade. After I won the coveted prize for most cookies sold in my scout troop, she'd ripped my heart out by refusing to let me go to camp. Instead, she'd sent me to a different type of camp. In New York. Couldn't enjoy weekends with my friends because I had to go to finishing school to learn the social graces.

I still remembered the day she pulled me out of the public school to attend Detroit Country Day School. I thought it was the end of my life at the time, but it turned out to be my salvation because I'd met my bestie there, my tribe. People who'd remained integral to my life since the fourth grade.

I had bonded with Bri over our mutual love of Destiny's Child. The day we met, we'd taken turns portraying Beyoncé during an impromptu mini concert in the school auditorium.

My best friend knew my family, at least all of the members that mattered to me. She'd also seen firsthand the trauma Allison had inflicted and had a few battle wounds herself for sticking her neck out for me.

"You do have other family," Bri pointed out. "Hear me out . . . I know you said no, but what about Ana?"

While my father never made it a priority to connect me with my mother's family, Grandma ensured I maintained a relationship with my mother's sister and extended family. Although Aunt Ana and her husband, Jax, were wealthy, and wouldn't hesitate to show up for me, I couldn't imagine hitting them up for a loan.

I shook my head, slicing a hand through the air. "Never."

"Sis, you love her. She'd do anything for you."

"I love her, too," I told my friend.

"Mo?"

Unfortunately, I wasn't the only child my father had with a mistress. My older brother, Moses, had been solid from the moment we met. Of course, he would help me, but . . . no. I loved Mo, but he would kill Darrell. Literally. "Bri, you know I can't do that."

Her shoulders fell, most likely in a mixture of pity and exasperation. "Albany, I—"

"No," I repeated, this time an octave higher. "I'm not asking anyone for help."

"Why be on the struggle bus if you don't have to?" she countered. "You won't call Grandma. You know she'll help if you tell her the situation. Your extended family is wealthy. Ana always asks how she can help. Didn't you just talk to her the other day?"

"We chatted about her grandbabies and cribs. Small talk," I argued. "Catching up about random shit. Having an innocent conversation about baby showers and asking for a loan are two different things."

Bri blew out a frustrated breath. "Fine, I'm just going to let you wallow in self-pity a little longer."

I sat up straight. "I'm not—" I sighed. "Okay, so I'm wallowing."

"And I'ma need you to stop that shit in two-point-two seconds. It's way past time for you to get your shit together."

Gaping at my friend, I said, "Wow. Tell me how you really feel." I tossed a paper plate at her, missing her on purpose.

"I'm just sayin'," she continued, "you would tell me the same thing. And you *have*."

I squeezed my eyes shut. "You're right. No more wallowing. Much."

"I understand. Trust me. I don't like asking for help either. But you don't have to do this alone."

"I'm not alone. I have you. Grandma Liv knows I'm getting a divorce, but I just don't want her to know all the details yet. You know how she is. She talks too fast. Love her to death, but she's liable to go on a rant and reveal everything to the whole world. Then, I'd have everyone all up in my business."

My friend let out a heavy sigh. "Fine. But I better not see that money on my nightstand in the morning."

I laughed. "I promise you won't." A couple of weeks ago, I'd stuffed a couple hundred dollars in her purse. The next morning, the money was on my bedside table. "I saw Wes today," I offered, needing a subject change. That encounter in the elevator earlier had rocked me. It had been years since I'd laid eyes on him, let alone stood close enough for my body to react to the warmth of his body, and I needed to talk about it.

Brianna raised a perfectly arched brow. "Really? With his fine ass."

"He's not that fine anymore," I lied. Truth was, Wes had transcended fine and morphed into something more than that. He was all man, smooth dark skin, intense light brown eyes, low-cut hair, and that beard . . . *Damn.* He was beautiful.

Brianna shot me a disbelieving look. "Oh please . . . Actually, I take that back. He's fine as hell. Did you forget I work in the city? I see him often and he gets better with time."

"Whatever," I grumbled. "He's alright."

Laughing, Brianna shook her head. "I call bullshit."

"What do you want from me? Okay, he's attractive. Still an asshole, but nice to look at."

"He's still *your* asshole." She stuck her tongue out after I tossed a pillow her way, missing her head by an inch. "You missed. Ha! So . . . ?"

"So, what?"

"How was it? It's been a long time since you've seen him. Did you talk to him?"

"Unfortunately, yes. And I hated every moment of it." *Even though my body loved it.*

Brianna stared at me intently. "I get it. It's a shame, though. As close as you were . . . Maybe you need to talk?"

My friend was right. Wes and I were more than friends. As far as I was concerned, he was my person back in the day. We did everything together, from playing tag in the field behind his house to attending every school and family function together. The connection was so intense, everyone thought it was a foregone conclusion that we'd marry. In fact, our families had campaigned for the ultimate Keyes-Batchelor merger.

After a while, I started to believe the hype too. Especially after our seamless transition from awkward kids to flirty young adults. It seemed to happen overnight, too. One day we were playing video games and the next evening we were making out in his car.

The joke was on me, though. Despite the years of endearing friendship between us, Wes had ruined everything with one selfish act on what was supposed to be the most special night of my life. After I'd finally confessed my love to him, he'd pulled the rug out from under me in the harshest way.

Grandma Liv had always told me forgiveness was for me, not the person who needed forgiving. Yet, I couldn't get over the fact that Wes had taken my virginity and promptly ghosted me. He promised to come back, and I believed him. Only to find out he left town altogether. No calls, no letters . . . Nothing.

It took years of therapy for me to even call him out on his asshole-ish behavior because I loved him so much. But once I'd written the words in my journal, Wes would always be The Asshole Who Broke My Heart. Not even Darrell's indiscretions had hurt as much.

"Tell me about the meeting with Mrs. Batchelor," Brianna said, bringing me back to the present. "Why did she contact you?"

When I woke up this morning, I had expected to wake up to unpaid bills, a too-much-wine hangover, and a ton of spam messages from random people. What I didn't expect was a voicemail from Joyce Batchelor asking for a favor. Even hours later, I still couldn't believe what the matriarch of the Batchelor family had asked me to do for her.

"A job offer"—I bit my thumbnail—"as her private investigator."

Brianna's eyes widened. "That's good. Isn't this what you've been waiting for?"

"Yes, but the first assignment . . . Apparently, there is an influencer intent on using the Batchelor family to get more views and reads on their platform," I explained. "She's willing to pay Keyes Investigations a hefty retainer to figure out who this anonymous blogger is and help with other things. Discreetly, of course."

"That's a job, girl!" She eyed me skeptically. "Why aren't we celebrating?"

Biting down on my bottom lip, I thought about the conversation earlier. I had never known life without Granny Joyce, as I called Mrs. Batchelor. She was family. After Cedric Batchelor was arrested and charged with embezzlement, my father and Allison had wanted to distance themselves from Wes's family. Ultimately, their efforts had failed because Grandma Liv had refused to abandon her best friend, her sister of the heart, under any circumstance.

"Albany?" Brianna called. "What's wrong?"

Pulling myself from my memories, I looked at my best friend. "Nothing. I didn't accept it."

Brianna frowned. "Why the hell not?"

"I need time to think about it."

"Your bank account is on life support. It doesn't have time. So again . . . why?" she prodded.

"Because the job involves Wes." I gave her a quick rundown on the job offer. Wes's ho-ish ways had caused a PR nightmare for the company. Weekly hit pieces had been released exposing his dirty deeds. Granny Joyce simply wanted to find the person targeting her family. "I mean, I understand why she needs the help. Her regular private investigator is retiring, and she needs someone to step into his role."

Brianna nodded her head. "All good things, right?"

"Right," I agreed. "I just don't know if it's a good idea to get involved with *this*. I'd have to work with Wes, to ask him about his personal life."

"But you mentioned she needed help with other things."

"True."

"Which is more work. *Consistent* work."

"Not necessarily," I argued. "It could be three times a month or three times a year."

My friend picked up a pad and paper and jotted something down. "I think we need a list of pros and cons. Actually, I can't even think of a true downside to this."

"But—"

"Give me a minute." It took less than sixty seconds for Brianna to hand me the list.

The top three pros should have sealed the deal—cash, opportunity, connections. But that fourth one . . . "Bri, I don't—"

She tapped the paper with her forefinger. "Those are the only reasons you need, to not only take the job, but accept *all* of the potential cases. The one con—*Wes*—is irrelevant."

Working for Batchelor Corp. could open countless doors for me. I'd be a fool not to jump at the opportunity. "I can't deny those are great reasons to take the job," I admitted. "That last one, though . . . Hate sex? Really, Bri? Yeah, no."

Brianna snorted. "Whatever. I don't think *you* even believe that. I say we place a wager."

"I thought we already established I don't have any money."

"Not money. I'm thinking food. If you somehow fall on his dick, you have to cook dinner for two weeks straight."

"And if I don't? You can't cook. What will I get for proving you wrong?"

Tapping her chin, Brianna peered up the ceiling. After a moment, she snapped and pointed at me. "If you win, I'll put gas in your car for two weeks."

With the price of gasoline high as hell, I considered taking the bet. Yet, the simple thought of sex with Wes flooded my body with a warmth I hadn't felt in months. No, years if I was being honest.

"You're thinking about naked Wes, aren't you?" Brianna waggled her eyebrows. "Told you . . . he's hot. Besides, it's completely appropriate for exes to fall into bed at least once after the breakup. I'd say you're about sixteen years overdue."

Clearing my throat, I sliced a hand through the air. "No. It's not going to happen. And, if it did, that would be a 'con' because nothing positive could come from that."

"Okay, then don't do it. Skip Wes's dick and take the job anyway," she said. "You need this."

Again, Brianna was right. I *did* need it.

"Do it now because you know Mrs. Batchelor doesn't wait

around," Brianna continued. "I'd hate for you to miss out on something that could be so good for your company."

The positives outweighed the negatives but . . . Was I ready to be in such close proximity to Wes? Could I put the past behind me to do a much-needed job? *Can I manage to keep my panties on?* Of course, I could. I had spent years in the industry gaining invaluable experience in the field. I'd survived shootouts, arrested high profile criminals, investigated top-secret crimes.

And shit . . . *I'm a muthafuckin' professional.*

A smirk formed on Brianna's lips. "Looks like you made a decision."

I nodded. "You already know. I'm good at what I do. Finding a mysterious influencer will be a cake walk. And she wouldn't have asked me if she didn't think I could handle this. I'm going to do this job with a smile on my face. Then, I'm going to do *all* the jobs."

A wide grin stretched across Brianna's mouth as she clapped slowly. "Finally. And if you decide to let your body talk you into bedroom or boardroom action, try not to fall in love again," she teased. "You know you're drawn to tortured souls and Wes is the poster child."

I scoffed. "Trust me, you don't have to worry about that. Never. Happening. Again."

"I don't know"—she hunched a shoulder—"I've learned to never say never, sis."

Even though I had my own doubts about my ability to not get sucked in by Wes's trauma, I couldn't afford to risk my heart again. Correction, I *wouldn't* risk my heart again. I held my head high and said, "Fuck Wes and his sad, sexy eyes. I'm getting this money."

# Chapter 4

## *Albany*

STAWWWPPP! Mr. Batchelor betta stop playin'. The streets are talking, and these women are talkin'. Join me later tonight for the scoop from a woman who says she spent a pretty forgettable night with the Batchelor heir. Perhaps, he's more like his father than we thought. Y'all know the history.

"I can't do this," I grumbled to myself as I scrolled for more Ms. Tea content. All morning, I'd plummeted down the rabbit hole of gossip content. And by the fifth video, I was officially tired of social media.

I nibbled on my thumbnail as I reviewed the notes I'd jotted in my planner. As much as I couldn't stand Wesley, I couldn't figure out what he'd done to warrant the attacks. While I wasn't a person who spent my days online, cracking up at videos, watching silly commentary about people I didn't know, I was familiar with some of the players. My job required me to know shit. Business shit. Celebrity shit. Random shit.

The Batchelor family was well-known in certain circles but

only a few of Granny Joyce's grandchildren used their status to be seen. Wes wasn't one of them. He had personal pages, but his last IG post was in 2019. And TikTok . . . It took me several minutes to track down his profile. Judging by the lack of activity, I assumed he'd only created a page to watch the chatter about him.

Sighing, I stared at the screen. Ms. Tea had posts dating back several years, but before that . . . nothing. The first post was a random share of another person's post. It wasn't until last year that she joined the Hot Topics hemisphere. She built her following covering national stories and shading other content creators. I could see why the viewers loved her. The influencer was witty. Her reads were thorough. And she gave zero fucks about clapbacks. But the question *still* remained . . . Why Wes?

Over the past month, the coverage of Wes had become increasingly hostile. Nasty. Almost personal. Hell, during the most recent post, Ms. Tea had dragged Wesley all up and through the streets of Detroit with her biting commentary. Despite her anonymity, it was obvious the influencer was from the "D." Her knowledge of the city rivaled my own, even her vernacular sounded distinctly like home. The way she talked indicated she was younger, maybe a millennial. Gen X?

The woman spoke like she knew Wesley, too. This wasn't a casual acquaintance. A jilted lover? Disgruntled employee? Or a devious family member? Knowing everything I did about the Batchelor family, I wouldn't be surprised if John or any of his spoiled offspring had something to do with this. There was no love lost between them.

The fact that the TikTokker brought up Wes's father didn't sit right with me either. Cedric Batchelor had died well before it was popular to post every daily activity on social media. His death had been the culmination in a years-long clusterfuck that threatened to destroy their family. Everyone had been affected. Including me.

*I can't do this.*

Even after all this time, I still hurt for Wesley. The circumstances surrounding his father's death had taken a huge toll on him, changed him. And not for the better. Which is why I knew taking this case would be a mistake. Because the last thing I needed was to feel sorry for the person who shattered my heart.

"You have company, Albany."

I glanced up from my laptop just in time to see my grandmother follow Brianna into the room. "Grandma?" I stood and embraced her. "It's so early. What brings you over here?"

Grandma set her cane down and gingerly took a seat at the kitchen table. "I was in the neighborhood because I have physical therapy. Decided to stop by and check you out."

"I wish you had told me you were coming by." I straightened up a bit, clearing the mail off the table, tossing my plate in the trash, and setting my glass in the dishwasher. "Would you like something to drink? Coffee? Tea?"

"No, Pooh." As a child, I was fixated on Winnie-the-Pooh. The nickname, short for Pooh Bear, had followed me from childhood to adulthood. "I'm fine. I just wanted to lay eyes on you."

"I'm sorry I haven't been by to see you this week. I've been busy."

"Busy working?"

I hated lying to my grandmother about everything that had been going on in my life. Scratching the back of my neck, I averted my gaze. "Yes. I got a job offer yesterday."

"I heard," Grandma said. "I had dinner with Joyce last night, and she mentioned you'd dropped by to see her. But she also told me you hadn't made a final decision yet."

After my conversation with Bri, I had drafted two emails. One thanking Granny Joyce for the opportunity but turning her down graciously. Another accepting the job with gratitude for the business. In the end, after I realized my checking account was overdrawn because I'd forgotten to cancel my home-owner's insurance, I'd sent the second message.

"I emailed her first thing this morning," I explained, choosing not to delve into my reasons.

Grandma met my gaze, all-seeing, all-knowing. She studied my face, assessing me from the top of my head to my feet. "You look skinny," she said finally. "Are you eating?"

Swallowing, I nodded. "Of course. Just had a bagel with lots of cream cheese."

"I can see we're getting nowhere." Grandma grimaced and shifted in her chair. "In life, we make decisions, Pooh. Those decisions are not always the right ones, but we have to deal with the consequences anyway. The good news is bad decisions don't define us. I can see you're not ready to tell me the truth, so I won't push. I just want you to know that I'm here to listen when you want to talk."

Tears burned my eyes and throat. "I'm fine, Grandma. Just trying to get settled."

Again, Grandma looked at me, through me. Without speaking, she pulled an envelope out of her belt bag and set it on the table. "One of the reasons I'm successful is because I know how to read people."

Olivia Keyes had amassed quite the empire since she'd purchased her first department store at the young age of twenty-five with the help of Albany's late grandfather, who also owned several strip malls in the Ann Arbor area. As an only child, she inherited his company and created Keyes Investments. Business had been good to the shrewd businesswoman and Grandma was currently in the process of developing a state-of-the-art shopping center in Downtown Detroit.

"Divorce final?" Grandma asked.

I paused, trying to remember how much I'd divulged to my grandmother when I'd told her I was leaving Darrell. "Yesterday."

"Good. It's never easy to divorce. Even if you can't stand the bastard you married."

Chuckling, Albany agreed. "That's true."

I had never known my grandfather, had only seen pictures of him. Essentially, Grandma Liv had erased his existence. She'd even changed all her kids' names to her maiden name because of the shame associated with being Donald Witherspoon's jilted wife.

The scandal was legendary in their small hometown of Ypsilanti, Michigan. I had made the mistake of asking my grandmother about the man she'd married and was promptly shut down. It wasn't until I was a teenager that I'd discovered the real reason no one dared speak of the man. Not only had he cheated on Grandma for years, but he'd also chosen to move in—and marry—his mistress while he was still married to Grandma.

"How did you move past it?" I asked.

"I took everything with me when I left that fool." She shrugged. "By the time I was done with him, he and his *wife* didn't have a pot to piss in."

"Do you regret it?"

Grandma flashed a sad smile. "I have to say . . . the best revenge is to live well and love better." She chuckled. "I tried, Pooh, but I can't even lie. Not even to help you feel better. The truth is, revenge was sweet. After what he put me through, I don't regret anything I've done to make his life hell."

"I'm done with love," I confessed.

Grandma patted my hand. "You're too young and too beautiful to say that. I have many regrets, but my biggest regret is that I let bitterness close my heart to new love for so long. Don't be like me. In a year's time, that asshole won't even faze you. He'll be a small dot on the larger map of your life. A landfill."

I cracked up. "You're hilarious, Grandma."

She sighed and stood. "I'm just telling the truth. Give me a kiss and walk me to the door."

Doing as I was told, I linked arms with her and led her toward the front of the condo. "I love you. I'm glad I'm home."

"I'll be glad when you finally tell me everything," Grandma retorted. Then she pointed at the envelope on the table. "In the meantime, take that blessing and stop being so damn stubborn."

"Thank you," I whispered, unable to stop the tear that fell.

Grandma dashed it away with her thumb. "I'm always here for you. No matter what."

As we walked toward the door slowly, we chatted about my plans for the weekend. "I'll stop by tomorrow," I announced. "We'll have lunch and watch a movie or something."

Grandma frowned. "Pooh, no. Tomorrow is poker night. I'm not watching no movie. We can do that Sunday. After you get your hair braided. They look a little raggedy."

Laughing, I nodded. "I'll make the appointment today. And Sunday it is."

A few minutes later, Grandma was gone. I peeked in the envelope and silently thanked God for my grandmother. I counted the cash, separated rent money, and set it on Brianna's nightstand. Then, I closed my laptop and headed to my first destination. No time like the present to shift my focus back to this case. The sooner I figured it out, the sooner I could move on, away from Wes.

To find the culprit, I had to figure out what Wes was doing when the videos started. I also needed to monitor his movements, observe his interactions, familiarize myself with his everyday contacts.

It didn't take me long to find him either. A quick call to his secretary told me everything I needed to know. He'd always been a creature of habit, so I was able to track him at his favorite breakfast spot. From there, I'd tailed him to the gym and watched him play basketball with Hendrix and some of his friends. Around lunchtime, he'd grabbed lunch at the café next to the fitness center.

Inside the café, I'd hunkered down at a corner booth. I tried not to pay attention to the way he smiled at the barista or flirted with the women seated near him. He seemed at ease there, like he knew the regulars and enjoyed the company. I made a mental note to speak with one of the women behind the counter, the only one who didn't seem affected by Wes's charm.

Pulling my cap down over my eyes, I tucked my phone in my purse. While I hated to leave in the middle of the day, I also didn't want to take a chance that he would spot me. After I finished my coffee, I hurried toward the door only to be blocked by the man that I was supposed to be hiding from.

He raised a brow. "Care to tell me why you've been following me?"

*Damn it.* So much for being incognito.

## *Wesley*

I stared at Albany. I told myself that I was studying her to figure out her angle, to try and throw her off her game, but the truth was I simply couldn't take my eyes off of her. The stress of the day, the buzz of activity in the café . . . Everything had faded away. Now, I was stuck in this silent bubble with her, unwilling to burst it for fear that our past would destroy the tiny sliver of peace I felt.

We sat across from each other, so close I could smell Albany's skin. Orange blossoms and vanilla . . . *Intoxicating.* Back in the day, her scent could simultaneously calm my nerves and drive me crazy with need for her. Even after all these years, that hadn't changed. Except, she no longer smelled like a teenager wearing Bath and Body Works body spray. Albany was a grown woman.

It wasn't until I'd left the gym that I noticed her. Not because she was sloppy, but because I sensed she was there. I couldn't explain it. Never could. When she was around, I was aware. It was like our small interaction in the elevator had awakened my Albany Meter. And I couldn't turn it off because I was tuned in to her.

Just being near her now was bringing up emotions I'd considered long buried. Over the years, I'd missed her. Although our relationship ended before we ever really got started, the friendship we once shared had meant everything to me. Until I got in my own way and fucked it up. Guilt washed through me as I replayed that night over and over in my mind. The way she'd looked baring her soul to me, the soft brush of her lips against mine, the feel of her body underneath me ... She'd given me a huge piece of herself that night, and I'd squandered it because I was so engrossed in my own pain. And I'd never forgiven myself for hurting her the way I had.

"Wes?"

Her voice brought me back to the present and I blinked. Shifting in my seat, I leaned forward, ready to talk.

She backed away. "Are you going to stop staring and say something?"

"I'm sorry," I told her.

At that point, I didn't care why she was there, why she'd been watching me all morning. I didn't even care that she hated me, that she wouldn't mind punching me in the jaw like she did when I broke her favorite doll. I just wanted to know her again, wanted to sit with her, even if that meant we sat in silence.

"How are you?" I asked, fighting the urge to hold her hand, to kiss her wrist the way I'd done countless times before.

Albany's lips formed a thin line. "You sat here like you have something to say," she said through clenched teeth. "Talk."

I shouldn't have felt offended by her abrasive tone, but I couldn't help but wish things were different between us. Since I didn't want to keep her where she didn't want to be, I said, "Why are you following me?"

Holding her chin high, she grumbled, "The gym, right?"

I nodded. "It's not your fault that old lady asked you to help her figure out the treadmill."

A small smile tugged at her lips before she steeled her expression. "She was cute. Reminded me of one of Grandma's friends."

"You had to help her," I said matter-of-factly.

"Exactly."

We sat in silence for a moment. Shifting in my chair, I pressed, "Well? You didn't answer the question."

Clearing her throat, she met my gaze. "I'm working."

"On?" When she didn't answer right away, I continued. "I assume your current job has something to do with me." She didn't react to my assertion, so I kept going. "I googled you yesterday."

The lie wasn't easy to tell—not to her. But I figured it would make matters worse if she knew I'd kept tabs on her all along. I wasn't a stalker by any means, but I'd made sure to check on her every now and then. And I used Hendrix's connection to Albany's best friend to my advantage. When Brianna was around, she'd inevitably bring her up in conversation.

"What did you find out?" she asked.

Over the years, I'd *found out* a lot of things, but I wouldn't tell her that. Instead, I decided to keep it simple. "You're a PI. Nice website, by the way. Complimentary reviews too. Who hired you to tail me?"

She sighed. "Technically, it's confidential. But my client gave me permission to divulge if necessary." Leaning back in her chair, she folded her arms over her breasts. "Your grandmother hired me to find out who Ms. Tea is."

Curious, I watched her intently for a moment before I said, "You know about that?"

"Who doesn't?" she retorted.

I tapped my thumb against the table. "What else did Granny tell you?"

She shrugged. "The only thing you need to know is she hired me to do a job. That's why I'm here."

"Is that the only reason?" I challenged.

"Why else would I be here? We're not friends. We don't talk. I have no reason to deal with you."

"Bug . . ." It had been years since I'd called her by that nickname. It felt good. *Right.* "I—"

She held up a hand. "Don't, Wes. We're not good. This isn't a catch-up session. And my name is Albany."

I didn't need a reminder of who she was. "Point taken," I conceded. "It's been a long time. I guess I have to get used to being around you and not being able to talk to you."

"Why is that a problem for you now? You didn't feel the need to talk to me when you moved to the other side of the state without even saying goodbye. You didn't feel the need to answer any of my calls or even write a two-sentence reply to one of my letters." She blew out a harsh breath. "I've wasted so much time analyzing that night, wondering if I did something wrong."

My heart squeezed in my chest as shame rolled through me like waves. I absolutely deserved her rage, but . . . the pain on her face combined with the searing guilt that had settled in my gut nearly broke me. "You did nothing wrong."

"Oh, I know that. Now." She cursed under her breath, but then she sat up, spine straight, eyes boring into mine. "But that's neither here nor there. The facts haven't changed. You hurt me. Fuck you."

I blinked. *This* Albany wasn't a stranger to me. She was feisty, secure, and strong. And that's why I loved her. "If I could go back to that night . . ." My words trailed off because there was no good excuse for the way I'd left things.

"Are we done here?" She arched a brow. "I have things to do."

But I didn't want her to go, and damn it, I was going to prolong this as long as I could. "Like what?"

She scoffed. "Seriously? Why would I tell you anything about my life?"

"You don't have to tell me about your life," I said lamely. Because, yep . . . I was acting like a desperate muthafucka fighting a losing battle to hold on to something that was lost to me forever.

"I'm glad you know that."

"What have you found out about Ms. Tea?"

Albany leaned forward, resting her elbows on the table. "She's local. She doesn't like you. Or she's *pretending* not to like you. She's familiar with your habits because you never change. This is why she's able to catch you doing your dirt. A former lover? Maybe a nosy neighbor? Family, perhaps? Someone with a definite axe to grind. And your head is her target. This is also why you're in deep shit if we don't unmask her soon."

"Granny told you my job is on the line." It wasn't a question because I already knew the answer.

"What do you think?" she tossed back with a hard roll of her beautiful, expressive eyes. Back then, I could always tell what she was thinking just by looking into those brown orbs. Obviously, she'd schooled herself to be less obvious in her reactions, but . . . *I know her.*

"So why accept the job?" Her phone buzzed and she glanced at the screen. As she peered down, I noticed the furrow that formed on her brow. "Albany?"

She muttered a curse and stood. "My reasons are none of your business anymore. If I have any questions about your influencer, I'll reach out. Otherwise, just let me do my job. Don't approach me, don't talk to me. Have a good day."

Then she left, taking my heart with her.

# Chapter 5

## *Albany*

*Ten minutes.*

My fingertips brushed the leather of the steering wheel, my nail catching on the short, frayed thread that I'd never bothered to cut off. My trusty car, my 2013 black Ford Taurus had carried me through blizzards, torrential storms, sneaky links, drive-thru collisions, silent tears, loud screams . . . and one precarious car chase. The mileage was high, the maintenance was expensive, but I couldn't bring myself to get rid of the first car I'd ever purchased with my own money. Even though I knew it was time.

*Eleven minutes.*

As the sun hung low in the sky, daylight lingered while time moved fast. Extended sunshine was the best part of June. Long days made dark nights seem less haunting, less lonely. Everything felt clean, almost perfect right around mid-month. The breeze, the smell, the city. The anticipation of summer had always made life better. Until it didn't. Until warmth became entangled and associated with crushing heartbreak.

*Twelve minutes.*

I was born on the twenty-third of the month. A true Cancer according to my grandmother. Unlike anyone I've known, Grandma read her horoscope daily. She studied birth charts and often talked about sun, moon, and rising signs. She knew who was compatible based on their birth date. As for her, Aquarius men and women need not apply for any sort of companionship.

Growing up, I loved that she wasn't a stereotypical grandmother. While she was into astrology, she still loved the Lord. But she wasn't preachy. Definitely preferred the quick, early morning church service as opposed to the longer afternoon service. Bible study? Nah. Choir rehearsal? The only person who ever heard her sing aloud was herself. Tithes and offerings? Every single week. Ten percent. Plus extra for the building fund and the mission department. But don't get on her bad side, because she could cuss as good as a sailor and had no problem telling anyone off if they crossed her. I loved her. I wanted her to be okay. Because she'd always made sure I was good. So . . .

*Fifteen minutes.*

I stared at the massive house in front of me. I still couldn't bring myself to get out of my car and walk into the house. Not because I had bad memories there. On the contrary, this place had been my safe space for so long. It was the only place where I ever felt at home. Still, I hesitated to go inside, choosing to park at the end of the circular driveway, closer to the mailbox than the front door. Because that text . . .

Over the years, Grandma had become surprisingly good with tech. Considering she'd once vowed to never even text because she preferred a phone call or a visit. Then, she'd promised to not fall into "that social media shit" that the "young, lazy people" were doing. Imagine my surprise when I received a friend request on all the platforms. And she wasn't just a casual lurker, she excelled at content. Thoughtful posts. Fun videos. She'd even done several dancing challenges with her poker friends. Crazy work, but if it made her happy, I loved it.

*Seventeen minutes.*

Sucking in a deep breath, I stared at the message again. Two words. Simple, but loaded with uncertainty, so many questions, and a little sadness.

I read it again. Then again.

After years of separation, the man my grandmother had married, raised a family with, then divorced, was dead. I'd never heard her say a kind word about him, but my heart hurt for what I imagined she was going through. Grief.

With a heavy sigh, I hopped out of my car and took the long walk up the driveway. Scanning the area, my gaze fixated on the small carriage house near the far end of the property, my old private den. Grandma had given me the keys when she'd brought me to live with her, instructing me to use it how I pleased since she no longer had live-in staff. I still remembered when we toured the small space. Her words echoed in my head.

*Every woman needs a personal, quiet space. Invite required.*

Grandma meant it. She'd never interrupted me there, didn't even give me an opinion on how to decorate. She'd simply given me a budget, told me who to call on to do any changes to the structure, and let me do what I wanted.

That space held so many memories. It was a top-secret teenage girl plot inlet, a book club sanctuary, a vision board haven, a silent oasis. It was my port in a storm. I'd retreat there when I was angry, sad, happy, or confused. And . . .

My mind drifted to the night Wes and I made love for the first and only time, the night he left me there. It was the moment my safe house ceased to be my happy place. It held the tattered remains of a broken heart. Because every time I walked in the door, I saw him. I felt him. I smelled him.

A long time ago, someone asked if it was even possible to love someone so much at such a young age. I never acknowledged the innocent question, but I knew the answer. Yes. I loved Wes in a pure, very authentic way.

My phone buzzed, bringing my attention back to the reason I'd shown up at Grandma's house unannounced. Well, not exactly. Because I'd responded to her message and told her I was coming by. Then I'd ignored her response telling me to stay home and came anyway. After all, I was *her* granddaughter. She never let anyone tell her what to do, so I wasn't going to let her steer me away from supporting her.

With a heavy sigh, I finally entered the quiet house. Nothing much had changed. *Except everything.* I smiled to myself as I smoothed my hand over the new dark wood table near the front door. Grandma used to always tell me she had no time for decorating. Yet, every year she seemed to transform the house while simultaneously insisting she didn't do anything different.

One thing never changed, though. Lavender. I inhaled, taking in the comforting smell, her favorite scent. I'd grown to love it, too. Even miles away, spraying a room with her favorite air freshener made me feel closer to her.

I walked through the kitchen, noting the lack of food on the stove. No dishes in the sink. Not even an empty glass on the counter. Peering upstairs, I wondered what she was doing. *Is she even home?*

It wasn't like her to stay out past seven o'clock, unless it was poker night. And Grandma watched game shows every day. It was her thing. *The Price Is Right* in the morning. Then *Wheel of Fortune* and *Jeopardy!* at night. Typically, she would be shouting answers at the television and cursing the contestants out for giving wrong answers. But there was nothing. No clapping from the studio audience. No sound effects.

As I ascended the stairs, I braced myself for what I might find. The last thing I needed was another tragedy. Once I reached the landing on the second floor, I frowned. The dimly lit hallway felt too still. Almost eerie. It was an old house, so there was always a creak here or a clank there. But I didn't hear anything.

The sliver of light under her bedroom door was the only indication she was actually home because Grandma didn't believe in leaving a light on in a room not occupied. Stopping in front of her door, I pressed my ear against the heavy wood.

Rustling?

*Is that a hiss?*

No, it was a moan. A knot formed in my stomach, but I didn't have time to wallow in dread or uncertainty. I turned the knob, pushed the door open, and barged into the room.

"Oh my God!"

"What the . . . ?"

Squeezing my eyes shut, I yelled, "Damn it, Grandma." I turned around and covered my eyes and tried to forget what I'd just seen. "Shit. Shit. Shit."

"What are you doing here?" Grandma screeched.

"Checking on you." I rested my head against the wall and took a deep breath. "I thought you were sad."

Behind me, I heard more movements. A swoosh. A zipper. Footsteps toward the en suite bathroom. Then finally a door shutting. I counted to twenty. I had been totally prepared to see her atop the bed, still, and maybe in need of medical help. But what I didn't expect to see was Naked Grandma with her legs up in the air while some strange man sexed her up. During *Jeopardy!* Which was on mute, by the way.

"Pooh."

I jumped, startled that she'd somehow inched closer to me without me realizing it. "Grandma!" I yelped.

She tapped my shoulder lightly. "Can you turn around so I can talk to you?"

Slowly, I did as I was told. "What?"

I felt her hand on mine before she tugged it from my face where it had been covering my eyes. "Open your eyes."

"Are you dressed?"

"I am."

Seconds later, I cracked an eye open. She wore an oversized robe, nothing familiar. Must've been *his*. Letting out a heavy sigh, I said, "You sent a death text. That's why I'm here."

"I told you I was okay." She pointed a finger at me. "And I told your li'l behind not to come."

"Grandpa died," I argued. "I thought you were sad. I thought—"

"Pooh, I told you I don't care about that man." When I gaped at her, she laughed. "Now you know I've never been nice when it comes to him. His death changes nothing."

I blinked. "I wasn't sure if you had some sort of epiphany. You were married to him for years. I wanted to . . ." I didn't bother finishing the sentence because I knew better. And I knew my grandmother. She was dead serious. "I overreacted. I should've listened to you."

Her shoulders fell. "Come on." She grabbed my hand, leading me over to the small love seat near the window. Gesturing toward the couch, she told me to take a seat. She joined me. "There are some things I probably should tell you."

The bathroom door opened, and the older gentleman emerged—fully clothed. *Thank God.* He grinned. "Hello."

I glanced at Grandma out of the corner of my eyes, noticing the way she lit up when she looked at the man. "Hi, baby," she said softly.

*Baby?*

He inched closer to us and held out his hand to me. "Hi, young lady. I'm Ace."

I stared at his outstretched hand. Eventually, I shook it. "I'm—"

"Pooh," he interrupted with a chuckle.

"Albany," I corrected.

He nodded. "Of course. I've heard all about you."

Eyeing my grandmother again, I wondered how long this man had been around. Forcing my attention back to Ace, I cleared my throat. "I wish I could say the same."

"I hope to change that," he offered. "I would love to get to know the young woman who makes my Old Lady smile with pride."

*Okay, he's good.*

Grandma gushed, averting her gaze for a second before she swatted his arm playfully. "Oh hush, Old Man."

*I know she's not blushing!*

I gave him a once-over. He was nice looking. *Fine*, actually. Salt-and-pepper beard. Well groomed. He was thin, but not in a frail way. While he walked with a limp, he had an air of confidence around him. A quiet strength. He was someone that should never be underestimated—or played with. Yet, he seemed sincere. And the way he looked at Grandma . . . I couldn't deny that his obvious endearment melted some of my ice.

"I heard you're back in the city indefinitely," he continued. "I'd love to take you and Liv to lunch."

While I still wasn't sure about any of this, I found myself nodding at the man. "Who are you?"

"Ace," he repeated.

Frowning, I shook my head. "No, I mean . . . what is your real name? Where did you come from? How do you know Grandma? When did you start spending time here? In this house. With her. In her bed."

He smiled. "You were right, Liv."

Grandma grinned. "Told you."

"Right about what?" I folded my arms over my chest. "What's going on?"

"She told me you were overprotective."

"Just as overprotective as she is," I tossed back.

"I think you have me beat, Pooh," she muttered.

"Ace is my real name," he explained. "My last name is Bond. I met Liv at Flower Day a couple of years ago."

"Years?" I croaked, glancing at Grandma before locking eyes on him again. "Are you from Detroit?"

Grandma was well-known and well-connected. I'd grown up surrounded by important people. It wasn't weird for her to have celebrities in attendance at her events. Singers, artists, rappers, athletes, actresses . . . Some of them even lived on our block.

*Bond* . . .

The name was familiar, but he didn't strike me as a typical famous Detroiter. He looked familiar, too. Not in a Motown-singer way or a city-government way, either. In a legendary way. As I stared at him, I tried to recall where I could've seen him. Then it finally dawned on me. "Wait, Bond? Are you—?"

A smile formed on his lips. "I am."

My mouth fell open. "Oh my God." I stood. "You're Ace Bond. The original Mr. Black Detroit."

He nodded. "Yes."

The Mr. Black Organization was founded at the height of the civil rights movement in America. Over the years, they'd expanded nationally. Thousands of Black men in every city represented the org, working to empower, educate, and enlighten our communities.

"It's an honor," I whispered, shaking his hand again. Because of all the celebrities, the important people I'd met in my life, this man was an icon.

He squeezed my hand. "I'd say it's an honor to meet *you*."

"I've read about your family. The Bond name . . . I heard so many stories growing up." I leaned in closer. "Is it true that—"

Placing a finger over his mouth, he shook his head slightly.

"Okay, enough," Grandma cut in. "Old Man, can you give us some time?"

Ace bent low and pressed a kiss to Grandma's forehead. "I'll call you later." He glanced at me. "Nice to meet you, Albany."

"You, too." Shrugging, I added, "I guess you can call me Pooh."

He barked out a laugh. "Got it. So long."

Once he shut the door, I turned to Grandma. "Really, Grandma? You're sleeping with Mr. Black Detroit."

"He's my man. *My* man. My *man*."

I cracked up at Grandma's use of the popular phrase. "You're too much." I sat next to her. "When did this happen? I expected you to be sad about Grandpa. But you're here getting busy."

"A woman has needs, Pooh."

I patted her leg. "Let's not talk about your needs, okay?"

She giggled. "Haven't I always been honest with you?"

"Maybe too much," I tossed back. "Seriously"—I squeezed her hand—"are you okay?"

"That man took years of my life from me," she explained. "He lied to me daily, cheated on me through our entire marriage, and then tried to steal my money. He doesn't deserve any more of my tears." She brushed her thumb over my cheek. "I just thought you should know that he died."

I let out a slow breath. "Is it sad that I have no feelings about this, other than concern for you?" After all, I'd never met the man. I'd only seen him in pictures. He didn't show up for birthdays, graduations. Not even for my wedding. And he was invited.

"Don't be. I'm good."

I smirked. "I can tell."

She beamed. "He's such a good man."

Tucking one leg under my butt, I turned to her. "Tell me about him. You met at Flower Day?"

"We both wanted the same plant," she explained.

Every year, on the Sunday after Mother's Day, Grandma ventured downtown to Eastern Market for Flower Day. It had been her tradition even before she'd moved to Detroit. Each time she went, she would return with a variety of flowers from the hundreds of vendors who attended. Then, she'd spend hours planting in her garden, listening to music and drinking wine. The fact that she'd met someone there seemed like destiny.

Grandma chuckled. "I tried to talk my way into getting it, but since he'd arrived first, the gardener gave it to him. Imagine my surprise when he gave it to me." She leaned in and added, "and it wasn't cheap either."

Smiling, I asked, "Is that when he asked you out?"

"Actually, I invited him to lunch."

My mouth fell open. This was the same woman who'd made me promise never to make the first move. "You did?"

"There was something about his eyes," she mused, staring off into space. "So kind. Genuine. I couldn't help myself. We sat at that restaurant so long that my hip was on fire." She sighed. "When he insisted that I go home and rest, I didn't want to leave. That's when I knew he was the real deal."

"I love that," I whispered.

"He took me home that day."

"On the first day?"

She shrugged. "I don't know why, but I knew that I didn't have to worry about anything with him."

"You felt safe." It wasn't a question because I already knew the answer. I'd only ever felt that way with a man once. Not since I was a teenager.

Eyeing me, she nodded. "I did. He took care of me that day. Stuck around to ensure I was actually resting. Then, made me call my doctor. When I had surgery, he was there. He stayed with me, made sure I ate, took me on slow walks around the property. Ace listens to me. He prioritizes me. When I'm in one of my moods, he knows to steer clear without holding it against me. He calls me on my bullshit. If I'm wrong, he holds me accountable."

Smiling at her, I said, "I've never seen you like this."

"Me neither," she admitted with a shrug. "I've never felt like this."

"I love this look on you." I squeezed her hand. "You deserve all the happiness you can stand."

"I want the same for you." Grandma cupped my cheek. "I don't love that look in *your* eyes."

Averting my gaze, I sucked in a deep breath. "Let's not talk about me."

"You know I can't listen to that, Pooh. I always have something to say."

That part was true. Grandma had never let the sun go down without speaking her mind. Even if her words hurt. Most of my friends' grandmothers spent their time cooking big meals, baking cakes and pies, giving good hugs, attending water aerobics, going on day trips to the casinos, and cruising to exotic destinations. Not mine. Grandma hated to cook for large groups, which is why she employed a personal chef for holiday get-togethers. The last time she baked a cake was on my sixteenth birthday. A pound cake. It was delicious, but when I asked for another one, she flat out told me "hell no." She rarely hugged anyone. If she did, it was usually because the person really needed it. While she knew how to swim, she considered water aerobics to be the next step before death, so she tried to avoid it. Cigarette smoke kept her from the casinos and she preferred all-inclusive resorts to overcrowded ships.

"I'm just waiting on you to talk to me," she said.

I peered up at the ceiling as tears filled my eyes. "I can't."

She tipped my chin, bringing my gaze back to hers. "What did he do to you?" she prodded. "If he put his hands on you, I'll set his ass on fire."

I gasped, then burst out in a fit of giggles even through the tears that escaped my eyes. "Grandma! You can't threaten people. Even Darrell."

"I'm serious."

"I know."

"Well?"

"He cheated on me. Lied to me. Stole from me. That's just the CliffsNotes explanation. Finally, I just couldn't take it anymore. So, I left. Then, he filed for bankruptcy, ruining my credit and leaving me with a ton of debt that I can't afford. As if that's not fucked up, he acts like it was my fault that our house went into foreclosure and his belongings were set out on the curb."

Grandma muttered a string of curses, but I could've sworn I saw something I didn't expect to see. Tears. But she turned her head before I could confirm my suspicions. Seconds later, she turned to me. "Sounds familiar," she confessed.

I'd heard the stories about Grandad, and I had to agree. Except, my grandmother ensured she left with everything she brought into the marriage. "Uncanny, huh?"

"I swear. I know people. I can have him—"

"Please," I interrupted, my chin trembling as emotion clogged in my throat. "The best thing I can do is forget about him. He doesn't matter anymore."

Before I could protest, she pulled me into her arms, wrapping me in the warmth of her embrace. Then, the dam broke. As I sobbed, she whispered words of affirmation into the air.

*I was worthy.*

*I was strong.*

*I was special to her.*

"And you are better without that stupid Jay-Z wannabe asshole."

Pulling back, I flashed a watery smile. "Grandma, stop."

She wiped my cheeks with her thumb. "I could rap better than that muthafucka," she continued. "His parents should've told him the truth instead of making him think he could do anything. I can't imagine a United States senator being okay with his son wasting all his money on a failed career in hip-hop. Sounding like a broke Kendrick Lamar. He's definitely not like us."

I laughed. "What do you know about Kendrick?"

Waving a hand, she said, "Girl, I know all about him." She

did a little shoulder shimmy. "I play his music all the time. I can barely understand the words, but I get the gist. Highly intelligent young—"

The door swung open, drawing our attention to it. Granny Joyce barged in. "Okay, Liv, what do you want me to do? I have that fundraising event tomorrow, but we can take a trip to Ypsi to handle that business."

Eyes wide and mouth open, Grandma stared at her friend.

Granny Joyce approached us. "What? I got your text." She glanced at Grandma, then at me. "Did I miss something? Was it a false alarm? Is the asshole still alive?"

"Fortunately for me, no." Grandma stood, giving her friend a quick pat on the back. She grabbed the folder on the desk in the corner. "Already called the lawyer."

"Good." Granny Joyce grimaced. "I'm sorry, Albany. I shouldn't have said that."

"You don't have to apologize," I assured her. "I know how Grandma feels."

The entire world knew how Grandma felt about her ex-husband. At any given moment, she would hurl a not-so-veiled insult at the man. It was no surprise that Granny Joyce hated the man just as much. The two had a strong bond and neither one of them hesitated to be there for the other.

"But you don't know this." Grandma handed me a piece of paper. "I'm now officially a widow."

Glancing at the document, I scanned it. Divorce papers. But . . . I peered at her. "It's not signed."

"No, it's not," she confirmed.

Granny Joyce grinned. "I'm prepared to be in attendance when you show up at that funeral and tell that homewrecker who the real wife is."

"Wait." I blinked. "I thought you divorced him years ago?"

Grandma raised a brow. "And give him my money? I don't think so. There's one thing my not-so-beloved husband always forgot. Never underestimate my petty. Your grandfather came into our marriage broke and he died broke."

"But—"

"It's okay, Pooh." Grandma pulled me into a quick, reassuring hug. "There's a lot you don't know. I want to tell you everything, but I don't have time right now." She shot Granny Joyce a strange look before extending her hand to me. "Come on."

I slipped my hand in hers. "Where are we going?"

She led me toward her bedroom door. "You're going home. It's past my bedtime, and I'm sure you have work to do."

"But—"

"No buts, Pooh. Besides, I have business to discuss with Joyce."

When I looked back at Granny Joyce, she grinned. "Are you okay?" I asked.

"I'm fine," she assured me. "By the way, have you made any progress on that crazy Ms. Tea?"

I shook my head. "I haven't."

My hesitation about the job intensified after I'd run into Wes at the café—until I received an overdraft alert from my bank in the middle of that tense conversation. I still wasn't convinced, but I was still broke. *So, there's that.*

"Albany?"

I blinked. "Huh?"

Granny Joyce approached me. "Are you okay?"

Nodding, I said, "Yes. I should probably get going."

Another glance passed between my grandma and Granny Joyce. Something didn't feel right. I heard what Grandma said, but . . . *Is she really okay?*

"What's wrong?" I asked, shifting my gaze between the two women. "It feels like there is something you're not telling me."

"Oh, baby girl"—Granny Joyce waved a dismissive hand—"we're fine. I did have something I wanted to talk to your grandmother about. Business. But that's all." She flashed a smile. "Do you need anything from me? I want to be sure that you have the necessary support to settle this assignment quickly."

The subject change would have been jarring had I not expected it. Granny Joyce was like my grandma in that neither of them could be swayed to have a conversation they didn't want to have.

Deciding to let this go, for now, I gave her a hug. "Thanks for asking. I'll let you know if I need something. For now, I'm good."

"Great," Granny Joyce said. "I'd like you to attend the fundraising event tomorrow. Everyone will be there, so it'll give you a chance to observe."

"I'll be there." Turning my attention back to my grandmother, I gave her a quick kiss on the cheek. "Love you, Grandma. I'll check on you tomorrow." I waved at them both before I left.

As I made my way back to my car, I thought about the interaction upstairs, the questions that didn't seem to have good answers. It was clear to me that something was off, and I was determined to figure it out.

Decision made, I grabbed my phone and typed out a text: **We need to talk.**

# Chapter 6

## *Wesley*

"*Did you hear the latest Ms. Tea blog?*"

"*Such a shame . . . I know Joyce is mortified.*"

"*He should be ashamed of himself seducing that poor, innocent woman.*"

"*Disgrace.*"

"*I always knew he'd turn out like his father.*"

The moment I stepped into the Batchelor estate, the stench of White Diamond perfume mixed with cigar smoke and a healthy dose of judgment destroyed any small sense of peace I'd had a few minutes earlier. I was used to being the subject of conversation when I walked into a room, but damn . . .

Negativity had fueled my climb up the corporate ladder, though. It wasn't the first time someone compared me to my father, but I'd worked hard to distance myself from his criminal legacy. And Candice Garland was neither poor nor innocent.

*I hate this shit.* Another fundraiser for one of Granny's charities. Around the room, members of my family were engaged, doing their part to raise the funds for the city's homeless population. They were all required to be there, dressed to the nines, ready to nod and smile for her guests.

As I snaked my way through the crowd, something in the corner of the massive ballroom caught my eye. A vision in a black formfitting but elegant dress. The high neckline, sleeveless dress had a ruffle detail cascading down the front, all the way to the hem below her knees. Her dark curls were thick and framed her brown eyes. *Stunning.*

Albany and Erica were huddled near the far end of the room whispering about something that seemed important judging by my sister's wide eyes and flailing hands. Curious, I made my way over to them just in time to hear my sister shush my ex-girlfriend mid-sentence.

"I guess I'm the topic of everyone's discussion today."

Albany glanced at me, her eyes unreadable. Dead, almost. "Hi, Wes."

Erica's gaze shifted from me to Albany, then back to me. "We weren't talking about you, brother," she explained unnecessarily. "It's just—"

I squeezed my sister's shoulder. "No worries," I assured her. "You're not the only ones whispering about the latest Ms. Tea post."

"Yeah, I saw that," Erica said. "Yikes. But I have to go."

Albany stood silently after my sister excused herself, staring at her fingernails. There was so much I wanted to say, but this wasn't the place or the time. The tension was thick, but I couldn't bring myself to walk away from her.

"Any new leads?" I asked finally.

She sighed. "We don't have to do this, Wes."

"Look." I stepped in front of her, tilted my head to meet her gaze. "I get it. I ain't shit. But this is my life. My career is at stake. I'd like to know what information you've gathered."

The ten-piece band segued into a ballad, and several people in attendance made their way to the dance floor. As the Duke Ellington song filled the ballroom, I thought about the first time I'd heard it. Immediately, I was transported back in time. It was Albany's birthday, and she'd determined the agenda.

Movies under the stars. I'd handled everything, rented a bunch of '90s movies and set up a makeshift drive-in theater on her grandmother's property.

The first flick was *Love Jones*. I'd never seen it, but I remembered the way she'd grinned when Larenz Tate appeared on the screen. I was jealous. And the movie was just alright, but there was one scene ... The main couple were dancing to "In a Sentimental Mood." For some reason, that song stayed with me for days afterward. Even now, whenever I hear it, I think of her.

Next to me, Albany swayed to the music, eyes closed, hand over her heart. She'd done that then, too. "I love this song," she whispered.

Staring at her, I agreed. "Me, too."

My voice must have ruined the moment because she blinked. Seconds later, the wistful look in her eyes was replaced with ire. "To answer your question," she mumbled, "no new leads. But I do think you should contact a PR person to handle the fallout from this smear campaign."

"Do you really think I need it?"

For the first time since I'd arrived, she peered at me with concern in her eyes before it disappeared. "We had this discussion. It could be anybody. Family, friends, colleagues ... You said you're concerned about your career, act like it." Her shoulders slumped. "Wes, I don't think you realize that *any* negative press can impact your career. Even if it's not true."

"It's not," I offered.

"It doesn't matter. People are going to run with the narrative. You need to get ahead of it."

Part of me felt that it was too late, that anyone who cared already formed an opinion of me. It had been that way for years. A few days ago, I didn't care what *people* thought of me. I cared what *she* thought. I wanted her to know I wasn't *that* guy. Except, I was. I'd hurt a lot of feelings, including hers, but ...

"Just so you know, I didn't seduce Candice," I explained. "We never—"

She held up a hand. "Stop. I don't want to know what you did with Candice. I don't care. But I do have a question."

Frankly, I was simply happy she didn't tell me to fuck off, so I nodded. "What is it?"

"Of all the women in the world, why her? Why risk Granny Joyce's wrath for *that* woman?" The fire was back in her eyes, and damn it, I liked it. Any emotion was better than none. "Is your dick so lonely that you can't find someone else? *Anyone* else."

Shoving my hands in my pockets, I replied, "Why wouldn't I like her? She's attractive, intelligent, sexy . . ."

"Oh, God," she grumbled.

"Why is that so hard to believe?"

"I've done my research. You're reckless. You're content to have meaningless flings with crazy-ass women just to prove you're manly. Mysterious. Unavailable. Which in turn attracts women to you. It's a trap."

I raised a challenging brow. "Are you speaking from experience?"

"Mostly. I know someone like you." She shot me a pained look and, suddenly, I wanted to hold her, to comfort her. But we weren't there. Not yet anyway. *Maybe never.* "Anyway, can you answer the question?"

"Is it going to help you uncover Ms. Tea's identity?"

She hunched a shoulder. "Maybe."

A host approached us, offering us one of the signature drinks—Granny's fave, French 75. Albany smiled, thanking him and grabbing one of the cocktails. I followed suit, slipping a tip onto the tray.

Once the man was out of earshot, I turned my attention back to her. "It feels like you're asking for details about my sex life," I teased.

She rolled her eyes and took a sip. "Trust me, there's not enough alcohol in this drink for that."

Folding my arms over my chest, I said, "I told you . . . she's a beautiful woman."

Scowling, she pressed, "Just admit it. Candice was a challenge for you. Forbidden fruit. You were only interested because Granny told you to stay away. It's a game, just like the one you're trying to play on me."

Stepping closer, I murmured, "I'm not playing you."

She nodded, retreating from me, putting unwanted distance between us. "You are. Teasing and flirting with me is only going to piss me off more. You've always been charming, but I'm not the same girl you left in the carriage house. Naked."

I scanned the immediate area, assured that no one was within earshot of us. "Bug, I know that. I'm not flirting with you," I lied. Because I absolutely was. And I'd done it intentionally and without regard for how she might feel. I was an asshole for that.

"Do you? Because it feels like you think you can just waltz back into my life, call me Bug, and smile at me. And smell good. Then, I'm what? Supposed to just giggle like a schoolgirl and drop my panties for you? Let you crack open the heart that you broke years ago, that I spent years trying to piece back together again?" She held her chin up high. "The only thing you're doing is insulting my intelligence."

Since she'd walked back into my life, I'd wanted to have a conversation with her that didn't devolve into harsh words. As crazy and delusional as it sounded, I wanted my friend back. "That's not what I think. Albany, please . . ." *Please what, exactly?* I couldn't finish the sentence because I had no idea what the hell I wanted to say. Because I had no good answer. I deserved her anger. I deserved her wrath. I *didn't* deserve her forgiveness. I didn't deserve *her*. "I just want you to know how sorry I am."

"I didn't hear an apology," she tossed back, fury in her eyes. "And stop looking at me."

I searched her eyes. "I can't stop."

Her eyes closed. "Just go," she whispered.

"I wish I could honor your wish, but I"—I sucked in a deep breath—"I don't want to walk away."

Albany arched a brow. "Again?"

*Shots fired.*

She set her still-full glass down on the cocktail table closest to us. "Like I said," she continued, "it doesn't matter. But just so you know . . . I'm not interested. I'll let you know if I find out anything new about Ms. Tea. Have a good night."

Before I could object, she breezed across the room, then disappeared out of sight.

The bartender slid another drink across the bar, and I immediately put the glass to my lips. The smell of the cognac soothed something in me, made everything feel better—even for just a minute. I took a sip, closing my eyes as the amber liquid burned its way down my throat, settling in my gut.

It had been a long week, an even longer month. My career was in temporary wait-and-see mode, Granny still wouldn't look at me without rolling her eyes, and Albany . . . Over the years, I'd thought about how it would feel to see her, to talk to her. I always imagined she'd be angry, but the reality of her disdain was a much harder pill to swallow.

"Drinking already?"

I'd already had my ass handed to me by Albany, but I wouldn't give Jackson the satisfaction of a reaction. "Don't you have someone's ass to kiss right now?" I grumbled.

My cousin Jackson stood next to me. "I wouldn't call networking kissing someone's ass, Wes."

I hated Jackson's voice, his mannerisms. Hell, I almost hated him. The only reason I didn't was because I felt sorry for him.

While Cedric's legacy had cast an indelible shadow on me and Erica, I considered myself blessed that I didn't have to grow up with my uncle. Every single one of John's children was fucked up. Trust-fund babies who didn't know how to think their way out of anything. They had no common sense and acted like entitled jerks.

"I'm networking," Jackson added.

I snickered, downed the rest of my drink, and quickly ordered another. This one would be my last. I needed to be on my toes during this event. "Good for you," I said, not even bothering to hide the sarcasm in my tone.

"You know"—Jackson turned to me, resting his elbow on the bar top—"you could be a little more grateful." He shrugged. "Especially since Granny rescued you from small-town obscurity."

My fist itched with the urge to connect to Jackson's jaw. My cousin never missed a chance to comment on the past. Whether it was during Thanksgiving dinner, Christmas brunch, or a work event. And each time, I'd had to grin and bear that shit. Well, except for that one time. The last thing I needed was to draw unwanted attention to myself. Especially since Ms. Tea was doing her best to discredit me.

*Family, perhaps? Someone with a definite axe to grind.*

Albany's words at the café filtered through my mind. She'd mentioned a lover, but I'd made it a point to never have seconds. Every woman I'd dealt with knew the deal because I was up front about my expectations *and* my limits. One-and-done. It had been that way for years, so I doubted it was a jilted woman angry with me for playing her. But family . . .

I eyed Jackson skeptically, my gaze locking on the scar just above his eye. The one I'd put there several years ago. The two of us were like fire and water, had never gotten along. And never would see eye to eye on anything. It would be so easy to tell his ass off, but more than likely, I'd come off the villain. *Story of my life.* "Walk away," I warned.

"Honestly, why don't you do everyone a favor and leave," Jackson suggested in a muffled voice. "The company, the state."

*And your head is her target. This is also why you're in deep shit if we don't unmask her soon.*

Suddenly, everyone was a suspect. Because my livelihood, my family, my *mother*, depended on me. And I would be damned if I let anyone—including Jackson—change that.

"And it's no secret that your activities have cast an unflattering light on the company."

I blinked, almost stunned that Jackson had still been talking. "I thought I told you to walk away," I said. Against my better judgment, I finished my drink and asked for another.

Jackson folded his arms and assessed me. Shaking his head, he muttered, "You're not even worthy of the Batchelor name. And neither was your mo—"

I must've blacked out because I heard Hendrix in my ear. "Bruh, let him go."

Everything in the room returned back to focus. The soft jazz played on the speakers, the low hum of voices around me, eyes boring into me, Granny's disappointed glare, and Jackson . . . My cousin was staring at me, fear unmistakable in his eyes, sweat on his brow, and my fists curled into the lapel of his suit.

Hendrix pried my hands away from Jackson. "Come on, man," he whispered. "Don't do this here."

Letting my cousin go, I stepped back and scanned the room again. Jackson scampered away from me, clutching his throat and swallowing rapidly. Thankfully, most of the people in the room were still engrossed in conversation, unaware that there was any commotion. I sent up a silent prayer of thanks that the bar was tucked off into a nook in the back of the event space, out of sight for most of the fundraiser attendees. But there were a few guests, the ones closest to us, that were watching intently.

Whispering.

Judging.

After all these years, I should've been used to disapproving looks, the sneers from people who'd automatically lumped me in with my father. And my mother . . . Jackson had hit a nerve when he mentioned her. The audacity of that muthafucka for even daring to talk about her—to me—ensured that I would lose it. Because she didn't deserve anyone's ire. She was the best person I knew, and she'd sacrificed everything to take care of us.

"What the hell is your problem?" Granny muttered under her breath. "You know how important this charity is to me. And you embarrass me?"

"Granny, I—"

"I don't want to hear it," she snapped, her eyes flashing with rage. "My office tomorrow morning. For now? Take your ass home and sleep it off."

Shame rolled over me and my eyes locked on Albany, standing near the entrance of the ballroom. The grimace on her lips, the slump in her shoulders told me she'd seen everything. Despite her words earlier, insisting she didn't care about me, she was disappointed. And I was too. *Because I knew better.*

Bile burned the back of my throat as the cognac I'd consumed threatened to come out. Unable to take that look in her eyes, I averted my gaze and told Hendrix, "Let's go."

Nodding, Hen said, "I'll meet you out front."

My eyes landed on Albany again. The disappointment was still there, but there was also something else. Sadness. Sighing, I made my way to the front door. There was a line of people waiting for the valet, so I took a seat.

Moments later, I heard the click of heels on the marble floor. Then I felt someone take the seat next to me. The soft scent soothed my tattered spirit—jasmine and vanilla. *Albany.*

"I'm sorry," I mumbled.

"Wes, please."

"No," I pressed, meeting her gaze. "Please listen to me. I'm so sorry. When I look at you, I see the hurt in your eyes, the pain that I caused. I can't go another day without apologizing to you for hurting you." I closed my eyes, grateful for this moment because it needed to be said. "I wanted to be the person who never hurt you. I knew everything—how your parents treated you, how you never felt like you belonged in that family. I promised myself that you would always belong to me. And I failed you."

"I don't know what to say," she said softly. "I guess . . . Thank you for the apology?" She smiled, bumped her shoulder to mine. "Not sure it changes much, though."

"You finally smiled at me."

She rolled her eyes, but the smile was still there. "I'm not smiling at you," she insisted.

"I hate it," I admitted after a long moment of silence. "I hate that I broke us."

"Yeah, you did." She picked at her thumbnail. "Things happened that changed me. I don't have much to smile about right now."

"Because of me."

She snickered. "You're so cocky. I just got a divorce, muthafucka. My world doesn't revolve around you."

I barked out a laugh for the first time today, and she joined me. That shit felt good. So good. And it sounded good, too. Almost like a love song, the perfect melody. Her treble to my bass. It reminded me of easygoing afternoons and Saturday mornings, taking walks in the park or playing video games at the carriage house. I missed it, the freedom of simply being me. She was someone who'd always accepted me with no questions.

"I guess I should thank you now," I suggested.

She eyed me skeptically. "Why?"

"For taking pity on me, coming to check on me. I know you didn't want to."

Albany swallowed visibly. "I don't believe in kicking people when they're down. Mostly. Besides, Jackson is an ass. Always has been. He must've said something pretty bad for you to react that way."

"He's predictable. I knew that and I . . ." I rubbed my face. Jackson only did what I allowed him to do, and I jumped into that conflict headfirst. No excuses. "I knew better."

"It's not too late to do better." She stood, squeezed my shoulder gently. "Take care of yourself, Wes."

I watched her disappear around the corner and rested my head against the wall. A few minutes ago, I considered the night a bust. But now . . . everything that happened was worth the time I'd just spent with Albany. I wanted more. And I wouldn't be happy until she was mine again.

# Chapter 7

## *Wesley*

I fucked up last night.

Drinking at the fundraiser, causing a scene, choking Jackson . . . Yeah, not my finest moment. And I didn't stop there. The urge to wreck my life had reared its ugly-ass head. Instead of taking the L and going to bed, I grabbed the fifth of cognac and drowned my sorrows. While I'd stopped short of taking home some random woman at the bar, I'd still done enough to find my activities on IG.

Ms. Tea's early morning post had skewered me over hot coals for my reckless actions. And I couldn't even be mad at her. I knew better, and I still fucked up.

The hot water rained down my back as I stood in the shower, as every small detail of the night replayed in my mind. Crazy looks from appalled guests at the fundraiser, Granny's disappointed eyes, the feeling of walking a plank as I was escorted from the room, Uncle John's knowing smirk on my way out . . . But it was that short conversation with Albany on the bench that stuck out to me.

For the first time since she'd returned to town, she wasn't

angry with me. She wasn't there to twist the knife. Instead, she'd applied a salve of sorts, with her soft laugh and concerned eyes. It felt like a glimpse of sun on an overcast day, and I appreciated her for it. Ultimately, it didn't prevent the wrong decision to go to the bar, but it helped.

The water ran cold, interrupting my thoughts. *Shit.*

Grabbing a towel, I exited the shower, dried off, and wrapped it around my waist. I milled around the closet for a while, mulling my day. Work? Home? Work at home. Decision made, I dropped the towel and slipped on a pair of joggers.

On my way to the kitchen, I grabbed my phone and sent a message to my assistant letting her know I wasn't coming to the office but would be online if she needed me. Then I started an email to Granny. Except I couldn't find the words to make anything I did okay, so I closed the app and opened TikTok. I'd already listened to Ms. Tea's latest video, but I was a glutton for punishment, so I did it again. And again. The comments sometimes gave me a laugh, but this time, I couldn't find the humor. It wasn't even noon, and there were thousands of people weighing in on my character as if they knew me.

Sighing, I stopped scrolling, poured a glass of water, and popped some ibuprofen. That was when I realized I wasn't alone. I swallowed.

"How long have you been here?"

Granny stared at me, a quizzical look in her brown eyes. She was seated at the kitchen table, a pitcher of water in her hands. "Good thing you emerged when you did. I was on my way to wake you up."

I gestured toward the pitcher. "With that?"

Standing, she approached me. "Since you like drama, I figured I'd be a little dramatic."

"Granny, I—"

"Don't bother," she commanded, refilling my empty glass with more water. "I don't need another apology, Wes. I need you to do better." The teakettle whistled behind me. "Have a seat."

The room descended into tense silence as she cooked a light breakfast. Once she was done, she brought over a plate of dry toast, an egg, and black tea.

"Eat," she ordered, sitting across from me.

It didn't take long to finish the food on my plate, but when I was done, I said, "I know you don't want to hear it, but I am sorry."

She tilted her head. "Are you, really?"

Shame settled in my gut. "I am."

"What's the reason for your behavior this time? Sad? Angry? What is it?"

I shrugged. "I don't have an excuse, Granny. I fucked up."

"You definitely did," she agreed. "I'm just trying to figure out why. You've had so many chances to get this right." Reaching out, she squeezed my hand. "You're excellent at your job, intelligent, intuitive . . . yet you still engage in these shenanigans."

"I don't know why," I admitted.

"You need to figure it out. If that means therapy, make the damn call."

It wasn't the first time she'd mentioned seeing a professional. I'd resisted because I felt like I didn't need a stranger to tell me what I already knew. My life was a series of unfortunate events. No matter how many strides I made, there was always a part of me that felt like I didn't deserve happiness, that I didn't deserve success. I didn't know how to change that.

Her expression softened. "I want you to win." Her chin trembled. "I want you to be better than him."

This conversation had suddenly taken a turn that I wasn't prepared for. I had no doubt that Granny loved my father, but she rarely talked about "him" like this. The tears standing in her eyes, the way her shoulders fell . . . The display of emotion was surprising because she rarely let her mask slip.

"Your father destroyed his life," she continued.

"He destroyed *our* lives," I corrected.

She shook her head. "No, he didn't. You're still here. You're still alive. *You* still have a chance to do something great."

My throat burned with unshed tears. "What if I'm not better than him?"

"You are," she insisted. "I wouldn't have invested in you like I did if you weren't."

Closing my eyes, I let her words wrap around my heart. "I don't want to let you down."

"Then don't."

"What do you need me to do?"

"Bishop Garland has requested a meeting this afternoon. For the record, I have no problem walking away from this deal, and I will, if necessary. I can't stomach his self-important ass anyway."

I chuckled.

"I'm not laughing," she said.

"She approached me."

Granny held up her hand. "I don't care. The only thing I care about is what I told *you* to do. And that's all *you* should care about, too."

"You're right. I messed up."

"I hope she was worth it."

"We didn't even—"

"I don't want to hear it," she interrupted. "I told you before, perception is reality. Act accordingly."

"But that's bullshit, Granny."

"It's business, Wes. What did or didn't happen doesn't matter. Bishop Garland has an image to uphold. His daughter has made herself out to be a beacon of virtue on these internet streets. Now, you're the Big Bad Wolf luring Little Red Riding Hood into his clutches. Which is why I told you to stay away from her."

"I can still close the deal, Granny. I—"

"I don't want you near him right now. Like I said, I'm prepared to walk away from this deal."

Frowning, I leaned forward. "Why?"

"Because I don't need him. Batchelor business is good. Thriving. And it's high time he recognized that. And, frankly, I'm sick of his whole family-matters schtick. I know too much about him to take him seriously."

Curious, I asked, "What do you know?"

"None of your business."

"I can still help behind the scenes."

"No, you can't. Your behavior at the fundraiser was unacceptable. If I can't trust you to be decent and sober at a work function, how can I trust you to do your job?"

*Ouch.*

"As much as I love you, I *will* fire you and not think twice."

"You've made that very clear," I said.

"I'm trying to teach you something, son. Learn the lesson."

I nodded. "Okay."

She leaned back in her chair. "I saw you talking to Albany."

Meeting her gaze, I waited for her to continue. When she didn't elaborate, I asked, "Did she say anything to you?"

Granny smirked. "Oh, she said plenty."

My stomach roiled as I thought about our interactions before and after the fight. "Are you going to tell me what she said?"

"She quit."

Confused, I asked, "Her job?"

"Yes."

"I still don't understand why you hired her in the first place."

"She's good at what she does, and she needs the job. She's family."

I snickered. "She can't stand me."

Granny swallowed, averting her gaze. "Well, we need to figure out who Ms. Tea is."

"Hire someone else," I suggested with a shrug.

"I don't want to. Albany is the woman for the job."

"You just told me she quit."

She stood. "But I'm telling you to hire her back." She cleared the table, rinsing the dishes and putting them into the dishwasher. "Since you have some time on your hands, I'm putting you in charge of the investigation."

"No."

Granny's eyes flashed to mine. "What did you say?"

I shook my head. "No, Granny. I'm not going to do that."

"Then, you're fired." She shrugged. "It's that simple."

"You know I respect you, but Albany has declared that she doesn't want anything to do with me and I don't want to make her uncomfortable."

With a heavy sigh, she approached me. "Sometimes we have to work with shitty people. Albany knows that."

"Are you calling me shitty?"

"If the shoe fits." She laughed, brushing her hand over my cheek. "I'm just kidding. What I meant to say was that we all do things we don't want to do to get to our end game."

Granny was up to something. Why was she so intent on hiring Albany back? What was *her* end game? I had questions, but I knew she wouldn't answer them. So, I agreed. "I'll talk to her."

"Good." She handed me a folder. "Instructions for you are inside. This is your sole responsibility for the day. I expect you to follow through." She walked to the door. "Don't call me until it's complete."

Granny didn't hug me. She didn't tell me everything would be okay. She didn't even tell me goodbye. She just left. Even so, I knew that she hadn't completely given up on me. Yet. And I was determined to make this right. With her. And with Albany.

# Chapter 8

## *Albany*

I was the type of woman who meticulously planned out my day. I usually woke with an agenda and methodically went about clearing every item off of my to-do list. It was my way of maintaining some control over my life after not having any for much of my childhood. Very rarely did I deviate from my schedule, and only for certain people, but today . . .

*I can't do this.*

Groaning, I covered myself with an oversized hoodie and draped my favorite blazer atop my throbbing head. My decision to drown my sorrows in vodka and simple syrup, then pass out in my rented bedroom—after I ate a gallon of rainbow sherbet and a full bag of potato chips—had caught up to me.

The door creaked opened, but instead of turning to it, I rolled over so that my back was facing it. "I know," I grumbled. "You told me to stop at one lemon drop."

Brianna had watched the train wreck in silence, nursing an ice water. A long time ago, we vowed that one of us would always remain sober. Since I was the inebriated bitch at the bar, she became my eyes and ears. I felt sorry for her, too. Because

I was a terrible, mopey, whiny, drunk friend. Now, I was the terrible, mopey, whiny, *hungover* friend.

"I'll get up soon," I continued. "I just need to lay here for another seventy-two hours." That was the subtle way of telling her I needed to be alone, because I couldn't kick her out of *her* second bedroom. I was in *her* space, using *her* shower, eating *her* food, and connecting to *her* internet for work. "Please," I begged.

Footsteps neared the edge of my makeshift bed. "Boo."

My eyes popped open because the voice was familiar, but it wasn't Brianna. I flipped over, throwing my blazer across the room. "Kay?"

Kayla grinned at me. "Girl, you look crazy right now."

I patted my hair, cringing when I ran my finger over a crunchy strand. "When did you get here?"

She picked up the empty tub of sherbet and set it on the desk. "This morning. Why are you still asleep at noon on a Monday?" She scanned the room. "Wait . . . Did you sleep on a pile of dirty laundry?"

"I couldn't make it to the bed. I'm broken," I mumbled.

"Aw, Pookie." She tossed a pair of jeans into the hamper. "You're going to be okay."

When I became friends with Brianna, I gained an extended family. *Her* big sister was *my* big sister, too. Our decision to attend Howard University had everything to do with the fact that Kay was already on campus. Which meant we had much-needed support.

"Okay." Taking a seat on the floor next to my pallet, Kay crossed her legs. "I'ma need you to get it together." She gestured to all the clothes. "Put a load in the washing machine, and get yo' ass in the shower because you look—and smell—like you consumed a fifth of liquor."

"Preferably sooner than later," Bri added, walking into the room with two mugs.

The smell of coffee and hazelnut wafted to my nose, while the steam coming off the mug lulled me into a trance. I held my hands out. "I hope that's for me."

She handed Kay one of the cups. "No, it's not."

Frowning, I asked, "Are you serious?"

Brianna took a sip from the mug she had in her hand. "As a heart attack." She pulled a bottle of water from the pocket of her robe and dropped it on my lap. "This is for you."

I muttered a curse as I untwisted the cap on the bottle. "I can't stand you right now."

"I don't care." Bri batted her eyelashes at me. "I'll have another lemon drop, please," she mocked with an exaggerated slur.

Gaping at her, I asked, "Is that how I sounded?"

"Don't worry, I recorded you," Bri assured.

Giggling, Kay set her mug down on the rug. "It's funny, too." Apparently, the video of my drunken stupor propelled her to book a last-minute ticket on the first flight this morning. "Anyway, what the hell is going on here, Pookie?"

She was the only person in the world that called me that. I wasn't sure why or even when it started, but it annoyed the hell out of me because it reminded me of Chris Rock in the movie *New Jack City*.

"I've never seen you like this before," Kay continued. "By noon, you usually have the first several items on your to-do list checked off."

"I do have something checked off," I lied.

She folded her arms over her chest. "Like what?"

"I woke up." *I'm full of shit.* "And I drank water."

Brianna snorted. "I'm glad you're here, Sissy." She leaned against the desk. "I needed reinforcements."

"You make me sick." I glared at my bestie. "I can't believe you recorded me."

"Sure did," Bri replied. "You should've seen Ma's face."

"You told Mama G?" I yelled. "Oh God."

My behavior was embarrassing enough without Bri sharing it with the woman who'd become a second mother to me. When were in college, Mama G checked in on me more than my parents did, and almost as much as Grandma. She'd sent us care packages of Detroit-made treats monthly. Better Made potato chips, original and red hot. Faygo Red Pop for Bri and Rock & Rye for me. A case of Vernors soda, which was a staple in most Detroit households and especially good to drink when sick. Kar's original Sweet 'N Salty trail mix. Several bags of Nick's Hot Sauce Corn Chips. Germack pistachios. Sanders chocolate candy. Everything that we could think of that reminded us of the D.

"She's going to call you," Bri added. "She's very concerned. So am I."

"Me, too," Kay chimed in. "You've been through so much. We want to support you."

The best part of being back home was getting to spend time with lifelong friends. Friends that had seen me at my best and my worst yet still loved me. Kay was engaged to her first love, Amir. She'd been in Milwaukee with his family, celebrating his great aunt's eightieth birthday. Now, she was here making sure I was good.

I glanced at my friends, so accomplished in their careers. While Bri's day job as a data manager for the local utilities company earned her a great living, it was her side hustle as a professional gamer that had increased her net worth. And Kay was a talented prosthodontist and had recently opened a private practice with her soon-to-be husband. I was happy for them. Really. But I'd be lying if I said I didn't feel like a complete failure around them sometimes. Especially now that I was unemployed again.

"You both have already supported me." I blew out a heavy sigh. "I had a moment last night. No more wallowing. No more lemon drops."

"It's okay"—Kay waved a dismissive hand—"I needed an excuse to come home early. I have so much to do before the wedding. The last thing I want to do is listen to Amir's mother drone on and on about their important family history. And you know they can't cook, so we had dinner at this hoity-toity restaurant. I felt bad for his auntie because all she wanted was a Big Mac." She sniffed her shirt. "Shit, I still smell like mothballs."

Bri winced. "I didn't want to tell you."

Kay tossed one of my bras at her sister. "Ugh." She glanced at me. "Do you smell it?"

I shrugged. "A little bit."

"A little?" Bri exclaimed. "She's being nice, Kay. It smells like you bathed in them joints."

Muttering a string of curses, Kay pulled her Howard Bison hoodie off and tossed it in the hamper. "Wash that when you wash your clothes, ma'am." She sighed. "Anyway, what is going on with you?"

When Bri spotted the empty sherbet container, she held it up. "You ate the whole thing? I just bought that the other day."

"I was hungry." I let out a loud burp. As much as I hated to admit it, I needed to wash my ass. "Fine. It's me." I struggled to stand, but Bri gripped my wrist and pulled me to my feet. But I didn't go to the bathroom. Instead, I climbed into the bed and burrowed into a pillow. "I'm the problem."

"Girl, stop," Kay ordered, fluffing her long curls. "Let's talk this out."

Sighing, I announced, "I fucked up." In my drunken stupor, I'd hastily sent an email, the *wrong* email to Granny Joyce. You know, the one declining the job offer. That was bad enough, but I'd added an extra paragraph at the end. It was so awful, totally unprofessional. I didn't want to read it out loud, so I grabbed my phone, opened my SENT messages and let them read it.

Kay read the first part in silence. She gasped, meeting my gaze before she finished reading aloud, "*P.S. Don't be mad at me, but Jackson probably deserved that beatdown at the fund-*

*raiser. He's an ass who always tried to look up my dress in middle school. And he used to try to trick me into playing Hide and Go Get It. He's probably a sexual predator. Anyway, Granny Joyce. I love you. I hate that I can't compartmentalize and do this job because I really need the money. My ex-husband broke me. Not my heart, but my bank account. Like I literally have no income, no money in the bank, no home of my own. I'm a bum. Thanks for listening. Love you. Bye."*

"Shit," Bri murmured. "You really went there, huh?"

I shot my bestie a sidelong glance. "Please take my phone away from me if get drunk again," I whined. "I can't believe I did this."

"You have to call her," Bri suggested.

Gaping at her, I shook my head. "No. I'm not doing that. I can't talk to her after this."

"Well"—Kay smacked her legs with her palms—"what else are you going to do? Like you said, you don't have the money. You can't wallow. You made a mistake, and now you have to fix it and get your job back."

"What if I don't want it back?" I nibbled on my bottom lip. "Yes, the email sucked. It was reckless. Stupid. But, I'm not wrong to want to quit."

"How do you figure?" Kay asked, raising a questioning brow. "You said it yourself, you need the money."

"Money isn't everything," I countered.

Kay squeezed my hand. "I know, but—"

I stood, pacing the room. "I'm a wreck. Between Darrell and my financial situation, I can't add Wes to the picture. Especially since I . . ." I squeezed my eyes shut, trying not to think about our last conversation at the fundraiser. The way he looked when he apologized to me, how I felt just being near him.

"What happened?" Bri asked, concern in her brown eyes. "You're worrying me."

"I don't hate him," I confessed. "I thought I did, but don't." The truth was I'd never hated him. Even through the pain, I'd always sensed there was more to the story, more to his abrupt departure back then. I still didn't know the answers, but I believed him. *That* was the problem, because it made me vulnerable to him, open to him.

Bri's expression softened, signaling she understood me more than she cared to admit out loud. Because she felt the same way about Hendrix, wanting to hate him, but realizing she never could. "You don't have to explain to me," she whispered. "I get it."

"I need to concentrate on me," I explained. "I know myself. I'll take this on and get wrapped up in his life, his family drama . . . him." I shook my head. "I can't do it."

"I still don't understand," Kay mused.

And she wouldn't. She was pragmatic and approached life's trials as a challenge. Under normal circumstances, I would've done the same thing, but it was okay to say no. As hard as it was to turn down the money, I had to do what was best for me.

"It's an assignment, sis," Kay continued. "Work. And that's what you do. You get the job done. You can do this."

In theory, yes. But the precarious state of my reality made this goal seem unachievable. And detrimental. "I don't want to. This isn't up for discussion anymore. I'll go see Granny Joyce today, apologize for my email." I grabbed a clean towel and headed toward the bathroom. "But I'm out."

When I emerged from my bedroom later, Bri and Kay were sitting at the kitchen table, bowls of Frosted Mini-Wheats in front of them. Cereal was my comfort food. When I was a little girl, my mother made me compete in every pageant she could think of. As a result, she'd restricted my diet to vegetables, lean meat, fish, and eggs. My mother also hated waking up before ten o'clock in the morning, so I became an early riser. It was the only time I had to myself, and I retreated to my hiding spot with a bowl of cereal. Somehow, milk and sugar made everything better.

Bri noticed me first. Smiling, she said, "You look refreshed."

Twisting in her chair, Kay nodded. "Perfect. We poured you some. Grab a spoon."

A smile tugged at my mouth, and I shuffled over to them, taking a seat next to the window. We ate in silence for several minutes. This was what I needed. Cereal and sisterhood.

"I fired Amir's sister," Kay blurted out.

Frowning, I asked, "From the dental office?"

She nodded. "And from the wedding."

"I told you not to hire her in the first place," Bri chided. "Samira always has been messy as fuck. She stays inserting herself into everyone's business."

I poured more cereal into my bowl. "Still?"

"Girl, she tried to break us up last year," Kay explained. "Now, she's begging Amir to let her be our wedding content creator."

My ears perked up. "What?" It wasn't like I cared about Samira. We never got along, partly because she'd exhibited several sociopathic tendencies. Including her obsession with Wes. While the group joked about it back then, it was downright scary sometimes, so bad that Amir had to get his parents involved.

"I hope you told her no," Bri said.

Nodding, Kay confirmed that she'd turned her future sister-in-law's offer down. "But Amir is feeling sorry for her. He wants her to be included, but I'm just not sure. During the bridesmaid meetup, she insisted on knowing the phone numbers of all the groomsmen."

While I was a member of the wedding party, I'd been unable to attend the group event. Which was a good thing because I was actively avoiding Wes. "I wonder if she still stalks Wes," I mused aloud. When I glanced up from my bowl, I noticed Bri and Kay looking at me with interest. "What?"

"Nothing." Kay tapped her finger against the table. "I'm just wondering why you asked."

*What the hell am I doing?* I quit. In the most inappropriate way, but still . . . Ms. Tea doesn't concern me anymore. *Right?* "No reason," I said.

Kay nibbled her bottom lip. "It's funny you ask, though. She asked about him last week."

"They don't even talk," Bri offered. "Hendrix told me she'd been trying to get a job with Batchelor Corp, but Wes nixed that idea."

*Shit.* So I couldn't simply turn it off. After all, I'd already spent hours on the case. Even if I wasn't going to work for Granny anymore, I owed this information to her—and maybe Wes. I glanced at my phone. "Damn it. The Lions traded McMahon."

"Amir told me about the job thing," Kay said. "She's pretty unstable. I bet she's still nursing that crush."

*Albany, don't say anything.* "I still think we have a chance at the Super Bowl this year." My attempt to appear engrossed in the Detroit Lions—and not Wes—was a front. In reality, I was scrolling Samira's social media pages, noting mutual friends in my private app, and mapping out her movements.

"Pookie," Kay called. "Did you hear me?"

I blinked, peering up at Kay, then at Bri. Both of them were staring at me like I'd missed an entire conversation. "Huh?"

Kay took her empty bowl to the sink. "I asked if you wanted to go to the mall today."

"We're looking for shoes," Bri added.

"Um . . ." Unfortunately, my thoughts had shifted to the case. I grabbed my laptop and booted it up. "I think I'll pass."

"What are you doing?" A knock on the door stopped Kay from sitting back down. She hurried to the door, shouting, "Who is it?"

Bri peered toward the door. "I'm not expecting anyone."

"Uh-oh."

I turned just in time for Kay to open the door, revealing Wes on the other side. Slamming my laptop closed, I tried to pull an errant strand back into the haphazard bun I'd hastily tried to create earlier. Hair was not my thing, and my decision to take my braids out and wear my natural hair for the fundraiser was as crazy as my decision to drink four lemon drops in one sitting. I'd spent the better part of my life going to the salon, so I didn't excel at hair styling. Hell, I didn't own a hairdryer or a flat iron.

Bri must've sensed my dilemma because she hurried over to me and fixed my bun. "You're good," she whispered once she finished.

"Thanks," I grumbled.

Seconds later, Kay entered the kitchen. "Guess who's here." She glanced at Wes, then back at me. "I tried to kick him out, but he wouldn't go."

Wes smirked, shaking his head in amusement. "She didn't try that hard," he teased, shoving Kay playfully. "Amir still in Milwaukee?"

Nodding, Kay gave us the rundown of everything she had to do before the shower. "I'll be glad when this is over"—she sighed—"because I'm tired."

"It'll be over soon." Glancing at me, Wes asked, "Can we talk?"

I tried to ignore the six pairs of eyes staring at me, waiting for me to respond. Standing, I tugged at my oversized T-shirt. "Outside?"

He gestured for me to lead the way. "After you."

The soft breeze against my face instantly settled my nerves. The small patio was perfect, and one of my favorite places nowadays. Michigan weather tended to be a little erratic, but now that the temps were steady, I'd taken to spending most mornings outside working.

I settled into one of the wicker chairs. "What's up?"

Wes took the empty seat next to mine. "How are you?"

Confused, I asked, "Why?"

He rested his elbows on his knees and dropped his head. "I had a meeting with Granny this morning." He peered up at me. "She told me you quit."

As heat crept up my neck to my cheeks, I wondered how much Granny Joyce had said to Wes. And since I didn't know, I figured it made no sense to lie to him. "I did."

"Can I ask why?"

"You can, but I'm not going to tell you."

He chuckled. "Got it. Well, I guess your email seemed a little off to her, so she wanted me to verify that you had indeed sent it."

"Oh, in that case, you can tell her I did." I stood, satisfied that the conversation was over. "If that's it, thanks for the message. And tell Granny that I'll be by to see her and explain everything."

He stretched his legs in front of him and leaned into the chair. "She is expecting you, but before you go, she wanted me to let you know that your letter of resignation has been considered but declined. Her exact words were *Albany is the woman for the job*."

I plopped back down, bumping the corner of the small table with a knee. "Ouch." I massaged my knee. "What?"

Shrugging, he added, "She also wanted me to give you this." He handed me an envelope. "I also have strict instructions to assist in any way I can."

"I don't need your help with anything."

"Open it."

I peeked inside the envelope, then flipped it over. A key fell into my lap. Holding it up, I asked, "What is this for?"

"Temporary housing, in one of the many Batchelor properties," he explained, glancing at his watch. "She's sending movers over around three o'clock."

Panic welled up inside me. "Wait, no. I'm not . . . No."

He lifted his hands up. "You tell her then."

Nibbling on my thumbnail, I paced the small area. "This can't be happening," I mumbled. "How do I handle this?" I squeezed my eyes shut. "Albany, think. Think." When I opened my eyes, he was watching me with interest. "What?"

"Oh"—he pulled out another envelope—"she also wanted you to have this."

I snatched it away from him and opened it. "Oh my God." My eyes flashed to his. "This is money."

"Really?"

"A lot of money." I counted the stack of hundred-dollar bills. "I can't accept this."

"You already know how Granny is."

My heartbeat pounded in my ears as I tried to come up with a plan of action. Except . . . nothing. I couldn't think of anything but the bills I could pay with all this money. I slumped against the patio door. "What am I going to do?"

"Are you asking me?"

Once again, I peered at him. "No."

"If you were"—he stood and approached me—"I'd tell you to take it."

"It's not a gift, is it?"

"Think of it like an advance," he suggested. "For services rendered."

I stared at the money. "Temporary," I muttered under my breath. "It's only for a short time. I'll work my ass off to earn the money, then find my own place."

"Good plan."

Frowning, I pushed past him and leaned against the railing, staring out at the park. I felt him next to me, the heat of his body against my skin. "I really needed this money," I confessed softly.

"Before we go any further"—he tilted his head to meet my eyes—"are you good?"

The sincerity in his eyes lulled me into a sense of security

I hadn't felt with anyone but him. He always had this gift of making me feel seen, even when I was purposely hiding from the world. Another of his superpowers was that he was a good listener. Honestly, our friendship was next-level. I'd be lying if I said I didn't miss that. But . . .

I couldn't share my financial woes with Wes. *Right?*

No, I didn't hate him. but I also didn't like him either. I definitely didn't trust him. Yet, there was a part of me that missed the effortless way we once were with each other.

Swallowing a lump in my throat, I averted my gaze. "None of your business."

"Okay," he relented. "I know the past is long and wide between us, but I never wanted to hurt you. And I don't want anyone else to hurt you."

"Wes, we can't talk like what happened between us didn't happen either. But like I said . . . I really need the money." Closing my eyes, I sent up a silent prayer of thanks. "Thanks for delivering the message."

"No problem."

I shot him a sidelong glance. "We're still not friends."

He chuckled. "I got it. Welcome back." He held out his hand. "Let's get to work."

Staring at his outstretched hand, I retreated a step. And only one step because the space was so small. "Wait a minute . . ." The half smile, half smirk on his lips made my stomach do an odd but familiar flip. "I'm back but not for you."

"You kinda are." He hunched a shoulder. "I mean, you're trying to find out who Ms. Tea is, and that directly impacts me."

"Even so, I work for Granny," I argued.

"Are you hungry?" he asked, ignoring me. "Did you eat cereal this morning?"

"No." I groaned. "I mean, yes. I had cereal. And I'm not hungry."

He walked to the patio door and slid it open. "Sure?"

"Did you hear me?" I followed him into the house. Bri and Kay were still at the kitchen table. "I just told you I'm not here for you."

"I'll meet you at the condo at three. I'm sure you already know where Batchelor Place is, but the address and the details of the lease are in the envelope I gave you." He glanced over my shoulder and waved at my friends. "I'll see you both at the wedding shower."

"Bye!" Bri and Kay sang in unison.

*Traitors.* "Wes, I mean it," I said. "I'm not working with you."

"Have you thought about an interview?"

"What interview?"

"The one you should've done with me a long time ago," he replied.

"I don't need to talk to you."

Ignoring me yet again, he said, "We should catch up. Not just in bite-sized interactions. We need to talk."

"Yeah"—I shook my head—"no. We don't need to do that."

"See you at three, Bug."

"But—"

The door slammed before I could finish my sentence, and I stood there for a moment. I clenched my fists, let out a heavy sigh, then turned around. When Bri opened her mouth, I held up a hand. "Don't say anything." I shook my head. "Granny didn't accept my resignation. I'm moving out today." I stomped toward my bedroom. "No questions."

As much as I needed to talk about everything, I wasn't sure I could because . . . *What the hell just happened?*

# Chapter 9

## *Wesley*

It was late.

She was late.

Three o'clock had come and gone, and I'd spent the day waiting for Albany to arrive. In that time, the only communication she'd sent was in response to *my* earlier message asking her ETA.

**Bug: I'll get there when I get there.**

To a stranger, it might have seemed like I didn't have my shit together. Especially considering the Ms. Tea situation. Yet, I thrived in my job because I kept a schedule. I had a routine that involved breakfast, work, gym, lunch, work, dinner, work. Sometimes, I ended my night with a no-strings hookup. Most times, I ended my night with more work. Rarely did I deviate from my routine.

"What are you doing here?"

"You're late, Bug," I grumbled, snapping my laptop closed.

Albany planted her hand on her hip. "I had things to take care of."

"What happened to three o'clock?" I stuffed my computer into my bag and stood. "You're two hours late."

"I never said that I'd be here at three," she retorted. "In case you forgot, I move on my own schedule."

My current predicament was my own fault. Anyone else who'd behaved the way I did at the fundraiser would no longer be employed by Batchelor Corp. Fortunately, Granny didn't go that far. *Un*fortunately, she put me on "Albany Duty" until further notice. Meaning my job duties now entailed overseeing the investigation into the mysterious blogger intent on ruining my life. It also meant that my only task for the day was ensuring my ex-girlfriend was settled into her new apartment.

Therefore, my office was the lobby of Batchelor Place today. My workstation was the sofa near the window. No dual monitors, no comfortable chair, no privacy. Sure, I could've gone upstairs, but I'd wanted to be on hand when she arrived. Things went from bad to worse when the concierge had a family emergency and had to leave. Since I wasn't the jerk people thought I was, I offered to watch the desk so he could go see about his wife. In essence, I was now doing three fucking jobs.

While I was the acting concierge. I tried not to think about all the work I wasn't getting done today. The contracts I had to review, the meetings I had to reschedule, the data that needed to be analyzed . . . everything was on hold.

*Hell, yeah, I'm irritated.*

Closing my eyes, I willed myself not to react in the way I would've if, say, Erica had pulled this shit. Albany was not my sister, though. Despite my irritation with her in this moment, I still wanted to fuck her. Possibly multiple times over a long period of time. *Maybe forever.* More than that, I needed her to get me out of this situation with Ms. Tea.

I took a few deep, calming breaths before I met her waiting gaze. *Damn, she's stunning.*

The oversized sweats and ratty T-shirt she'd worn earlier had been replaced with black leggings and a thin gray tank under a ripped blue jean shirt. The brim of her Detroit Tigers baseball cap covered her eyes. I wanted to pin her against the wall and unwrap her like a fragile gift on Christmas morning. Slow. Careful.

"Wes?" She snapped her fingers in my face. "You can go now."

Hendrix emerged from the elevator, his attention on his phone as he walked past the concierge desk.

"Hey, Hen," she said.

My cousin glanced up and smiled. "What's up, Albany?" When he noticed me in my little office space, he frowned. "What's up, brotha? What are you doing down here?"

"What do you think?" I asked.

"Actually, I'm curious, too," Albany chimed in. "I asked him the same question and he's yet to answer."

I pinned her with my gaze. "Why does it matter to you?"

Albany folded her arms over her breasts. "Still didn't answer my question."

"I do live here," I replied.

Hendrix snorted. "Barely."

A couple of years ago, Granny purchased the commercial property. While it was once an office building, she'd made the decision to transform it into residential space. Once the project was done, she'd offered all her grandchildren units, which I'd accepted with no hesitation. However, I'd declined to live in the condo full-time. I preferred to get out of the city to my place in Novi, Michigan. The northwestern suburb of Detroit was close, yet far enough to create much-needed distance from my family.

The proof was in the interactions I'd had with certain family members today. It was Monday, so I knew I'd see many of my cousins. What I didn't expect was most of them to walk over and strike up a conversation, mostly about my actions at the fundraiser. Jackson wasn't a favorite cousin by a long shot—for anyone.

Even his siblings didn't seem to care for him—or anything else for that matter. When my cousin, Amelia, strolled through the lobby, she spent the entire time cackling with her friend, on speakerphone, about the guy she'd had sex with last night. Common courtesy wasn't her strong suit, and just like her brother, she spent most of her workday getting paid for bullshit tasks doled out by their father.

The only person I hadn't run into today was Jackson. Good thing, because any interaction would've ended with my fist against his jaw. It was bad enough that he'd goaded me into losing my temper, but he'd continued acting like a damn victim all day. According to Erica, who stopped by to see me on her way to her apartment, he'd shown up for a meeting with a turtleneck on. During a heatwave. Of course, when sweet Mrs. Jeffries from Accounting asked him why he was wearing a sweater in eighty-eight-degree weather, he'd given her a whole sob story about being choked for simply asking me if I was okay.

*Fuck him.*

"I know you keep an apartment somewhere else," Albany said. "There's really no need for you to still be here. Boston told me he dropped my stuff off an hour ago."

Our classmate, Boston, owned the moving company Granny had contracted. He'd always had a crush on Albany and never missed a chance to show off when he thought I wasn't looking. Earlier, his punk ass casually mentioned he wanted to take her out. No surprise he called her after finishing the job. Probably talked her ear off about his new Range Rover and condo on the Detroit River, too. That's just how he operated.

"He also mentioned you had a bad attitude," she added, a mischievous gleam in her brown eyes. She knew what she was doing, just like she knew I couldn't stand that snake-ass mutha-fucka. "I can't believe you slammed the door on him."

Hendrix barked out a laugh. "He probably deserved that shit, Albany. You know Boston is a damn clown."

*My guy.* It didn't matter what happened, wrong or right, Hen was going to have my back. "Exactly," I agreed. "You should be thanking me for making sure he didn't drop anything valuable. You know he's clumsy as fuck. And he was hanging around waiting to ask you out."

"And?" she said with a shrug. "I'm single. Maybe I wouldn't mind going out with someone like Boston. He owns a success-ful business. He's not a fuck boy. He's—"

"A clown?" Hendrix asked.

Albany rolled her eyes. "No." She punched Hendrix's shoul-der. "He's a gentleman. He goes to church every single Sunday, serves on the usher board and everything."

Hendrix cracked up dramatically, nearly falling on the small couch he was leaning on. "That's funny. I just saw him at the strip club last week."

She arched a questioning brow. "What were you doing at the strip club?"

"Minding my own business," Hen replied nonchalantly.

"Still," she pressed, "Boston was paid to do the job. You shouldn't have treated him like that, Wes."

"Batchelor Corp values Black and local businesses," I re-torted. "That's the only reason he got the job."

Albany blew out a frustrated breath. "Whatever. You can go home now."

"I *am* home," I insisted. And I was sure I'd be staying down-town for the foreseeable future.

"I hope you don't think you have unlimited access to me now that I live here. I'll walk out that door and take my chances with Granny."

"I'm sure you will." I folded my arms over my chest. "We

have to make the best of this situation, though. The sooner we figure out Ms. Tea's identity, the sooner you don't have to be around me."

*Who am I kidding?* Now that she was here, I had no intention of letting her go again. I knew it the moment she'd taken pity on me at that fundraiser, offered me an ear, and a little understanding. I wanted Albany Latia Keyes. And I was willing to walk through fire to make her mine again.

"Excuse me?" she exclaimed. "We? How many times do I have to tell you? *We* don't work together."

"Do me a favor?"

"I know you fuckin' lying," she said incredulously. "Why would I do anything for you? Because I was nice to you one or two times?"

"Humor me."

She narrowed her eyes on me. "What?"

"Can you let your guard down for a few seconds? You're so stiff right now. Back straight. Chin up. It looks painful."

"I don't—" She glared at me. "What does my posture have to do with anything?"

"If we're going to work together, you—"

"We're not. This is my job. I told you I don't need your help."

"And I told *you* that your job impacts my livelihood."

"Maybe you should've thought about that before you slept with your client's daughter," she tossed back.

I stretched my neck to relieve some of the tension that had set in. "I told you I didn't sleep with her," I muttered. "And we're working together on this."

"I work for myself," she said, clapping her hands together with each word. "Hired as a contractor by Granny. Not you."

"Semantics."

"Truth."

Hendrix cleared his throat. "Just a quick reminder that we're in a public building. Inside voices." We both glared at my cousin, and he lifted his hands in surrender. "Anyway, I'ma let y'all finish this conversation. I need to meet your friend out front anyway. She recruited me to bring the rest of your stuff in, if you care."

"We're not talking about this anymore," she muttered under her breath.

"That's what you think," I grumbled.

Ignoring me, she asked Hendrix, "Aren't you two on a break?"

Hendrix snorted. "I never said that. *Your girl* said she was done with me around nine this morning because I told her to order her own breakfast," he explained. "Then, she asked me to help get the rest of your things from the car."

My cousin had a love-hate, no-one-else-would-ever-really-be-right relationship with Brianna Cobb. He pushed. She pulled. It was a constant tug-of-war between them. I was convinced they loved it that way, because they were never really done with each other.

Chuckling, I said, "How long are you going to keep doing this?"

"I know, right?" Albany giggled. "When are y'all going to stop playing around?"

"Probably until the wedding," Hendrix mused, rubbing his beard. "I am her plus-one."

It was the first time she'd smiled at me tonight. And it felt like the sun had shone down on me, bathed me in light. I wanted to bottle the feeling up, the overwhelming sense of peace I felt, the calm that washed over me.

"How long has it been?" she asked Hendrix. "Fifteen years?"

"Twenty," Hen corrected. "We were twelve when we sat together on the bus for a Cedar Point trip."

Albany lit up. "Ah"—she clutched her chest—"I remember those days."

Growing up in Detroit, we could count on one activity every

summer. A trip—or two—to Cedar Point, the world-famous amusement park in Sandusky, Ohio. Back then, it was about thrill rides, roller coasters, thick-cut French fries, and funnel cakes. Although the group was smaller, we still tried to make the hour-and-a-half drive annually.

"I haven't been there in so long," she continued, a wistful smile on her face. "Do they still have the Top Thrill Dragster?"

The year that particular ride opened, Albany had insisted we go on opening day because she wanted to be among the first to experience it. We continued that tradition every year afterward, until . . . Well, until we didn't.

Hendrix frowned. "I think that closed a couple of years ago. But they have some new ones you'd probably like."

"We're going next month," I offered.

Her smile fell then. "Oh?" She glanced at me under the brim of her hat, then averted her gaze again, tucking a strand of hair behind her ear.

"After the Fourth," Hendrix added, his gaze flitting from me to her.

"Sounds like fun," she responded flatly. "Anyway, I should probably head up to my new place. Thanks for helping with my stuff, Hen." She looked at me again. "Thanks for helping earlier."

It was a small gesture, but it was something other than ire. So, I responded in kind. "To answer your question from earlier, I'm here because you are."

Her lips parted. "What?"

"On that note." Hendrix stretched his arms above his head. "I'll just take your stuff to your place, Albany." Then he excused himself without another word, leaving us alone in the lobby.

Once I heard the soft click of the door, I cleared my throat and hefted my bag on my shoulder. "I can walk you to your apartment. Give you a short tour of the facilities."

Nodding, Albany said, "Okay."

As we headed toward her new condo, I gave her a quick run-down of building services, explaining everything from con-cierge hours to common areas and community amenities. The building was equipped with a fitness center, an indoor pool, a rooftop deck, two multipurpose rooms, a mail room, and even a coworking space for remote workers. Each unit boasted high-end finishes, including modern kitchens with high-end smart appliances, hardwood floors throughout, and bathrooms with spa-like fixtures. Parking was a commodity in the city, so Granny had purchased the secured lot next door and offered valet parking during certain hours of the day.

"I'm sure Grady introduced himself to you before you entered the building," I said as we neared her fifth-floor apartment. "He's head of security, and his team works twenty-four-seven. If you have questions or concerns, he's the one you need to talk to."

"Yeah, he mentioned it, gave me his card, along with the access codes for the common areas." She stopped in front of her unit. "He also gave me instructions on setting up the smart lock."

"Good. He stayed late because I told him you were coming."

She let out a dramatic sigh. "Fine, I was wrong for that. I'll apologize to him."

"Only him?"

"I'm sorry," she grumbled, unlocking the door with the key I'd given her earlier.

"Thanks."

Albany walked into the apartment and I followed behind her, flicking the light on. The apartment was one of the few fully furnished options in the building. Granny had kept it for important clients or consultants who were in town for a longer period of time.

"Wow." Albany did a three-sixty turn in the middle of the living room. "I can't believe this."

"We call it the J Model," I explained.

She grinned. "After Granny Joyce."

"You got it." I set my bag down on the couch.

Albany walked into the kitchen, inspecting the cabinets, the refrigerator, and dishwasher. She ran a hand over the granite countertop before she turned the faucet on then off. Seconds later, she ventured into the dining room, before making her way to the second bedroom.

She smoothed a hand over the wall. "I have an office again," she murmured. "But I need . . ."

She carried on a whole conversation about supplies, computer monitors, and a special chair for her desk. With herself. It was almost like she forgot I was there. And that was okay with me. I just liked to watch her.

Finally, she turned to me. "Can I contact the concierge for a maintenance request?"

"Yes, they'll coordinate it for you. They can also assist with reservations, manage deliveries, and recommend restaurants. We even have someone on staff that will run short errands for residents. Colby Thomas is the lead concierge. He usually handles the move-in service, but he had an emergency. When he gets back, I'll introduce you."

She tilted her head, surveying me. "How do you know so much about this?"

The question caught me off guard a little, but I replied, "I worked here before I went to work at Batchelor Corp."

Nodding, she set her purse down on the desk. "You were the concierge?"

"Only part-time," I told her.

When I returned to Detroit, I transferred to Wayne State University to finish my undergraduate degree, then promptly enrolled in an accelerated MBA program there. Maintaining a full-time job wasn't going to work, and instead of doing some made-up job at Batchelor Corp, I'd chosen to work close to home. Being a part-time concierge was convenient because I could study while I was on duty.

"That's cool," she said after a moment.

Albany left me in the office to finish her tour. I didn't follow her for one reason. Eventually, she would end up in the master bedroom. I didn't want to enter that space until she invited me in. While she was gone, though, I took the opportunity to respond to some of my emails.

"Wes?" She poked her head inside the office. "I think I'm all set."

I closed the email app on my phone and walked toward the front door just in time for Hendrix to haul some of her things inside. I really should've helped him with that, but . . . yeah, I didn't want to.

He pushed a suitcase into the condo, then another one. "Bri figured you were hungry, so she's getting food," he announced.

Albany rubbed her hands together. "That's perfect."

A rumble of thunder caught my attention, and I stepped onto the balcony. Leaning against the railing, I peered at the sky. The sun was still bright, but dark, towering cumulus clouds loomed in the distance.

"Think it's going to storm?"

Albany's voice pulled me back to the present. I glanced at her over my shoulder. "Maybe."

She joined me, staring at the wall of clouds forming to our east. "Looks scary."

"It'll probably pass over." I stared at her profile. She still had on that baseball cap. Back in the day, she'd gone through a period of hating her hair. She'd purchased hats in every color, for every Michigan team. Unable to help myself, I reached out and tapped the brim. "Are you going to take this off?"

She snickered. "You don't want to see my hair right now."

"Still hate your curls?"

Shrugging, she replied, "No. I've grown to embrace them. I still don't know how to style my own hair, though."

I fought the urge to touch her soft hair. Even after all this time, I remembered how it felt against my skin, the way her curls wrapped around fingers like vines. "Why did you take the braids out?"

"Grandma told me they were raggedy." She giggled. "And a few of them fell out while I was working out."

"We really should sit down to have a conversation."

She raised a questioning brow. "Isn't that what we're doing now?"

I glanced back at Hendrix, who'd plopped down on the sofa and stretched out like he wanted to go to sleep. "In private."

Albany walked to the patio door and pointed at it. "See this?" She closed it. "I can open it." She slid it open. "And close it." She shut it again.

"Away from your house," I clarified. "At a restaurant or something."

"No." She shook her head. "I don't think we should confuse things. We're not friends. I don't want to be your friend." She nibbled on her bottom lip. "In fact, I'm going to actively avoid you unless it's related to the case. I've said this so many times already, but you refuse to listen. I'm really only doing this to help Granny."

*And because you need the money.* The sentence was on the tip of my tongue, but I couldn't say it. Even though I meant it in gest. After this afternoon, I sensed her financial situation was a sore subject for her. I'd already hurt her so much. I couldn't do it again, whether joking or not.

At the same time, I wasn't going to let her keep telling me we weren't friends. Deep down, she knew it wasn't true, which was why she kept saying it. "You've never lied to me before," I said. "Why start now?"

She sighed, hanging her head. "Why are you doing this?"

"Bug, you're fighting this."

Albany flinched. "What?"

"Every time you tell me we're not friends, it's after we share a calm moment together."

"That's not true."

I gestured to the space around us. "So, we didn't just have a nice conversation?"

"Talking about the weather is polite, yes, but it wasn't special."

Closing the distance between us, I reached out to touch her. She didn't move, didn't even attempt to step away from me. Searching her eyes, I grazed my hand over her jawline. "You can't stop this," I whispered.

"Stop what?" she breathed.

"The pull that makes you want to be near me. The inevitable connection we have. It's still there."

She swallowed against the thumb I'd pressed against her throat. "I don't want to be your friend."

A smile tugged at my mouth. "You already said that."

"You're not listening to me."

"I heard you." I inched closer, brushing my nose against her cheek. "You don't really believe what you're saying, though."

When she opened her mouth to talk, I took the moment to trace her lips with my finger. "Oh God," she mumbled. "You can't do this."

"I promise I won't do anything you don't want me to do." I flicked her hat off, sank my fingers into her curls, enjoying her sharp gasp. I wanted to kiss her more than I needed to breathe in that moment. We were so close I could feel her breath against my mouth, smell the hint of cinnamon mixed with hazelnut. "But I'm going to let you set the pace."

"You're so full of yourself." She shoved me away, scrambling to pick up her hat and place it back on her head. "You think you're funny, huh?"

"No, I'm dead serious. But since you want to change the subject, you're going to need me if you want to get this job done sooner than later. Set up the interview. I'll tell you who I've interacted with. Answer any questions you have about the company I keep."

She waved me off. "I already know what I need to know."

"Well, like I told you earlier, I'm here because you are. As long as you're here, as long as Ms. Tea is wreaking havoc, I'm not going anywhere." Before she could protest, I straightened her hat, ran my fingers over the brim. "Sounds like Bri is here."

Albany blinked, glancing into the house. When she cracked open the patio Hendrix and Bri were arguing about whether feta cheese belonged on pizza. She smirked. "It absolutely does."

I couldn't stop staring at her. "What?"

"Feta cheese?" she said, her voice low. "It definitely belongs on pizza." She froze when she stepped inside. Turning to me, she said, "Since you're here, you can grab a piece."

Laughing, I said, "Only if you have another non-feta cheese option."

# Chapter 10

## Albany

*Picture this* ... A sex-starved woman whose last orgasm was the night before she filed for divorce months ago, fueled by visions of the man who broke her heart, a smutty romance novel, and a drawer filled with sex toys.

*Yep, that's me.* And I'm fucked.

I stared out of the window at the slew of people walking down the street. Outside the restaurant, blue skies and mild temps set a vibrant mood, made me want to soak up the energy. The fun vibe of Campus Martius Park, an area in the heart of downtown, was electric. Buildings that were once vacant had been restored, shops were full of customers ... the city was lit with excitement. It felt like another world, a melting pot of diverse cultures, trendy restaurants, and one-of-a-kind experiences.

"Albany?"

I tore my gaze from the fountain in front of the restaurant and met Bri's concerned gaze, before turning my attention to the waitress. "I'm sorry, what?"

The woman smiled. "Would you like to see the dessert menu?"

"No, thanks." Once the waitress walked away, I took a healthy sip of my third mimosa. "So good."

"What the hell is going on here?" Kay asked. She snatched my drink away from me. "I thought we were past your drunk phase. Not another sip."

Brianna snorted. "Too late. She's already gone, Sissy." She snagged one of the brunch potatoes off of my plate.

I let out a loud hiccup. "I told you . . . it's me. I'm the problem."

Kay fluffed her long curls before meeting my gaze. "What did you do?" She glanced at her watch. "And make it quick because we don't have much time."

I took my time answering the question because saying it out loud would make it real. Instead, I ate a piece of the glazed cherrywood bacon. Groaning, I held it up. "This is delicious."

"Babe"—Kay squeezed my hand—"I love you, but the wedding shower is in an hour. And I need you to be there and be the amazing person you are." She glanced at Bri. "Do you know what's wrong with her?"

Bri hunched a shoulder. "Just that she needed to get out before the wedding shower."

"And because I missed you," I added. It had been a few days since I was forced to move. While we'd spoken several times, I hadn't seen Bri since the night I moved in to the new place because she'd been on maid-of-honor duty.

Kay pulled the plate away from me. "Stop stalling. What happened?"

"Nothing," I assured them. "I just wanted to brunch with two of my favorite people."

Raising a challenging brow, Kay said, "On the day of my wedding shower? When I've spent hundreds of dollars on bite-sized food, cucumber sandwiches, and pastel-colored drinks?"

Brianna giggled. "That's exactly why brunch was a good idea, Sissy. Crustless bread and watered-down cocktails are not my idea of a good time."

I held up my fork. "That part."

Kay leaned back into her chair. "It doesn't matter. But I swear if I don't see either of y'all with a plate of stuffed mushrooms, veggie tartlets, caprese skewers, and bacon-wrapped dates, I will kick both your asses."

"Bacon-wrapped dates?" Bri swallowed. "Yuck."

Frowning, I finished my pancake, which by the way was delicious. Roasted apples and cinnamon-spiced maple syrup. *Yum.* "Wait a minute, what happened to the chicken wings, meatballs, deviled eggs, and the fruit table?"

"I'm compromising." Kay grumbled, glaring at Bri. "You already know this."

"Still"—Bri finished my potatoes—"it's bad enough I have to wear pastel colors. You know black is my aesthetic."

Kay twisted her neck, and for the first time I took a good look at my friend. While her makeup was flawless, I noticed the cracks in the foundation. Her shoulders were stiff, her jaw was clenched, and her eyes . . . lifeless.

"It's almost over," Kay breathed, her chin trembling with emotion. "It's almost over."

"Sissy?" Bri's expression softened. "Are you okay? If you don't want to do this, say the word, we're out."

"I'm fine," Kay exclaimed. "Please. I'm already hearing this from Mom. I can't talk about it with you."

Bri leaned forward. "But, Sissy, you don't look happy for someone about to walk down the aisle in a couple of weeks."

The last several months, Bri had been dropping hints that something wasn't right. Amir's mother was one of those society types, like Allisifer. Nothing was ever good enough for her. She'd made the entire wedding planning experience unpleasant with her lofty expectations. This shower compromise seemed to be the tip of the iceberg for Kay, and I definitely understood where she was coming from.

Concern took over, and I slid into the side of the booth with her, wrapping my arms around her shoulders. "Are you okay? I can't believe Mama G hasn't told Amir's mother off yet."

"Oh, she did," Bri chimed in.

That wasn't hard to believe. Genie Cobb grew up in one of the toughest neighborhoods on the East Side. Now, she was deputy mayor of Detroit and the third Black woman to serve in that role. Before that, she helped run Cobb Law LLC with her husband, Marc. Needless to say, she didn't play. Not about her business, her husband, or her kids. *Or me.*

The difference between Ma and Pop, as I called them, and Amir's parents was stark. They were prominent members of the community, but they didn't flaunt their wealth. They were down-to-earth and never forgot where they came from. And it showed in their community work. That wedding shower menu? It had to be Amir's mother who'd come up with it because Mama G hated that high-brow food, as she called it.

Sighing, Kay thumped my hand away.

I rubbed the sore spot on my knuckles. "Ouch," I muttered. "Can I be concerned about my friend?"

"This conversation is supposed to be about you." Kay bumped my shoulder. "Move."

Returning to my seat, I bit down on the last piece of bacon. "Fine. But I refuse to eat bacon-wrapped dates."

Kay laughed finally. "Girl, will you stop with the bacon-wrapped dates. Yo' ass better eat everything else, then."

"What is a veggie tartlet?" I asked.

"Enough." Kay sliced a hand through the air. "Talk. Is this about Wes?"

*Yes.* I pointed my fork at her. "No," I lied.

It wasn't my fault that I'd reverted back to drowning my sorrows. In my defense, Wes's charms had waged a full-on assault on my emotions. So much that I'd spent the last few nights dreaming about him. Our last interaction had only made my desire for him stronger.

Bri's eyes widened. "Uh-oh." She smirked. "She lost our bet."

"No." My denial was as lame as a cucumber sandwich because as much as I wanted that to not be true, she was probably right. I was going to lose the bet. "Shut up."

"What bet?" Kay asked.

"I'm just sayin'." Bri shrugged, ignoring her sister. "You look flushed. Just like you did when you and Wes came back in the house from the balcony."

"Stop," I hissed. Glancing at Kay, I grumbled, "Get your sister."

"*Our* sister," Kay corrected with a smirk. "I have to say, though. You're glowing."

I muttered a string of curses as I waved the waitress over. To sober up, I placed an order for coffee and waited until we were alone again before I put their suspicions to rest. "I did not fuck Wes." *Yet.* Although the thought did cross my mind several times since I moved in. It was a big part of the reason I'd gulped down three mimosas in less than an hour. Because I wanted to forget. I'd even skipped a potential client meeting in favor of bacon, pancakes, and scrambled eggs.

Bri rolled her eyes. "Girl, then why are we here getting day drunk?"

"I know why I'm here drinking," I retorted. "Why are you?"

Bri's mouth fell open. "Solidarity. And Hendrix gets on my fuckin' nerves, so there's that."

Shaking her head, Kay massaged her temples. "This is stupid. Just answer the question, Albany."

"Work is stressful," I offered.

The legwork involved in any case was rejuvenating. Yet, being so close to Wes, interacting with him on a daily basis, was torture. I ran into him in the hallway on most mornings, and I found myself looking forward to seeing him in his gray sweatpants after a run. I liked watching him interact with Erica and his cousins.

Despite everything that happened between us in the past, he was still a pretty awesome guy. The proof was in his willingness to do small things that mattered. Bringing me coffee from the shop around the corner in the morning before he left for the office. Assembling my new ergonomic office chair. Helping me set up a few security cameras in my place. Just in case.

*Our banter.* I swear, I couldn't get away with anything. He called me on my bullshit every time. Lord, he stayed on my last nerve. I liked it, though. *I kinda like him.*

And he was right . . . I picked arguments on purpose when I felt like we were getting too close. Yesterday, I yelled at him for not getting my Big Mac without pickles. He didn't even have to buy me anything, but he did because I told him I was craving McDonald's.

The Wes he'd been for the past several days was the Wes I'd always known, the man that would burn the world to the ground for me because he cared so much. Hard shell. Soft, chewy inside. Like Skittles. It was difficult to reconcile that person with the one who broke my heart. And I reminded myself of that every time I saw him. Still, the more time I spent with him, the more I wanted to spend with him.

Then, there was that almost kiss. The way his gaze had dropped to my lips, the smell of his skin, the stubble on his jaw. The lean, the way he'd slowly inched closer. So close I felt his breath on my mouth and the heat of his body against mine. And damn it, as much as I hated to admit it, I had wanted him to kiss me that night.

My phone buzzed. I glanced down at the screen.

**Wes: Not looking good, Bug. They fumbled the bag not holding on to the Bama running back.**

See! It was little shit like this. He knew I was a diehard Lions fan. And I liked that he talked to me like he respected my opinion on the game. But it wasn't just messages like this. I'd grown accustomed to random texts in the middle of the day. About the weather, about sports, about politics, and even about my favorite TV shows. Yesterday, he sent me an old song we used to listen to, and it immediately transported me back to a time when a copy of the latest Pretty Little Liars novel was my idea of the perfect romantic gift.

Bri leaned forward and whispered, "Do you know who Ms. Tea is?"

I shook my head. "No." While I had a strong suspicion of Ms. Tea's identity, I wasn't ready to divulge that information to anyone—not even Wes. Because the truth could have far-reaching implications for his family relationships.

"Hendrix thinks it's Jackson," Bri said with a shrug.

"It's not," I told her. "He's not smart enough."

Kay glanced at her phone, then groaned. "Now I have to go back home to grab Amir's glasses. I swear . . ." She tapped at her screen, then dropped the phone on the table. "Okay, you've stalled long enough, Albany."

My dominant emotions teetered between dread and embarrassment. *Dread*, because since this morning, my sole focus was his infuriatingly handsome face, his hooded eyes—and his dick. And that was a *me* problem. *Embarrassment*, because I'd vowed to not let him affect me.

The hits kept coming, too. I'd missed an important phone call with my divorce attorney, stubbed my toe on the way to the bathroom, and suffered through an acute allergic reaction to the tiny piece of pineapple that fell in my late-night smoothie. As if things couldn't get worse, I couldn't even make myself come—not even with the big rubber dildo I'd recently purchased from my favorite Black-owned naughty toy company.

The waitress returned with my coffee. I stared at the table, still torn about how much I was willing to divulge. Telling my homegirls everything that happened felt like an act of terrorism against myself. What would it accomplish exactly? Other than highlighting that I was a horny bitch. Correction, I was a clumsy-as-fuck, desperate-ass, horny-ass bitch. And that was the sad part.

Explaining to them that I felt the need to masturbate after one almost-kiss made me feel all kinds of things. Pitiful. Weak. *And still horny.* Then there was the act of admitting it out loud. I loved Bri and Kay, but there was so much they didn't know about me, so much I'd kept hidden from them. Still, I felt the need to unburden myself.

Kay nibbled on her bottom lip. "I'm worried about you, Pookie. You've been so erratic, not like the Albany I know. Honestly, sometimes I wonder if you've fixated on Wes because you can't deal with the end of your marriage to Darrell."

Like a faucet, I slipped into anger mixed with overwhelming regret. And I decided to embrace it. "I have to face my choice to marry Darrell every single day when I look in the mirror," I grumbled, trying to keep my voice even. "My bank account was on life support because of him. I had to sleep in Bri's bedroom for months because of him. The only reason I'm not there right now is because Granny took pity on me after I wrote a sad, rambling, inappropriate email about how my life is a shit show."

"Hey, I—"

I cut Bri off to continue my rant. "My credit is shit because of him. Trust me, I don't need an excuse to think about Darrell and everything that he's put me through. And, no, I don't need to transfer that negative energy onto Wes. They both suck." *Except Wes doesn't suck.*

Kay raised her arms in surrender. "Okay, sis. I got it. I just want you to be okay."

"Well, I'm getting better every day," I confessed. "Sometimes, I'm not okay. Sometimes, I'm a mess. But I'm not defeated. Right now, I'm just embarrassed because I"—I leaned closer and lowered my voice—"broke my dildo trying to fuck imaginary Wes in the shower this morning."

Still unable to meet their eyes, I fumbled with a napkin. When I didn't receive a response, not even a snicker of laughter, I glanced up at them. Only to find both of them staring at me with wide eyes and mouths.

Kay blinked, then snapped her mouth closed. "How did—"

Shaking her head, Brianna blew out a slow breath. "I'm at a loss for words right now. And I'm wondering how . . . I'm sorry. I got nothing."

My cheeks burned with embarrassment. "I know. It's crazy, huh?"

"Very." Kay grabbed Bri's mimosa and finished it. "I'm going to assume you and Wes had an argument or something."

Sighing, I confessed, "No. He's still an asshole and everything, but he's a nice asshole. Every time I see him, I'm hit with these warring emotions. I hate him, but I don't hate him. He's not my friend, but he kind of is. I don't like him, but I do. He sucks, but not really. I told you I'm a hot-ass mess. I can't control my emotions."

Kay narrowed her eyes as if in deep thought. "When is the last time you saw him? I'm just trying to figure out what prompted this."

"He bought me a Big Mac!" I snapped.

"How does that translate to masturbation?" Bri asked, confusion etched across her brow. "'Cause I'm still trying to wrap my brain around this."

"Ugh." I dropped my head against the table. "I haven't had an orgasm from a real dick since the night before I filed for divorce."

Kay fell back against the seat, shoulders shaking with silent laughter. "Really?"

"This is so much information," Bri added. "Whew, chile. So why you don't just get some?"

My gaze flashed to her. "Sure. Why don't I just go out and ask some random guy to give it to me?"

"I don't think she's talking about a stranger, boo," Kay suggested. "You live in the same building with the man you want to fuck. So just pin him against a wall and rub yourself on him."

"Actually, I don't even think she needs to do that. Wes looked like he wanted to devour her the last time I saw him."

I let out a wistful sigh. "That was the night."

"The night you what?" Bri asked. "Because I was there, and you were sitting on the other side of the table eating your pizza in silence."

"Silence because you and Hendrix kept arguing about stupid shit," I tossed back. "Seriously, you can't talk about anything, sis."

"We're not talking about me and Hendrix, though," Bri argued.

Kay cut in. "Anyway, what happened?"

"He almost kissed me," I admitted.

"Why didn't he?" they both asked simultaneously.

"He said he wants me to set the pace."

Bri lifted her hands in the air, before she pounded her fists against the table. "Girl, will you hop on his dick so we can move this party along?"

Nodding, Kay agreed. "I mean, you deserve a good sexcapade, Pookie." She traced the rim of her mug with her finger. "We all do."

I stared at Kay. My heart hurt for her because *her* heart didn't seem to be fully invested in her upcoming marriage. I didn't want to say anything, but if not being ready for marriage was a person, it would be Kay. I wanted more for her.

Bri must've been thinking the same thing because she said, "Look, Sissy. I meant what I said. You don't have to get married."

Kay waved the waitress over. "We're not talking about this. Let's get out of here. Wedding shower time."

THE EX DILEMMA / 127

After we paid our bill, we walked out of the restaurant arm in arm. The ride to the hotel was silent, each of us consumed with our own thoughts. It almost felt like we were walking individual planks into an unknown abyss of our own making. Would this wedding actually take place? Could Bri and Hendrix make it an entire day without arguing? *Will I be able to keep my panties on around Wes?*

Just our luck. When we pulled up to the venue, all three men were waiting outside. Kay slowed down as we neared the front entrance, but then she sped up again, putting them and the hotel in the rearview mirror.

After we'd ditched the shower, I opened my door to find Wes outside. I rested my head against the frame.

"Hey," he said, holding up a bag of food. "Can I come in?"

Sighing, I held the door open, letting him in. I headed to the kitchen. "Thanks for coming. How's Amir?"

Wes set the bag down on the countertop and slid onto a barstool. "Not good. What's going on with Kay?"

I opened the fridge and handed him a beer. "I'm not sure."

"Where is she?"

I glanced back at my bedroom and nodded. "Sleeping. Bri's in there with her."

"Did she say anything earlier? Give any indication that she didn't want to go through with this?"

"No."

After we pulled a Thelma, Louise, and Tamika, racing off to an unknown destination, we were bombarded with phone calls from everyone. From Mama G and Hendrix to Amir and Wes. Kay had refused to talk to Amir or her parents. We drove around for a while before we came here.

It had been hours, and Kay still hadn't said much. Tears were shed, wine was consumed, but she'd yet to offer an explanation. Not that she needed to. I was going to support her no matter what she decided.

"I am worried about her, though," I added. "Something's not right."

"How much do you know about Amir and Kay?" he asked.

I rested my elbows against the countertop. "Why? Is there something I *should* know?"

He shrugged. "He mentioned something to us about a month ago. Said that Kay wanted to postpone the wedding for some reason."

"Hm."

Leaning forward, he cracked his knuckles. "Just doesn't seem like her to do this."

He was right about that. Runaway Bride was more in line with Bri's personality. Kay wasn't an emotional person. She rarely cried, always maintained her composure. In college, she'd stuck to her plan, graduated with an undergraduate degree in three and a half years and went straight into dental school. Amir had proposed three years ago, but she wouldn't even set a date until they started their practice.

"I don't know," I mused. "I hope they can talk, though. They have a practice together, years invested in each other and their relationship. Anyway . . ." I peeked in the bag. "Coney Island?"

"Lafayette. I got a few of everything. Hot dogs, loose burgers, plain fries, and chili cheese fries for you. And a couple of doughnuts."

I opened the box, peered at the mound of fries covered with heavy chili, cheese, and onions. Again. He'd done something so small. Remembering my greedy ass loved Lafayette Coney Island. "Thank you."

He stood. "No worries. Let me know if you need anything else."

I followed him to the door. "I'm sure we'll be fine for now."

"Colby is off work, but I let Grady know that you wouldn't be accepting visitors."

Before he could leave, I rushed ahead of him, stepping between him and the door. "Wait." I placed a hand against his chest, right over his heart. "I really appreciate this."

His gaze dropped to my lips. "You know I'll do anything for you."

I searched his eyes. "You mean that." It wasn't a question, but a statement of fact.

"I do."

Inching closer, I was acutely aware of his reaction to me. He wasn't stiff, but he didn't retreat. He didn't speak. He didn't meet me halfway either. When he told me he would let me set the pace, he meant it. And tonight, I wanted to . . .

Without a word, I reached up on the tips of my toes, clutched his shirt in my fist, and pressed my lips to his. He smelled so good—like sandalwood and spices, citrus and a hint of vanilla. Sensual. Sexy.

I groaned when his strong arms encircled my waist, holding me to him as he deepened the kiss. And damn . . . It was better than I remembered. The perfect balance of tongue and teeth. It was supposed to be a simple, thank-you kiss. Something to test the waters, but not fully immerse myself in him.

Not yet.

Maybe never.

His mouth was so soft, his body was so warm. I knew I should let go of him, pull back, step away, but my emotions were at war with each other over the best course of action. In the end, though, he made the decision for me when he broke the kiss, taking his body heat with him as he put some distance between us.

"Bug, I—"

Nodding rapidly, I blurted out, "You don't have to say anything. I already know." I placed a hand over my mouth. "I was just . . . I don't know what I was doing."

His tongue darted out, and I was laser focused on the movement, transfixed by the dimple on his right cheek, the tiny creases on his mouth. His beard. His diamond earring. Everything.

"I should probably go," he suggested.

"Yes, get out." I opened the door. "Don't call me."

He chuckled, and the sound went straight to my core. I flattened my hand on my stomach as he brushed past me into the hallway. But before I could close the door, he turned to me, gripped my jaw with his massive hand, and pulled me into a quick kiss.

*Damn it.* That was good, too. Maybe it was the force of it, the way he claimed my mouth, or the way his thumb swept down the column of my neck? So gentle. Sweet yet demanding. My knees nearly buckled, but I managed to hold on to the door frame.

He pulled back again, and I was struck by the heat blazing in his eyes. His hungry expression. "When you're alone"—he circled my nose with his and kissed the tip—"I'll have my way with you the way *you* want. Remember . . . you set the pace."

Then, he was gone.

Closing the door, I slumped against the wood and slid down to the floor. It felt like I'd opened a box that couldn't be closed anymore. He said he would let me set the pace, and now that I'd tasted him, now that adult me knew what it felt like to be kissed by him, the question was . . .

Hard and fast, or nice and slow?

*Or both?*

# Chapter 11

## *Wesley*

Ooo wee . . . it's being alleged that Mr. Batchelor
is treading on thin ice. IG is buzzin', but I have it
on good authority that his dalliance with a certain
#PreachersDaughter has landed him on someone's
shit list and possibly the unemployment line. Join me
live at 7 pm for the tea.

The latest post from Ms. Tea followed me from breakfast at the
Hudson Café with Hendrix, all the way up to a few seconds
ago when someone's grandma called me a dirtbag as she waited
at a red light. A few days ago, I probably would've told her off,
respect be damned. But today, I simply waved at her and kept it
moving because Ms. Tea had just performed a good deed, albeit
at my expense.

For three days straight, it had been one thing after another.
The emergence of another blogger who claimed to have exclusive information about me and my family kicked things
off on Monday. Fortunately, this person wasn't anonymous. I
knew her.

Samira Jackson debuted her new gossip page, The Tea Whisperer, hinting that she'd be sharing inside knowledge about the elite Black families of Detroit. Since she'd positioned herself to be direct competition for Ms. Tea, she'd teased an exclusive Batchelor story in her first post.

The breaking news about my family was, of course, about me. It had started sweet enough, with her contacting me to set up an interview to tell my side of the story before it aired. Things took a turn when I declined her offer. Moments later, she released a video "revealing" that I had a three-year-old daughter in Wellspring, Michigan, and had never paid a dime in child support.

All hell broke loose shortly after my attorney got the video taken down before it gained traction. *Thank you, Albany.* She had been tracking Samira's social media activity for days and received a notification that Samira had gone live before it gained traction.

Samira doubled down on her attack by interviewing my so-called "baby mama" to prove that I was a deadbeat father. She'd also uploaded a second video about the wedding shower with scathing commentary about Kay, Brianna, and Albany.

Countless content creators latched on to the drama, dragging Kay for being careless with Amir's feelings—and me simply because it was popular. The ensuing drama pitted several families against one another, and long-term relationships were strained under the weight of the scrutiny.

A lawsuit was filed. *Batchelor versus Jackson.*

Kay called off the wedding.

Granny banished me to my home office until the drama simmered down.

Another lawsuit was filed. *Cobb versus Jackson.*

Hendrix and Brianna called it quits again.

Amir left the dental practice.

Kay disappeared to parts unknown with Brianna.

And Albany limited contact with me to short texts. No mention of the progress we'd made, the kiss *she'd* initiated.

Then Ms. Tea posted her blog. And all the other influencers, including Samira, switched gears to cover yet another episode in the nonexistent Wesley Batchelor drama.

*Is it totally untrue?* No. According to Granny, I could get fired any day. How did Ms. Tea know that?

Even though the "breaking news" kept me in the spotlight, I was glad Kay wasn't the topic of discussion. But the timing was strategic. It posted thirty minutes after the Garland contract was finalized. Too late to impact the deal. Too convenient to be a coincidence. Which begged the question . . .

*Is Ms. Tea someone close to me?* Absolutely.

Albany must've thought the same thing because she called.

"Hey," I answered.

Her voice filled my car over the Bluetooth speaker. "Did you see the latest post?"

"I did."

"I told you it was someone you know."

"Very likely," I agreed.

She grumbled a curse and let out a heavy sigh. "So, we should probably sit down and talk about it."

Unable to help myself, I laughed. "Will it kill you?"

The sound of her soft, airy giggle settled into my heart and squeezed it tightly. "I didn't mean it like that."

"I don't know. You've been acting funny."

She gasped. "What?"

"Do I have to elaborate?"

The line was silent for a moment, before she murmured, "It was too much. I couldn't confront it, so it was easier to avoid you."

My stomach roiled. "And now?"

"I still don't know, Wes."

There was a part of me that needed answers to the questions

that continued to form in my mind. About her past, about our future. *If* we had one. However, I needed her to feel comfortable with me, to be sure *of* me. I had to let her control our movement, whether it was two steps forward or three steps back. "It's okay, Bug. Let's just focus on this case."

"The baby in Wellspring—"

"There is no baby," I interrupted. The last thing I ever wanted was to be someone's deadbeat daddy. My father wasn't the best example, and I would never willingly put another human being through what I'd gone through.

More silence.

"If you would've let me finish," she said, "I was going to tell you that I reached out to your supposed baby mama."

I let out a humorless chuckle. "Ah, you got jokes. What did she say?"

"She told me that she reached out to Ms. Tea as well."

Intrigued, I asked, "When?"

"Months ago."

The pieces were starting to click. "But Ms. Tea didn't post about it."

"Exactly," Albany said. "She picks and chooses what she divulges about you on her platforms. She's a gatekeeper of information about you and your family, which—"

"Could be another indication that she's close," I mused. "Who's on your suspect list?"

"I've already crossed your cousins off the list. Besides Jackson, no one hates you that much. And Ms. Tea uses a VPN, so it's been difficult to track her location. But I know what I'm doing. Now that I've been able to order the equipment I need, it shouldn't take long to unveil her identity. In the meantime, social engineering. I've been analyzing her social media interactions, taking notes. Trying to piece clues together."

Albany had always been interested in cyber security. We used to tease her about her multiple monitors, network mappers, and other software she used to hone her skills. It made sense that she'd majored in psychology and minored in computer science, then taken her talents to the FBI's Behavioral Analysis Unit.

She didn't know it, but I'd followed her career, checked in on her over the years. I knew that she'd earned several promotions while she was at the Bureau and was well respected amongst her peers. Although I suspected she would've left her job to start her firm eventually, the divorce forced her hand before she was ready. I was grateful that Granny had an opening and a reason to hire her.

I checked the map displayed on the touchscreen, turned down Kensington Avenue, and drove a quarter of a mile until I made it to my destination. "What about John?" I parked in an empty spot in front of the building. "Have you talked to him?"

"No. I've tried to catch him, but he's avoiding me. And I haven't been able to rule him out either. At the same time, I don't think it's him. I should know more this week, though."

Turning the ignition off, I asked, "What are you planning?"

"I'm planning to mind my business." She chuckled. "Anyway, I'll let you go. Just stop by when you get back."

"Will you be ready when I get there?" I challenged.

"To discuss the case? Yes. To discuss anything else? Time will tell."

I smiled to myself. "Got it."

"Bye, Wes."

Before I got out of my truck, I scanned the immediate area. Elijah Moore lived in a quiet suburb of Detroit, close enough to keep his ear to the ground yet far enough from the drama and danger he'd once thrived on.

When I stepped into his small apartment, I paused at the threshold. It had been years since I'd seen him in person. Time, too much liquor, and hard living had taken its toll on him. He bore the telltale signs of prolonged medical steroid use for his condition. His once chiseled jaw was swollen, his eyes blood-shot. He was a shell of the man who'd controlled the block back in the day, the man who'd been there for me more than my own father had.

"What are you staring at?" he growled. "Bring yo' ass in here."

Grinning, I walked over to the kitchen. "Some things never change. You still like talking shit."

"I can only be me." He shuffled over to me, pointed his cane at a chair. "Sit down."

"After I put this shit away."

I emptied the bags, organizing his cabinets while I put stuff away. "You like it here?" I opened the refrigerator, checked the date on the milk and the cheese. "They treating you alright?"

"I can't complain." Elijah crossed his legs. "Beats a jail cell."

Elijah had recently been released from federal prison. While my father lived the corporate lie, Elijah was doing the dirty work for their criminal organization. After his conviction and my father's subsequent death, their criminal empire crumbled, leaving Elijah to take the fall.

"Thanks for making the call," he added.

The small senior living community provided the comforts of home with access to dedicated staff support. His apartment had plenty of living space, a master bedroom and bathroom, a fully equipped kitchen, and a balcony. Elijah could live an independent life, while taking advantage of the many services offered to their residents.

"No worries." I joined him at the small table. "Glad I could help."

"It's good to see you." He patted my hand. "It's been a while."

"I wanted to be here when you moved in, but work is pretty busy."

He waved me off. "Don't worry about it. Erica helped me out."

Over the years, I kept in touch with Elijah through letters. Initially, I wrote because I wanted to know information. The police had tied a convenient bow on my father's death, and I still didn't believe the sequence of events leading up to that day. The timeline wasn't right. Eventually, my anger wouldn't allow me to continue my search for the truth, so I gave up my investigation. But I'd never stopped communicating with Elijah.

I tapped the table with my thumb. "Erica told me what the doctor said."

Elijah was estranged from his adult children. My sister and I had stepped in to fill in the gap, splitting duties. Erica handled his health care, while I took care of his finances.

"I don't want to talk about that shit. Tell me what's going on with you," he asked. "I've been hearing some things about you."

I met his waiting gaze. "What did you hear?"

He lifted a curious brow. "A baby in Wellspring?"

Laughing, I shook my head. "You know that's not me, Unc."

The man in front of me, even though we weren't blood related, was the only man I'd ever considered my uncle. He was far from perfect. Never held down a real nine-to-five job. And he was always involved in some shady shit. But when I needed him, he showed up. Even from jail.

"Sure?" he asked.

"Positive."

"Well, that social media page keeps telling all your business. Sounds like you keep fucking up to me. Every time I look online, I see something about you. Public altercations at bars, random women claiming to have your baby, and then that whole craziness with Bishop Garland's daughter. That Ms. Tea got you looking like a no-good asshole. You're on thin ice with Joyce."

I froze. "What?"

"If you're not careful, you're going to get fired."

Granny couldn't stand Elijah. There was no way she'd tell him anything about Batchelor Corp. "How do you know that?"

"I know people. I always told you . . . jail don't stop nothing."

Again, Albany's words came back to remembrance. Elijah still had connections in the city. Even when he was in jail, he always seemed to know when I was fucking up. Almost like he had a tail on me or something.

*He can't be . . .*

Nah, it was impossible. One thing about Unc, he loved me like a son. He wouldn't do anything to hurt me or Erica.

"How is Albany?"

Once again, I glanced at him. "What do you mean?"

"I heard she was back in town."

I rubbed my head. "Yeah, she's home."

"When were you going to tell me?"

"I wasn't," I admitted. "We live separate lives."

"Is that what you call it?"

The feeling that something wasn't right amplified. It was one thing to know online gossip. Anyone with a smartphone could find out information, but Albany hadn't even told her own parents where she'd moved. She kept a low profile, barely left the house unless it was work related. She moved like a ghost, seemingly disappearing into thin air sometimes. I knew that because I'd tried to follow her after we ran into each other at the café.

Leaning back in my chair, I surveyed him. "How did you know she was back?"

He hunched a shoulder, but didn't answer. Instead, he said, "Her divorce is final, right?"

"I guess."

"Don't you think you need to make your move?"

A grin tugged at my mouth. "What makes you think I want to?"

"I know you." He chuckled. "Some things never change. You've loved that girl practically your entire life."

He wasn't wrong. My feelings for Albany were as strong as

they were the day I left her. Even after all this time, I still only knew two things to be true.

My family was fucked up.

Albany Keyes was everything.

"I hurt her," I murmured.

"We all mess up good things. Your father loved your mother, but he didn't deserve her. If he would've lived, they wouldn't have lasted because he was a flawed man."

Snorting, I said, "That's an understatement."

"Wesley," He squeezed my hand. "You have so much anger toward your father, and I understand why. There are things you will never know, things you should never *want* to know. But you should never doubt that he loved you. And he would've never left you on purpose."

The rumors of suicide had fueled my anger over the years because it made sense. The possibility of life in jail could've made anyone want to end it. But Elijah had always maintained there was something more to the story. Still . . . "I don't care. He's not here now. He wasn't shit before he died."

Elijah's shoulders sagged. "You'll never be able to move on if you keep holding on to this."

"I'm not angry," I said. "It's just the truth. *Cedric* cared more about his business—all of them—than his family. We lived in fear for months because of him."

"No. There was plenty of reasons for your mother to leave town. One of them was John Batchelor. If I've never told you anything, remember this. Never trust him. *Never.*"

Frowning, I stood up. The change of subject was abrupt. One minute we were talking about Ms. Tea. Next minute, he was talking about Albany. Now, John. I tried to remember that he was old and sick, but damn. "What are you trying to tell me?"

"So much," he confessed softly. "Maybe one day you'll hear what I'm trying to say."

"Are you telling me John killed my father?"

Elijah used his cane to push himself to his feet. He placed a hand on my shoulder. "I'm telling you not to trust your uncle"—he gave me a strong hug—"and make sure you keep your business offline." His expression softened. "And move heaven and earth to get your girl back. Life is hard enough. You definitely don't want to grow old alone."

Without a word, he shuffled toward his bedroom, grumbling something about salmon patties and dirty towels.

"Where are you going?" I called after him.

"To use the bathroom. I'll talk to you later."

Once I heard the bedroom door close, I took his empty glass to the sink, washed it and set it on the drying cloth. I cleaned the table, swept the floor, then left.

On the way out, though, I pulled out my phone and typed out a text: **Meet me on the roof. Eight o'clock.**

# Chapter 12

## *Wesley*

I was four years old when my mother told me I ran to her bedroom and said I wanted to be Superman. I didn't remember that particular conversation, but I remembered wearing that damn red cape everywhere. Until I flew my ass down the stairs and knocked my tooth out. I threw the costume away that day.

On my sixth birthday, I knew I wanted to play in the Major Leagues. I worked hard to land the starting spot on the team. Short stop. During one of our games, we were caught in a thunderstorm, one so severe we had to take cover. I was transfixed by the flying debris, the wind, the large hailstones falling from the sky, unable to move because I was so mesmerized by the scene. It was the first time my mother yelled at me. Through her tears, she'd begged me to move, to run. My father wasn't there, but my coach hoisted me over his shoulder and carried me to the shelter.

The tornado touched down less than a mile away from the baseball diamond. After the storm passed, and we emerged from the shelter, I couldn't look away from the damage, the miles of destruction left in its wake. Uprooted trees, shattered glass, shredded homes . . . Mom's brand-new Lexus GS 400. I recalled her scream when we spotted it, overturned near the concession stand, damaged beyond repair due to the wind and hail.

The experience changed me. From that moment on, I wanted to be a meteorologist. For some reason, my interest in atmospheric science made my father angry. He hated the thought of his son being a scientist instead of a business mogul, but I was resolute. He'd never hesitated to tell me how much of a disappointment I was to him either. I didn't care, though. I'd spent hours in the library, reading books about cloud patterns and climate trends, and analyzing and interpreting weather data. I watched videos of storm chasers every day, learned how to anticipate risks.

Of course, I didn't end up doing that shit, but I still loved storms, I still found myself watching the sky, looking for signs of calamity in the clouds.

I excelled at science because I was a wizard with all those things that made me excellent in business now. Since I joined Batchelor Corporation, my keen observation skills, ability to think critically, and solve complex problems had helped Granny expand into new markets and avoid bad business deals.

My success proved one thing. *Basically . . . my father didn't know shit.*

The one aspect I always struggled with, though, was patience. At the NOAA Middle School Science Camp, I'd failed the part of the exam that required me to wait for the weather pattern to materialize. I had to fight the urge to run to the danger, not from it. My need for instant gratification had tripped me up often—in business and in my personal life.

Like now . . .

It had been hours since I'd left Elijah's house. His words turned over in my mind on an endless loop. More questions. No answers. Yet, I couldn't stop thinking that the conversation was somehow connected to the social media drama. Specifically, Ms. Tea's identity.

I'd retreated up to my safe space almost immediately, grabbing a bite to eat and putting a couple of beers in a cooler. The music coming from my speaker was low, just soft enough that I could hear it and the sound of the approaching rain.

When Granny let us pick the apartments, she'd given me first choice. My place was the only unit with direct access to a private enclave on the roof, which infuriated Jackson, who thought he deserved the space because he was the oldest grandchild. While I suspected she couldn't stand some of her offspring, she'd never played favorites. She literally picked my name out of a hat.

Although the roof was a common space, my tiny slice of heaven was private. I installed a gate, which shielded the area from view. It had served me well when tenants were using the roof for events. No one knew I was there most of the time, and I'd gathered a lot of intel because of it. Which I'd used to my advantage often.

Lightning lit up the sky and the rain started, but I didn't move. The forecast predicted scattered thunderstorms. Nothing severe, though. I'd taken the precautions before I came outside.

For a brief moment, I considered going to her. Albany hadn't called or responded to my text earlier to meet me here. I thought about sending her another message, luring her up by teasing more information about the case. But I'd promised myself that I would move at her pace no matter how much I wanted to demand her attention.

Albany was *my* storm—a destructive yet transformative force. She was all-consuming, so beautiful I couldn't look away even when I knew I should. The damage was done years ago. My feelings for her were overwhelming with intensity. Passionate. Turbulent. Sometimes chaotic, sometimes calm. Always vulnerable. At the same time, nothing felt better than the connection, the perfect combination of her warmth with my cold front. It was everything.

Closing my eyes, I inhaled the earthy scent of rain. When my phone buzzed on my lap, I peered down at the screen.

Tapping the screen, I said, "What's up, Ma?"

"Hey, son."

I kicked my legs out, stretching in the oversized chair. "Long time."

"I know, I know. We just got back from the cruise a few hours ago."

It had taken a long time to move on after my father died, but when she married Morris Walker, she'd finally started to live again. "Did you have fun?"

She chuckled. "Lord, yes. It was so nice to get away."

"Where did you go?"

"We did the ABC islands," she replied. "I told Morris I wanted to move to Curaçao. It was so beautiful, Wes. You would've loved it."

Admittedly, I hadn't traveled much. Before I moved back to Detroit, I spent most of my time doing stupid shit. Now that I was here, I mostly worked. "Maybe I'll make a trip there soon. Not on a cruise, though."

"I'm telling you it's like a big city in the water."

I enjoyed the excitement in her voice. For years, she didn't smile, and I would forever be grateful to Morris for making her happy. "I'll take your word for it."

"Erica told me about Joyce's ultimatum." She cracked up. "I'm not surprised she lit a fire under your behinds."

The past several weeks had been so hectic, I hadn't really thought about the whole marriage thing. "For them, maybe," I said.

"Your sister is freaking out."

The last time I'd seen Erica, she had scheduled several dates with old friends. Her plan was to marry someone she didn't love, someone with shared goals for success, and someone who wouldn't want her to "pop out a baby."

"I told her to relax," Mom said. "Your grandmother would not want you to marry someone you don't love."

Another bolt of lightning cracked the sky, followed seconds later by a roll of thunder.

"Is it storming there?" she asked.

"Not right now."

"Are you outside, boy?"

I was sure my behavior had given my mother heartburn over the years, but I'd never lied to her. Not even if I thought it would help me. "Yes."

She groaned. "Oh, Lord. I need you to take your butt inside the house."

"I'm safe."

"I worry about you. When are you coming to visit?"

We moved to Wellspring, Michigan, after my father died. My mother was born and raised in the small town on the western side of the state. She had a supportive family, friends, and a safety net she didn't have here.

Wellspring was supposed to be a short stop on the way to something better. She'd suggested she wanted to move south, somewhere like Charlotte or Atlanta. Then, she'd rekindled a flirtation with the county sheriff and declared she wasn't going anywhere.

"I don't know, Ma," I admitted truthfully. "I'm pretty busy."

"Erica told me Albany is back in town."

My sister talked too damn much. "Did she?"

"Yeah. She also said you seem to be enamored."

I barked out a laugh. "Did she say that exact word?"

"No." She giggled. "She said you looked thirsty."

"Figures."

I heard the alert for the rooftop door and glanced at my watch. *Nine thirty.* Albany was late, which meant she wasn't coming. She was as anal about timeliness as I was, and if she was running behind, it was usually on purpose.

The only people with access to the common area were residents and maintenance. Since I was the only one who didn't mind sitting outside in the rain, I figured it was an employee of the building doing a security check.

"Well?" Mom called, pulling my attention back to her.

"What are you asking me, Ma?"

"I'm asking," she said in the singsong voice she used when she was about to get in my business, "are you trying to rekindle your love affair with Albany?"

"What?" I rubbed my face. "I don't want to answer that question."

"You know you can always talk to me," she pressed. "You're so closed off."

"Maybe, but talking about love affairs with my mother is not what's up. Anyway, I may come out and see you next month."

"Oh, good. You can come to the Fourth of July parade. It's a highlight."

If I recalled correctly, the parade was just like any other. Boring. Hot. And long. "I may come after the holiday. More likely it will be mid-month, around your birthday."

"That'll work, too. Maybe you and Erica can come together."

"I'll ask her." I looked up just in time to see Albany at the entrance to my gate. I'd left it open in case she dared to show up. She waved at me. My eyes lingered on hers, but I told my mother I'd talk to her later. "Love you, Ma."

"Sorry I'm late," Albany offered. "I wasn't going to come."

A smile tugged at my lips. Her honesty was both frustrating and refreshing. "Why did you?"

She shrugged, stepping closer. Standing before me, she looked down at me. "I couldn't stay away."

I raised a brow. "Because of the case?"

"Maybe." She plopped down into the chair next to mine and glanced at me. "Maybe not."

Passing her a beer, I stared out at the night sky. "How was your day?"

"Long."

Although I wanted to delay the conversation, just to be able to sit with her, to talk to her about anything other than this, I figured it would be best to get business out of the way. "Remember Elijah?" I asked.

"Of course." She took a long pull from the bottle. "How is he?"

Sighing, I gave her a rundown of the talk I'd had with him earlier, leaving out the talk about her. "Maybe I'm a little paranoid, but something's not right with Unc. Then, I got to thinking. . . . What if Ms. Tea is not one person, but a group of people?"

Albany shrugged. "I'll admit it's crossed my mind more than once. I just can't imagine the Elijah I knew doing this. He's a muscle man. If Ms. Tea threatened to kill your ass, then I'd consider it. Besides, isn't he sick?"

"He's still sharp, though. He knows a lot for a man that's been in prison for over a decade. Even told me to watch out for John."

"Well, that's not a surprise. Your uncle is a horrible person."

Turning to her, I said, "This is going to sound crazy, but I've always thought John had something to do with my father's death. Unc basically confirmed it."

"What did he say?"

"I told you. *Don't trust John. Watch your back.*"

"Say he's right," she speculated. "What are you going to do about it?"

I felt her staring at me, but I kept my eyes trained on the sky. Once again, the rain picked up as fat drops pelted the awning above where we were seated. Leaning forward, I rested my elbows on my knees. "My feelings about my father are so complicated, I don't even know."

"I understand why you would want to find answers, but I'd caution you to be careful. When people feel like they have something to lose, they get desperate. Dangerous. If you open that door, you have to be prepared to deal with the fallout."

My eyes flicked to hers. "I can't not find out, though."

"How about we concentrate on Ms. Tea. Then we can deal with John."

"What if John is Ms. Tea?"

She paused. "We'll cross that road *if* we get there."

I smirked. "You said *we*."

"You won't leave me alone, so I might as well give in and let you feel like you're helping me." A bolt of lightning illuminated the sky and split it into pieces. Thunder followed, the loud snap echoing in the air. "Would it be too much to go inside during the severe thunderstorm?"

I glanced at her while she watched the fast-approaching storm. She was luminous. Even in the dark, she was stunning. Her hair was pulled into a messy bun. She wore loose-fitting, but still sexy-as-fuck pink fleece shorts and a white hoodie over a thin T-shirt. Instead of gym shoes, she had on a pair of white Crocs.

"You're so beautiful," I whispered.

Her eyes flashed to mine. "What?"

Absently, I registered the song playing on the speaker. An Isley Brothers joint. The words fit the moment. She was like an angel. "When we were kids, you were like my own personal angel."

"Wes," she whispered.

"Even after I left. We weren't together, but you were always with me. At my worst moments, when I was so low I could barely think straight, I thought about you. Your eyes, your voice, your smile."

"I don't know if we should . . ."

She was right. Every instinct I had to protect myself was

screaming at me to shut the hell up. But I couldn't leave this roof without telling her my truth. "Can I finish?"

She shook her head. "It doesn't matter."

"It does to me."

"No, for real. It doesn't. I'm glad that you have good memories, that I could help you when you needed to conjure up a vision of me, but I'm not that girl anymore. I'm not an angel. I'm definitely not *your* angel."

"Why do you say that?"

"Because I don't want to be in this space with you. I don't want to travel down memory lane. It's bad enough we're sitting here right now having a beer like I didn't spend years trying to hate you."

"You said *trying*. Does that mean you don't hate me?"

"I could never hate you, Wes. Not really. But it did take me a long time to get over you, to be able to think about you without feeling like I did something wrong."

"You didn't."

"It doesn't change how I felt then. Or how that feeling shaped me into the woman I am now."

"What can I do?"

Her shoulders fell, then she peered at me. "You can accept that we can't pick up where we left off."

"Then where does that leave us?"

"What do you want from me, Wes? I'm trying here. It's taking a lot for me to even have this discussion with you."

"Tell me why you kissed me."

"I wanted to," she revealed. "I just needed to see if . . ."

Her confession was the sliver of hope that I wanted to hold on to. I studied her, noticed the way her gaze dropped to my mouth, the way her hooded eyes assessed me. Even if she didn't like me, she wanted me. And I would give her what she wanted.

"What else do you want?" I slid off my chair onto my knees. Grabbing her chair, I turned it to face me. "Tell me."

Albany's eyes fluttered closed. "Stop."

"Is that what you really want?"

"No."

I glided my hands up her legs, under her shorts. My thumb swept over her core and she shivered beneath my touch. "Tell me," I pressed.

"Please."

Gripping her thighs, I pulled her closer. With my eyes locked on hers, I tugged her shorts off and tossed them behind the chair so they wouldn't get wet. The downpour intensified, spattering on my back, on her legs. Slowly, I slid her panties down, inhaling deeply. Her scent drove me crazy, made me want to set up residence inside her, to consume her.

"Oh shit," she murmured.

I pushed her legs apart. "Is that a yes?" My gaze drifted down to her core. *So beautiful.* Running my fingers over her slit, I found her wet. Ready. I parted her slick folds, pressed my thumb against her clit, enjoying her sharp intake of breath.

She nibbled on her lip, offering me a slight nod.

Then I bent down and tasted her, dragging my tongue from her clit to her entrance. *Shit.* She tasted good, too. Like a sweet treat. And I couldn't get enough. I repeated the motion, licking her from bottom to top before I sucked her clit into my mouth.

It didn't take long for her to come on my tongue, but I didn't want it to end. I wanted to savor her like she was my first cup of coffee in the morning and my last meal of the day. Lifting her legs above my shoulders, I pressed my mouth to her, more licking, more sucking until she cried out my name into the dark.

Damn. I couldn't get enough. I went in for more, bringing her to the brink of another orgasm before I stopped, pulling away from her to stare down at her.

Frowning, her eyes popped open.

"Finish," I commanded. "I want to watch you."

Albany slid her hand to her pussy, sinking two fingers deep inside. Our gazes locked on each other as she fucked herself. I unbuttoned my jeans, shoving them down to free my dick from its cage.

When I pressed myself against her, she gasped. But her surprise was short-lived because she gripped the base and tugged, silently begging me to come inside.

*Not yet . . .*

"Shit," I murmured, resting my forehead against hers as I tried to gather my composure.

Then, her lips were on mine. I cupped her face in my hands and took over the kiss, deepening it. I'd dreamt of her mouth, of her body, of her soft moans. But this was different. Nothing in my wildest dreams prepared me for the flood of emotions that threatened to choke me.

"Are you sure?" I murmured against her mouth. Because if I crossed this line, if I made love to her, I wouldn't be able to stop myself from wanting more.

"Shut up," she breathed. "If I wasn't sure, your ass would be on your back and my foot would be on your neck."

Chuckling, I sucked her bottom lip until she purred. "Then tell me . . ." I wanted to hear her say the words. "Tell me you want me."

"Wes, I—" She gasped when I pressed my dick against her again. "Shoot."

The sky opened up, drenching us as the storm raged on. Unfazed, I kissed my way down her neck as I lifted her soaked tank up. I dipped my tongue in her belly button before descending further. Once again, I pressed my tongue to her, flicking her tiny nub until she fell over the edge again.

She convulsed beneath me, grabbing for me, tugging at me until I stopped. Once her trembles subsided, I kissed my way back up her body, sucking on a nipple through her bra.

"I can't," she whined.

"You can't what?" I murmured against her skin.

"Please."

I pressed my mouth to hers again. "Please, what?"

"Fuck," she grunted.

"Fuck?"

"Me."

I smirked. "As you wish."

My eyes rolled in the back of my head as I buried my dick inside her. *Shit*. She felt so good, so warm. So perfect. I held myself still, just so I could capture this feeling in my memories forever. The feel of her around me, the way we fit together.

As the storm intensified, our movements grew more frenzied. Slow and steady morphed into hard and fast as we raced toward completion. I felt her lips against my face, kissing my cheeks, my nose, my eyes, and finally my mouth. It was demanding yet relenting, give and take, push and pull. It was us, the way we'd always been with each other.

Albany fell over the edge first, groaning my name as she came. And I followed her over, my body shuddering my release.

I felt her pull away before I was ready to let her go, so I cradled her in my arms and stood. I expected her to buck against me, to demand that I put her down, to pretend that this didn't happen. Instead, she kissed me.

"Take me inside," she whispered against my mouth.

I smiled at her choice of words.

Giggling, she dropped her head to my shoulder. "I meant that literally, in every way you could imagine."

Winking at her, I said, "Good to know."

# Chapter 13

## *Albany*

*Warning.*

I pressed my hands against the cool gray tile and ducked my head under the rainfall showerhead, reveling in the feel of the hot water against my scalp, flowing down my back.

*Danger.*

The man behind me coaxed me to yet another orgasm with his fingers. One massive arm wrapped around me, holding me close to his hard body.

*"Don't stop."*

"Never," he muttered against my skin, sinking his teeth into my shoulder.

*Damn, I didn't mean to say that out loud.*

It was the truth, though. In this moment, when the storm was raging outside and inside, I never wanted him to stop. His hands were everywhere, gliding down my back, over my ass, cupping my breasts. His mouth . . . He was a wizard. He must've licked every inch of my body, kissed every wrinkle, every stretch mark.

And his dick . . . so thick, so hard. Admittedly, I hadn't had a good look at it because I was preoccupied with how he filled me up. The perfect fit, like I was made for him and him for me.

Then, he was gone, taking the heat of his body with him.

Yes, I whimpered, reaching for him like a damn fiend.

Before I could turn around, he was back, pressing his erection against my back, assuring me that he wasn't going anywhere. He flicked his tongue over the back of my neck, then kissed a trail of wet kisses over my shoulders.

My head fell forward on a sigh as Wes inched inside, winding me up again with his impressive fuck game. Time and experience had been good to him. Sixteen-year-old Wes was sweet, but he wasn't like this Wes. Virile and demanding, yet gentle and giving. In a few short hours, he'd mastered my body, in every way I could imagine. We'd made love from the kitchen counter to the wall in the hallway, now in the shower.

After tonight, I'd never be the same. That much I was certain. But the past between us was complicated. My heart was under lock and—

I groaned. "Shit."

He'd fucked me out of breath, because it was a struggle to take in air, to see, to hear, to feel anything but him. My knees gave out when he slammed into me hard. But he was quick on his feet, turning me around, lifting me up, and sinking inside again.

I cried out as pleasure rippled outward from my stomach to my extremities.

"So good," he muttered. "Tell me . . ."

I knew what he wanted. I knew it the first time he asked me outside. Which was hot, by the way.

Us.

A damn thunderstorm.

My arousal had reached a pinnacle, something I couldn't come down from. I felt the same way now, like I was floating on a cloud of bliss, ruined for anything or anyone else.

"Oh God," I whispered, digging my nails in his scalp as he moved, slow, then fast, then slow.

He was tearing me apart, driving me crazy in the best way, then fusing me back together. I'd lost all control, and I was hopeless to stop the destruction. But . . .

"I'm coming," I announced, as my orgasm ripped through me, shattering me into tiny pieces.

Wes gripped my chin with one hand, sucking my tongue into his mouth as he succumbed to his pleasure. We stayed like that for a moment, tangled in each other. Seconds later, the shower stopped, and I was flying. Soon I was lying flat, engulfed by the soft fabric of his comforter as he dried me off with a plush towel. Slowly.

The simple touch of his hands to my body lit the smoldering fire between us again. But instead of making love to me again, he climbed into bed and wrapped his arms around my waist.

"Sleep," he commanded against my ear.

His words had the opposite effect as my body tensed. The haze was fading fast and my mind started drifting to tomorrow. What would happen when I woke up? Could I handle it?

*I need to go.*

"Bug," he muttered against my skin. "Tomorrow is another day. We don't have to make any promises."

I swallowed against the hard lump in my throat. The tenderness he'd shown, the way he'd taken care of me tonight, nearly made me lose my composure. But . . .

*I'm so sleepy.*

Torn, I considered slipping out in the middle of the night—after he fell asleep. There would be no awkward goodbyes, no weird solution to the problem, no morning wood, no repeats.

As my eyes fluttered closed again, I cemented the deal with myself. Sleep now. Escape later.

I woke with a start, my eyes frantically searching in the dark for anything that seemed familiar. Glancing over my shoulder, I noticed the bed was empty. *Where the hell is Wes?*

The bathroom door was ajar slightly, providing a sliver of

soft light in the massive bedroom. Scanning the area, I took in the rich mahogany wood, tall ceilings, floor-to-ceiling windows, and dark furniture.

Briefly, I wondered if a woman had decorated the space. It felt too sleek, too modern. Jealousy flared to life, starting low in my belly and spreading upward to my heart.

I let out a heavy sigh, raked my fingers through my still damp hair. I didn't need a mirror to know I looked a hot mess.

*Where are my clothes?*

My eyes caught the white fabric of my hoodie draped over a chair in the corner. I scooted off the bed and tiptoed to the chair. My shorts were nowhere to be found, so I slipped my hoodie on and zipped it up.

"Where are you going?"

I jumped, clutching my chest. "Oh shit." I tried to steady my breath. "You scared me." My eyes landed on him, seated in another chair on the far side of the room. "What are you doing over there?"

He stood, setting a glass of amber-colored liquid on a small table. "Waiting for you to wake up and try to leave."

A blush worked its way up my neck as I assessed him, looking like a glorious specimen of lean muscle. The low light from the bathroom gave me a view of his large, naked frame.

"Do you just drink liquor without any clothes on?" My voice came out raspier and more unsure than I'd hoped. "I mean, I'm sure you have some joggers or something."

His low chuckle awakened the part of me that wanted him to throw me on the bed and make love to me again. "I prefer to sleep like this."

Swallowing, I nodded, fingering the edge of my hoodie. "Okay, well . . . I better go."

Wes disappeared into what I assumed was a closet and returned seconds later in a pair of black joggers.

*Damn, he looks just as good in those.*

I stiffened as he approached me. "Wes, I—"

He handed me a pair of shorts. "Take these. I don't want you walking down to your place like this."

Without a word, I slipped the basketball shorts on. "Thanks," I grumbled.

Strangely enough, I couldn't look at him. I couldn't even muster up a fake smile. Because if I talked to him, then I wouldn't want to talk. I'd want to stay. I'd want to spend more time wrapped around him.

"Bug," he said, his voice low and dangerously seductive.

Damn it. It should've repulsed me, to hear him call me that name. Instead, it made me feel everything good about us and none of the bad.

All those years of resentment. All the anger, the hurt . . . I still wanted him. Tears filled my eyes, and I plopped down on the bed. "When you left, I was sick," I confessed. "I literally couldn't eat. I couldn't sleep. I couldn't function. It wrecked me, Wes."

He kneeled in front of me, squeezed my thighs. "I'm so sorry, Bug."

The first tear fell, giving the others permission. I didn't bother wiping my face, though. "I don't want to be in that position again." I wet my lips, tasting my salty tears. Evidence that I was still fallible, that I'd willingly walked into this hell because I wanted to know what it felt like to be with him again. I'd betrayed my vow to myself, and now I was paying for it.

"What can I do?" he asked, searching my eyes.

I shrugged. "Nothing."

He brushed a thumb under my eye, cupped my face in his palm. "I want to say so much to you, but . . ." He kissed me tenderly, almost reverently. "Excuses don't change what happened."

"Exactly," I agreed. "I enjoyed tonight. But this can't happen again. I'm just starting to feel like myself after my divorce.

Being with you will only hamper my progress. I've fought too hard, too long, to move forward. I don't want to look back."

He nodded. "If that's what you want."

The way he'd acquiesced so quickly irritated me. Because he'd just literally transported me right back to the carriage house. Naked. Wanting him. Ready to give him every part of me. Only for him to walk away without a fight. The difference was, I would've fought for him back then. But not today. Never again.

My shoulders fell on a sigh. "Yeah." I stood, staring down at him. "It's what I want."

When Wes peered up at me, I was struck by the fire in his eyes. He frowned. "Is that it? You're going to walk away."

Something had shifted in the atmosphere. We were at the point in the conversation where we would either start fighting or start fucking.

"You don't want to go," he added, tilting his head to the ceiling as if he was angry. *He* was angry?

Brushing past him, I muttered, "I need to get the hell out of here. Bye, Wes."

"I get it," he called.

I froze. "Get what?"

"You don't want to get hurt. But don't run from this."

Whirling to face him, I yelled, "Stop. I"—I smacked my chest hard for emphasis—"am the not one who ran away."

He approached me, unfazed by my rage. "You're afraid."

"You're damn right I'm scared. And I don't like feeling that way."

"Then don't. Bug, we can work—"

I shook my head. "No. This can't work."

"It will work. It worked tonight."

"Sex. Sex works. But other than that . . . I don't trust you!" As if I wasn't vulnerable enough, a sob broke through as more tears streamed down my cheek. "You broke my heart."

His eyes connected to mine. The emotion shining back at me was unmistakable. Shame. It was so real, so raw, I almost went to him. Almost. "Please," he whispered.

"After I gave you everything I had," I shouted. "It's been sixteen years. And my body, my soul, my heart still feels that pain as if it happened yesterday. The loneliness. The self-doubt. Why would I want to put myself back in the position to go through that again."

"It won't happen again." He reached for my hand, but I pulled it from his grasp. "I'm not the same person I was then."

"And despite what you think, *I'm* not the same person I was then."

"Tell me who you are, then. Because I want to know you."

Squeezing my eyes shut, I willed the tears to stop falling. "That's where we differ, then. Because the only thing I wanted to know about you was how good your dick would make me feel."

He rocked back on his heels, his eyes wide. "Wow." To my surprise, a slow smile spread across his lips. He stalked toward me, pressing his erection against my stomach. "Is that so?"

*Shit, he still smells good.* Like soap and sin, and something unmistakably Wes. And my body reacted to him, to the heat of his skin. "Move."

"Nothing can match what we feel for each other." He nipped my ear lobe. "No one."

My heart raced as my body skipped ahead to the potential orgasm. I was burning up, consumed with need for him. But I was also a stubborn bitch. Taking a deep breath, I backed away. "Maybe so. But I'm willing to risk never feeling it again."

"Why deny it? I'm part of you, just like you'll always be part of me. You used to say we were meant to be, that we were soulmates."

"I was a teenager, obsessed with *Dawson's Creek*."

"You were #TeamPacey."

The fact that he remembered that made me want to rethink my earlier position and throw myself on him. "That's neither here nor there."

"So you say."

"Last night, you said we didn't have to make promises. You told me to set the pace. Now, you're playing dirty."

He lifted his arms up. "You're right. I meant everything I said. I never want to make you feel pressured. If you want me, you have to tell me."

Searching his eyes, I fought the urge to lean into him, to wrap my arms around him. *Where would that get me?* "This was a mistake. I thought I could do this, but I . . . I can't."

I walked to the door, pausing at the threshold. Turning around, I walked back to him, stood in front of him. Even now, I wanted to drown in him. I stepped closer, so close I felt the steady beat of his heart against mine. He brushed his thumb over my cheek.

*Damn tears . . .*

He placed a gentle kiss to my forehead, trailed his mouth down the ridge of my nose and over my mouth. "Bug, stay."

I pressed my lips to his one more time. "Bye, Wes."

I didn't mean to laugh.

Well, it was more like a tiny snicker. In my defense, though, I was hot—and a little hungry. The church thermostat had been set to hell, and I wondered if it had been done to scare us into accepting Jesus as our Personal Savior.

"Look at him," Grandma muttered, gesturing toward the huge picture of my grandfather in front of the sanctuary. "What did I see in him? Looking like a broke Barry White. Hair looking thin and greasy. I should call him Slick Back. Yep, that's my new name for him."

I tried to hide my mortified yet slightly amused facial expression under a handkerchief. Grandma had been like this all morning, making little comments with a straight face while I . . . Yeah, my poker face was still asleep.

"I just don't understand how he cheated on me with his small ding-a-ling."

I snorted—loudly. Several pairs of eyes landed on me, and I sunk into the pew. It was already bad enough Grandma called me at five o'clock this morning, after I'd spent the night fucking Wes, to tell me we were coming to the memorial for a man I'd never met, a man *she* couldn't even stand.

The pastor's wife glared at me. The older woman had been terribly rude since we walked into the temple. Of course, that was probably because Grandma swatted her hand away when she attempted to hug her.

"You have to stop, Grandma," I murmured. "They're going to kick me out of here."

"They could try," Grandma said, just loud enough so that the women in front of us could hear. "I will own this church before the day is out. Bishop Matthews is a charlatan anyway. He was a drug kingpin from way back."

"What?" Okay, so that came out louder than I expected. Three old women in nurses' uniforms shushed me simultaneously. To my right, I saw an usher inching closer to us, but he froze in place when Grandma glared at him. "Are you serious?" I whispered.

Admittedly, I hadn't visited my grandmother's hometown much. I kept in touch with some of her family on social media, but I tended to stay close to Detroit on the rare occasions I'd visited home.

"As a heart attack," Grandma responded. "I've known Floyd for years and, let me just say, he's more likely to end up sipping margaritas in hell than praising God in heaven."

The woman in front of us gasped, craning her neck to glance at us. Grandma smiled sweetly. "Turn around, Mabel. I'm not talking to you."

Granny Joyce shook her head. "I can't take you anywhere, Liv."

I cut her a sideways glance. Like Grandma, she was stone-faced, her eyes fixed on the minister who was still praying for my grandfather's soul.

*I don't even know why I'm here.* I didn't know him or the people sitting in the front row accepting hugs and kisses from people offering condolences for their loss. I didn't recognize anyone. Except for my parents, who were seated a few rows ahead of us.

It was the first time I'd seen them since I'd been in town. Luckily, they hadn't seen me yet. And I was hoping to keep it that way. My plan was to exit stage left as soon as the eulogy was complete.

Ram in the Bush Tabernacle was filled with people, though. The old church had seen better days. The ceiling looked like it could use some patchwork, the white paint had faded to a dull yellow, and the muted stained-glass windows were dirty.

*Did I mention, it was hot as hell?*

"What happened to air conditioning?" I mumbled to myself.

Grandma snickered. "Knowing Floyd, he probably purchased his new Benz with the repair money."

The minister hollered, "In the name of Jesus!"

The organist started to accompany him, playing to accentuate the message.

One of the men in the pulpit responded with, "Gon' head, Passa. Preach."

I glanced around at the various people. Some were crying loudly, others were scrolling on their phones. One woman was fanning herself frantically while the man next to her was snoozing.

Growing up, I used to love going to church. *Not this church.* When I met Bri, her parents invited me to their church on the West Side of Detroit. My first visit was quite the experience, definitely different from the Catholic church Allisifer dragged me to on Christmas and Easter Sunday.

*This church, though?* The atmosphere was all wrong. It made me uncomfortable. "Can we go now?" I asked hopefully.

"Not yet, Pooh."

A loud wail caught my attention. Several people were circling grandfather's fake widow, as she crouched in front of the picture, holding an urn in her hands. Except, there were no tears, no streaks in her heavily caked foundation. Her quick weave was frozen in place like the permanent scowl on her face.

The old paper fan I'd been using snapped right before she broke out in an off-key rendition of Teddy Pendergrass's "When Somebody Loves You Back" in the middle of the twenty-minute prayer. Usually that would've been my cue to leave, but one sideways glance from Grandma kept me rooted to my place at her side.

"Isn't that something?" Granny Joyce grumbled, shifting in her seat. "That must've been their song."

"I think 'As We Lay' would've been more appropriate for the occasion," Grandma muttered. "Or 'Part-Time Lover.' Half the women in the first two rows were his hoes."

Yep, I laughed again.

This time garnering the attention of Fake Wife, as I called her. She paused the theatrics to glare at me. But then her gaze shifted to Grandma, who tilted her head forward and grinned.

I half expected the woman to wail on us, accuse us of disrespecting my grandfather's memory. Instead, though, she just stared. The look in her eyes wasn't anger, not even hatred. It was fear.

I glanced at Grandma. "What's going on here?"

Granny Joyce patted my knee. "Everything is going to be alright, Albany."

Standing slowly, Grandma scanned the room. I braced myself, prepared for the worst, but silently hoped for the best. I wasn't dressed to fight. Not in this tight-ass dress I'd slipped into or my three-inch heels. Hell, my body still ached from last night. I needed a heating pad, not a potential melee at a memorial service.

The sanctuary was silent. My father stood and made his way back to us. When he finally noticed me, he frowned. Once he reached us, Grandma held up her hand and he stopped in his tracks.

"Grandma," I whispered.

"It's okay," Granny Joyce assured.

"Do I need to take my shoes off?" I asked.

She shook her head. "No." She turned to my father. "Sit down, Gregory."

My father obeyed, sliding into the pew behind us. Up front, I noticed Allisifer staring at me. *Everyone* was staring at me, at us.

Finally, Grandma sighed. "Let's go. I've done what I came to do."

Confused, I scrambled to grab my purse and followed her out. As we breezed down the long aisle toward the door, I felt someone close on our heels and briefly wondered if it was security. Or Fake Wife.

But it was neither of them. It was my father.

"Mother," he called softly. "Why did you do that? You embarrassed yourself and me."

As usual, it was all about him. "Dad, please." I stepped in between them. "Just let it go."

Grandma and my father had a contemptuous relationship, partly because of how he'd treated her when she left my grandfather, but mostly because of me. He resented her for advocating for me, for insisting that he take care of his responsibilities when my mother died.

"When did you get back?" Allison asked, stepping into the foyer.

"I've been back," I replied.

She folded her arms over her chest. "Care to explain why you haven't called us? Darrell has been looking for you."

"Wait a minute," Grandma said. "What you won't do is come at her in front of me."

This was our dynamic. My father and Allison ganging up on me and Grandma defending me. I knew it would happen eventually, just not now. Not in the middle of a church in Ypsilanti. Not while a funeral service was going on in the sanctuary.

An usher approached us and ordered us to leave the grounds. Once we cleared the doors, all hell broke loose. Everyone talked at once. Dad accusing Grandma of being performative. Grandma yelling at Dad for being a traitor. Allison shouting at the top of her lungs about my disrespectful nature. Granny Joyce defending my grandmother.

I stood there, watching the scene unfold and wishing I could blink myself back to my apartment. Overwhelmed, I turned to leave and ran into someone's hard chest. "I'm sorry," I grumbled.

The argument stopped.

I peered up at the man I'd nearly bulldozed during my attempt to flee. "Moses?"

My brother grinned, pulling me into a tight hug. "What's up, sis?"

# Chapter 14

## *Wesley*

*B*oom.

I turned up the television, hoping to drown out the sound. Seconds later, another knock followed. Then, another.

One of the reasons I preferred not to stay at Batchelor Place was the unexpected but not surprising visits from family members. Everyone had access to me through a short elevator ride or a trip up the stairs. If it wasn't my sister bringing me family drama or my cousin, Cyn, with her wild puppy, it was Hendrix eating all my food.

Make no mistake, it was someone from my family. An outsider would've had to go through Colby or whoever was working the concierge desk today.

*It could be Albany.*

On second thought . . . Burrowing into my couch, I flipped the channel to Syfy. Today was *Sharknado* marathon day.

Albany had made her position perfectly clear when she left in the wee hours of the morning—even though I begged her to stay. Turnabout was fair play, right? I'd left her, so she left me. But she wasn't that type of person. At least, she didn't used to be. She kept telling me I didn't know her anymore. Yet, as much as she'd tried to tell me she'd changed, she still seemed like the Albany I loved beyond reason—except everything about her was better.

Something had passed between us last night, something deeper than sex, something deeper than the past. Despite what she'd said, our connection was as strong now as it was then. I felt it in the way she responded to me, the way she'd started to leave, then came back. And she *was* running from it.

*I promised to let her set the pace.*

She was scared. I couldn't blame her, though. When she'd described how she struggled after I moved away . . . my heart shattered at her confession. Because I would've done anything for her, I would've moved heaven and earth to protect her. I never thought I'd have to protect her from me.

After she left, I couldn't sleep. I couldn't unsee the look in her eyes, the devastation that I'd left there. Since then, I'd been in the same position. My phone was on DO NOT DISTURB, and my laptop was closed.

*Boom.*

"Wes," Erica called. "I know you're home."

I finished the beer I'd opened moments earlier and made my way to the door. I still had no intention of letting her in, but I needed to be sure she was okay before I could sufficiently ignore her.

"Please," she whined. "I'm having a panic attack. I don't know what to do."

*Shit.*

"That guy I went out with last night . . . He did something and I—"

I tugged the door open and yanked her inside the house. "Did he hurt you?" I studied her face, looking for signs of abuse. "Where is that muthafucka?"

Erica sighed. "No, he didn't hurt me."

"Then, what?"

"He turned my proposal down."

Grumbling a curse, I walked away from her and plopped back down on my sofa. She was still talking, but I'd effectively tuned her out. The tornado just touched down in fictitious Manhattan and the sharks were wreaking havoc in the subway tunnels.

Eventually, she sat next to me. "What are you doing?" she asked. "Did you hear a word I said?"

I glanced at her. "No."

"Wes, I don't know what to do. I thought he was a good prospect. He's successful, works hard, and he's celibate."

"What?"

"I figured the best person to marry was someone I wouldn't really fall in love with. I don't want to deal with heartbreak. I'm not ready to be invested in someone like that. But he turned me down, called me high maintenance. Said I wasn't his type. His type for what? Separate bedrooms, a shared dinner here and there, and companionship?"

"Could that be the reason he turned you down? Most men would consider separate bedrooms a deal-breaker."

"It shouldn't be. He told me he was asexual."

I choked on the water I'd just gulped down.

"I figured it was a win-win scenario," she continued, oblivious to how uncomfortable this conversation was for me. "I didn't have to be intimate with him, but we could've built an empire together."

I blinked. "I guess I'm just confused why you thought this was a good idea."

"Wes, you know me. You know what I've been dealing with. My last relationship ended with flat tires, court dates, and hard feelings. I just wanted this marriage thing to be easy."

"Don't you have some friends to talk to about this?"

"Cyn is holed up in some bungalow with one of her boyfriends." She pouted. "Besides, you *are* my friend."

At four, my sister declared that I was her best friend. Through the years, she'd maintained that stance. No matter what she was going through, she typically came to me first.

A night out with the girls? I held her hair up while she hurled in my toilet.

Dreary mood? Dinner at her favorite restaurant followed by a rom-com movie night.

Bad breakup? She used my shirt as her Kleenex as she bawled her eyes out.

Shitty boyfriend? I beat his ass. Period.

*But . . .*

Today, I wasn't in the right headspace to deal with Baby Sis. I didn't have the energy to comfort her or help her come up with a plan. Today, I was in my own little funk. Rejected. Dejected. A little angry. Mostly sad.

"I'm gonna fail at this, too," she mumbled, her voice so low, so small.

Frowning, I peered at her. "At what?"

"The test." She shrugged.

Still confused, I asked, "You have to help me out here, Erica. What are you talking about?"

My sister sniffed into a tattered piece of tissue. "I feel like damaged goods. I'm never going to find someone to marry me."

Erica was diagnosed with obsessive-compulsive disorder about a year ago. Up until that point, she'd hid it well, but then the pieces started to click together. The anxiety, the compulsions she'd waved off as being careful, the way she obsessed about everything. Her house was pristine, not a single thing out of place. Her cabinets were organized by color and size.

After her last breakup, though, things spiraled out of control. She'd become abusive to herself, overly consumed with morality. Her condition started to disrupt her work life to the point where she'd refused to come out of her office for a meeting.

Seeing my sister curled into a fetal position behind her desk, crying her eyes out, begging me to tell her what the hell was wrong with her, haunted me. I still remembered carrying her out of the building and bringing her to the hospital. She sobbed for three weeks straight. I moved her in with me and took care of her.

It had been a long, slow road of therapy and internal work. But since then, she'd been laser focused on working through it, taking her meds, and continuing her sessions with her psychologist. She was better. But I still worried about her.

Sitting up, I rubbed her back. "Baby Sis, you got this."

Tilting her head toward the ceiling, she let out a tiny whimper. "I'm glad you think so. It's just . . ." She dashed a tear from her cheek. "I've been doing the work, but there are times when I just want to hide, when I feel like I'm sinking, when I feel like the worst person in the world. And I can't shake it off. It's hard to stop obsessing about it, asking myself all the questions. What if I fail this assignment? What if Granny is disappointed in me for not rising to the occasion? What if there is no man willing to be with me knowing about my OCD? What if I mess up?" Another sob broke through. "I feel I'm already so behind on everything. I can't think, I can't focus. Now this . . . I'm a wreck."

I wrapped my arm around her shoulder and pulled her to me. Kissing her brow, I whispered, "You're not a failure, and I promise you, Granny would never be disappointed in you. I swear you're her favorite."

She let out a watery giggle. "I think you're it."

"Nah"—I shook my head—"she loves you. She *knows* you."

"What if you're wrong?"

"I'm wrong about a lot of things, but not this. I really feel like you're putting too much into this whole marriage thing. Granny isn't going to disown you if you decide to stay single."

"She sounded so upset," Erica said. "I've never seen her like that."

"Yes, you have."

She rolled her eyes. "You're right, I have."

"But you've also seen her dedicated, kind, and giving."

The woman who'd given us that ultimatum was the woman who ran a multimillion-dollar corporation. That woman had single-handedly taken Batchelor Corp to new heights. But Granny was also generous, loyal, caring, and understanding in ways the average person wouldn't expect.

I'd seen her empty her wallet to an unhoused person on the corner, witnessed her cancel contracts with companies with discriminatory hiring practices. She didn't simply donate food to the shelter on Thanksgiving, she worked there, too. Every year. She'd purchased housing for employees down on their luck, bought cars for people so that they could go to work, and paid the tuition of countless Detroit public school students.

Granny had been there for me. She'd pulled me out of my personal gutter and encouraged me to assume my rightful position in the company she built. Even now, after everything that had happened recently with Ms. Tea, she sent texts every day to check in on me.

Yes, she was stern.

Of course, she had high expectations for us.

She absolutely would cuss us smooth the fuck out if we disrespected her.

But she also wouldn't hesitate to do anything to help us out of every nasty situation we found ourselves in. She would burn the world to the ground to protect us. I had no doubt she would do the same for Erica. Especially knowing of her personal struggle.

"I wish you could see how awesome you are," I murmured. "I'm not saying that because you're my little sister. You're an amazing human being. Everyone who knows *you*, knows *that*. Everybody else is just the shit you step over on your way to the top."

She hugged me. "Thank you for being the best big brother."

"Erica, I need you to do something for me." When she met

my gaze, I continued. "Every time you feel like you're drowning, call me."

She raised a questioning brow. "Will you actually answer the phone?"

I nodded. "Every single time."

"Why didn't you answer today?"

I sighed. "I was being an asshole."

Erica smiled at me. "That's an everyday occurrence."

Chuckling, I nodded. "Call it my love language."

"Are you okay?" she asked.

Talking to Erica about Albany was a disaster waiting to happen. I loved my sister, would do anything for her, but she talked too damn much. If I shared with her what happened, she would definitely tell someone. Whether it was Cyn or Ma—or Albany herself.

"I'm fine," I lied.

Erica studied me, her eyes searching mine. "I don't believe you. You're watching *Sharknado* for the umpteenth time."

I glanced at the TV just in time to see a falling whale shark crush Pepa, from Salt-N-Pepa. I muted the volume. "It's a comedy," I replied with a shrug.

"I saw Albany this morning."

"Oh?" I reached over and grabbed the bottle of water I'd brought over earlier, aware that I was being watched like a hawk. "What was she doing?"

Erica eyed me skeptically. "She was leaving."

I shifted against the tightness in my gut. My stomach roiled as I considered my choice of words. If I let on that I cared, my sister would latch on and take it as a personal challenge to "help" me. If I acted like I couldn't care less, she'd accuse me of being a jerk, then try to "help" me find my conscience. Either way, I was fucked.

Clearing my throat, I said, "I'm sure you're telling me this for a reason."

"Well, I didn't get a chance to talk to her, but she looked out of it, frazzled. She was wheeling out a few boxes on the cart. What if she doesn't come back?"

I rubbed my forehead, tried to force a smile. "Maybe she's just going away for a couple of days." *Because of me.*

"I don't think so. She didn't stop when I called her name."

My mind turned over all the possible scenarios. A case, a trip back to the east coast to handle some business . . . *Did she quit again?* Aside from the ramifications of that, I didn't particularly want to deal with Granny asking why I'd run her PI away before she completed the job. Because that's exactly what would happen. She would blame me, and I wouldn't be able to deny it.

"Then again, she did tell me the other day that she had to return some packages."

I slumped back into the cushion as relief washed over me. "That's probably it."

"Brother, you want Albany back, right?"

"What makes you say that?"

"Well, for one, you're here."

"I live here," I argued.

She waved a dismissive hand. "Boy, please. You can say that shit to her, but not me."

"Why don't you talk to that one guy who asked you out?" I asked, changing the subject. "The one that lives in Ann Arbor? What's his name?"

"Asa Young," she grumbled.

"Yeah, what about him?"

"I already asked about him," she admitted. "He's off the market. Besides, that would defeat the entire purpose of my plan to marry someone I don't want to have sex with."

"On that note . . ." I stood and took my dirty dishes to the sink.

Erica followed me into the kitchen. "Can you introduce me

to one of your homeboys? I take that back. You don't really have any friends, besides Amir. And he's off limits. And Hendrix. We're related. I'll ask him."

I lifted a brow. "Be my guest."

She bit down on her thumbnail. "Wait a minute . . . Hen doesn't have any friends either. What's wrong with y'all?"

"Says the person who calls her big brother her best friend."

Erica cracked up. "Oh, shut up. I can't help that we're an insulated group."

My sister wasn't wrong. I kept my circle small because I learned a long time ago that maintaining friendships was hard when your last name was Batchelor. Being the son of the man who'd nearly destroyed that legacy added another layer of hardship.

"I feel a lot better," Erica blurted out, "so thank you. Are you hungry?"

Nodding, I washed the few dishes in the sink. "Not really." I eyed her skeptically. "You must be hungry."

She beamed. "I am."

When she didn't say anything else, I sighed. I knew what she wanted, but honestly, I didn't want to leave the house. "No."

"Wes!" She gaped. "We should go out."

"Nah, I'm good. And you just said you felt better, which means you don't need me."

"I always need my brother."

It didn't matter how adamant I was when I started a conversation with my sister. She had the ability to get me to abandon most plans for her. Typically, all it took was her big, teary doe eyes, and the sad pout she was currently sporting. The only other person that could do that was . . . *Albany.*

"We can eat a nice dinner, have a few drinks," she cajoled. "Then, you can tell me all about Albany."

"Nice try," I muttered. "There's nothing to tell."

"I wish I believed you." She flashed a sad smile. "Since you've given me your ear, allow me to give you some advice. From a woman who's been around my fair share of dirty bastards."

Advice was the last thing I needed or wanted. This thing with Albany had to be handled by us. Only us. As much as I wanted to move forward, I couldn't get around how I'd hurt her. My actions had consequences. I'd apologized to her, and I would happily do that every day of our lives if she'd . . .

Dropping my head, I stared at the countertop. "Well. . . ?" I prompted.

"Remember when you told me you wanted to marry her?"

It wasn't often that I discussed my personal life with anyone, let alone my sister. Yet I recalled the moment. Albany and I had known each other practically our entire lives because our grandmothers were best friends, more like sisters.

Our first interactions were forgettable, mostly innocent run-ins in the backyard during elaborate picnics or social events. We were toddlers, but I distinctly remembered she carried around an old doll with her. I hated that thing. For one, it was ugly. Add to that, the eyes didn't close. I was scared as fuck. Ran every time I saw it.

When she started attending my school, we became *real* friends, not just forced friends. I started to seek her out at the functions. Not gonna lie, it helped that the doll was gone. It also helped that she was cute. She had a little chip on her shoulder, probably because her stepmother was so hard on her. But she was the smartest girl in class, always on time, always talking shit.

One year, we had a Santa's Secret Shop at school. We went crazy that year buying cheap gifts for our parents and siblings. Albany presented me with a gift right before Christmas break. A book. More specifically, it was *The Kids' Book of Weather Forecasting*. And although I already had the book, the fact that she'd thought of me at all sealed the deal. I knew then she would be Mrs. Wesley Batchelor.

Although I was smitten with Albany, I was also popular.

Other girls wanted my attention, too. Since I was still a cocky asshole, even as a tween-slash-early-teenager, it took me a while to get my shit together and tell her how I felt. But once I did, it was over for me. I only wanted her. *I still do.*

"I remember," I murmured. "But we were kids."

"Still, even at that age, what you two had was special."

"It doesn't matter now."

She squeezed my shoulder. "I don't think that's true. If you're sincere, if you are willing to place your heart in her palm, she'll keep it safe."

"But will she give me her heart?"

"I hope so. I always told you to use your words. A simple conversation, a confession, goes a long way. Tell her the truth."

There was no way around this. My sister was a great lawyer for a reason. She had the badgering the witness piece down pat, but I was done talking about my feelings. "Give me an hour or two," I relented. "Then we can grab something to eat."

She sighed, grabbing her purse and walking to the door. "Fine. I'll pick the place."

"You usually do."

"I'm the youngest." She stuck her tongue out. "It's my prerogative."

"Get outta here." I tossed a dish towel at her. "I'll meet you downstairs in about an hour."

After my sister left, I turned my phone back on. No missed calls, but there were two messages. From her.

**Albany: Thank you for keeping your word. I know it was hard.**

**Albany: Last night was nice.**

A smile tugged at my mouth as I reread the texts. The despair I'd felt seconds earlier morphed into a sliver of hope. I'd told her to set the pace. It was hard as hell to let her go, to not go after her, to not camp out in front of her door. Now, I was confident I'd done the right thing.

In business, I'd perfected the art of closing a deal. Every day, I navigated complex transactions, negotiated pricing, and handled conflict. The key was persistence, transparency, strategy, and a little finesse. I also knew when to walk away. In this case, my decision to give up would depend solely on her. I wouldn't push her, but I wasn't ready to throw in the towel yet.

# Chapter 15

## *Albany*

*Failure is for everyone else, not you.*

The first time Allison said that to me, I'd lost the local spelling bee. I was six years old. Those words had been drilled into me for so long, I thought that giving up made me weak. Hence my penchant for remaining in unhealthy situations for far too long. That doubt, the nagging feeling that I wasn't good enough had nearly crippled me.

I'd avoided my parents purposely because my life was better without them. I was healthier without their lofty expectations. I didn't want to talk, and I damn sure wouldn't explain any of the decisions I'd made.

The waitress hurried over to the table and set our food down. We'd been at Grandma's favorite hometown restaurant for a good thirty minutes. The scene in the parking lot at the church was cut short by the arrival of my brother. And my grandmother when she'd nearly fainted because she hadn't eaten anything.

"We could've stopped at Burger King, Grandma," Moses suggested, breaking the long silence.

Grandma happily ate her pancakes. "No, boy. You know the Bomber is my go-to place when I come to Ypsi."

At least, she didn't take us on the same tour of Ypsilanti we'd been on several times already, visiting her old hood. I loved to listen to Grandma's stories. Typically, we would start at Depot Town, a shopping district within the town. While there, we would visit the Farmer's Market, take pictures at the Ypsilanti Freighthouse, and shop at the many businesses lining Cross Street. The antique store was Grandma's favorite. Except she never bought anything, just perused. Finally, we would pay our respects to my great-grandparents who were buried at the Highland Cemetery.

Today, though, we'd skipped the tour and just stopped to eat. The restaurant was a staple in town and often had a long wait to be seated. But the owners knew Grandma and always ensured we'd have a space, even when we arrived just before their early closing time.

"Aren't you going to eat, Albany?" Granny Joyce asked. "It looks delicious."

Granny's presence here was the reason my parents were on their best behavior. Probably because the last time they'd acted a fool in her presence, she'd threatened to absorb my father's company by hostile takeover. All because Allison had questioned her ability to run a business at her age. Grandma had told me the story through a fit of giggles.

I stared at my plate of homemade corned beef hash and eggs. It looked good enough, and I would've devoured the food any other day, but I had no appetite. Especially since Allison was staring at me the entire time.

Pushing my food away, I shrugged. "Not really hungry."

"You seem distracted, Pooh," Grandma said.

"Just thinking about all the things I have to do." Like dawdle, watch Netflix, file my nails . . . anything but this.

Grandma smirked. "Oh? Do you have a date?"

Allison snickered. "Is the ink even dry on the court order yet?"

Ignoring my stepmother, I mumbled, "No date, Grandma."

My grandmother knew me. She knew I didn't want my parents to know anything about my personal life. She also knew that a date was the last thing on my mind. *And* she knew that I was a homebody. I preferred my own company to crowds any day of the week.

Granny Joyce cut into her waffle. "What about you, Moses?"

My brother waved the waitress over. "I already ate." He asked her to top his coffee off. "I don't really eat greasy food."

I eyed Moses skeptically. "Really?" The last time I'd seen him, he had a plate full of bacon. However, I did notice that he was more bulky than lean. Like a chocolate Jason Momoa with long locs pulled into a ponytail and a confident swagger.

He bumped my arm with his elbow. "Sure."

I smiled inwardly, convinced he was lying because he simply didn't want to talk about his reasons for not being comfortable around our father and his wife. If we weren't here, I would've been grilling him about his life, asking him why he'd never texted me back when I told him I needed to talk.

Grandma mused about the latest construction project on Michigan Avenue while I busied myself checking emails, and rereading the texts Wes sent, multiple times.

**Wes: I'll be here when you're ready.**

**Wes: You should know . . . I can't walk away from you. From us.**

After our emotional conversation early this morning, I'd contemplated saying anything to him. My body was still on fire, still steaming with the remnants of desire. He'd loved me thoroughly, bringing me to new heights with every touch, every kiss.

Despite my best intention to appear unaffected, but sure of what I wanted, I was swimming in indecisiveness. I didn't want to be with him, but I did. I was up and down, sure but then unsure. Simultaneously free yet bound. I hated feeling so out of control. I also loved it.

*Maybe I'm just going crazy?*

I knew it wasn't a good idea, but I tapped out my text, smiling to myself: **Again?** 😂

**Wes: I deserve that.**

**Me: You definitely do. But why?**

He questioned my last message, then said: **Why, what?**

Sighing, I responded but I couldn't bring myself to hit SEND. I cursed myself because I shouldn't have opened the door to more honesty, because his honesty was like catnip to me. I was so drawn to him because he'd always been truthful with me. *Until he wasn't.* My thumb hovered over the message, warring with myself on whether I wanted to ask the question. In the end, I left him on READ and set my phone down.

"You look sloppy, Albany," Allison said. "Your skirt is too tight, and that hair . . ."

My eyes flashed to her, then cut to the rest of the table. Grandma and Granny Joyce had excused themselves and were currently talking to someone familiar on the other side of the dining room. Moses was gone, too.

I couldn't remember exactly, but I had to have been around seven years old when I overheard a heated discussion between my parents. The subject? Me. And my refusal to participate in the Miss Michigan Pageant. At that youthful age, I had listened intently as Allison berated my father for defending my right to have autonomy over my own body, to have my own schedule and my own desires. During that conversation, she'd called me his illegitimate spawn, an ugly reminder of his indiscretions. I knew then that I'd never belong to her, that I was her daughter in name only. Our relationship never recovered. The part of me that wanted her approval, the piece that wanted a mother's love, had been destroyed.

"Where's Moses?" I asked.

I listened as Allison picked apart my appearance. My hair was too short and the color was dull. The shoes I wore were from two seasons ago and not nearly feminine enough. My clothes . . . Well, apparently my *sloppy* attire looked cheap.

"Why do you insist on walking around here looking like a tack head?" Allison continued. The insult was her way of belittling me, calling me both stupid and tacky at the same time.

"Allison, keep your voice down," my father grumbled.

"Seriously." She crossed her arms over her brand-new breasts, her blue eyes piercing. I wasn't sure until now, but it was clear, she'd finally received the enhancement she'd wanted after all. She flipped her blond extensions from her shoulders, sat up straight. "I can't believe you."

I frowned. "Believe, what?"

My father leaned forward, resting his elbows on the table. "Imagine our surprise when I received a call from Darrell asking me where his wife was."

"*Ex*-wife," I corrected curtly, just at Moses reappeared. "And what did you tell him?"

I felt my brother's eyes on me as he slid back into the booth, but I didn't dare look at him. I loved Moses, but we operated on a strictly need-to-know basis. Once I needed him to show up, that's when he *needed* to know my business. Other than that, we barely talked about relationships.

"We told him we didn't know," my father explained. "I also mentioned that if I got in touch with you, I'd send you home."

"That's unfortunate, Dad. Even if you had the power to send me anywhere, there is no home to go back to. Your precious son-in-law gambled away—or smoked—our savings, took the mortgage money to do other shit, and the bank foreclosed."

Moses glanced at me again. "What?"

"Need to know," I reminded him.

Allison shook her head, disgust on her face. "How dare you embarrass us like this? To find out that our daughter had divorced her husband—the senator's son—from someone else? Foreclosures? You're ridiculous. You've always—"

"Wait," Moses interrupted, "what the hell is wrong with you, Allison? Do you really think I'm going to let you talk to her like that?"

"I'm not talking to *you*," Allison retorted. "Stay out of it."

My brother never got along with my father, and he couldn't stand Allison. Unlike me, he had never fallen prey to her machinations because he'd never been forced to live with us. Even though his mother wasn't present, she had a large extended family. He was able to move in with an uncle.

"It's fine." I placed my hand on his arm before I shifted my gaze back to them. "I don't have to clear my activities with you. I'm a grown-ass woman. You should be glad I left that muthafucka. He stole from me and cheated on me with every available woman he could find, and here you are . . . blaming me for finally leaving him?"

"What you should've done was be a good wife," Allison continued. "Instead, you were too busy working when you should've been making a home. I told you a long time ago that your job was to serve your husband, but no . . . You chose to go everywhere except where you were supposed to be. Now, you're divorced. Who's going to want you now? Your best bet is to talk to the senator and beg for their forgiveness."

Despite the evidence presented to her of Darrell's indiscretions, her only concern was the scandal surrounding it, the gossip among her friends. After all, her daughter was divorcing the son of a United States senator. It didn't matter that the senator himself—along with the rest of Darrell's immediate family—had given me the blessing to leave. As long as I agreed to keep the sordid details quiet. They'd even offered to pay for the court proceedings and give me a monthly stipend, which I declined.

I shifted in my seat. "That's never going to happen."

"You're not even worth the time I spent to get you into shape," she spat.

"Are you just going to let her talk to your daughter like this?" Moses growled.

When I turned to my brother, his eyes were trained on my father. *Oh Lord.* "Mo, please don't—"

"Like my wife said, this has nothing to do with you, son," my father said.

Gregory Keyes was a successful musician who'd seemingly read the tea leaves and left his popular boy band in the late '80s and became an award-winning music producer. Then, a successful businessman in the tech space. To this day, he was still sought after by industry legends and up-and-coming artists looking to sample one of his iconic tracks. Despite his accolades, though, he sucked at fatherhood.

My father only stood up for me one time, and it didn't go well. After that, he'd closed himself off to me. Most of my childhood memories of him consisted of cheap gifts on Christmas and a little cash stuffed inside impersonal cards. We didn't have heartfelt father-daughter conversations. We never went fishing together. He'd failed to teach me how to perform routine maintenance on my car, how to shoot a gun, or even how to land a punch. He didn't show up for birthdays, and he missed my high school graduation. My life wasn't his concern. At least until I met Darrell. Then, he just pretended to care.

"This is some bullshit," my brother grumbled. "I swear. You always sit back and let her talk shit about us, treat us like shit, act like a shitty person."

"Shut up," Allison hissed.

"No, you shut up," Moses interrupted.

"Don't talk to your mother like that," Dad said.

"She's not my mother," Moses reiterated. "She never was a mother to me or Albany. Shit, you weren't a father either."

Allison scowled. "You always have something to say, Moses. You were the problem. In trouble all the time. Talking back. Disrespecting me and our house." She glared at me. "And you? I—"

"Allison, watch your words. You got one more time to disrespect my sister."

"Or you'll what?" she taunted.

Moses chuckled. "You better get her, Dad," he warned. "Somehow, I don't think you want her to find out your secrets." He leaned forward, lowering his voice. "Don't test me."

My father sat up straight. "Allison, let it go."

A hint of fear flashed in Allison's eyes. "What is he talking about, Greg?"

I wanted to know the answer to that question as well, but I was content to let this play out.

My dad shifted uncomfortably. "It's nothing. This is not the time or place to entertain him."

Moses pressed his palm against the table. "That's what I thought."

My father let out a heavy sigh. "Albany, your mother's right. You can't just walk away from your marriage without trying to fix it."

"So I can end up like her?" I pointed at Allison. "Bitter?"

"How dare—"

"Allison, stop," I said. "You know what, I'm done. I don't need this. And I don't need you." I glanced at my father. "Or you. I've been living my life without you practically my entire life and I—" My phone buzzed. I glanced at my screen.

Ms. Tea posted again. I quickly scanned the post and my blood ran cold. She'd posted three pictures of Wes—and an unfamiliar woman. They were smiling at each other. His hand was draped over the back of her chair. They were at a restaurant because food and drinks were on the table. The caption was simple.

Busted? #HarpoWhoDisWoman
#BatchelorShenanigans

I hated it. Worst of all, I hated the way I felt in that moment. Jealous.

"You alright?" Moses asked.

Counting to ten, I blew out a calming breath. "I'm fine." I turned my attention back to my parents. "My life is none of your business. I don't have to explain my actions to you. I don't care what you think anymore." I stood, dropped my napkin on the table. "Let's go."

Grandma approached us, eyeing us hesitantly. "What's going on?"

"Mo is going to take me home." I gave her a hug. "Love you." My gaze drifted over to Granny Joyce, who was tapping furiously at her phone screen. I tilted my head and studied her movements. She was so engrossed in her phone that she didn't seem to realize Grandma had come over here.

"Pooh?" Grandma called. "Are you okay?"

Forcing my attention away from Granny Joyce, I glanced back at my parents again, before addressing Grandma's question. In the past, I would've made up a nice excuse to leave, but I didn't have it in me to lie. "No," I admitted. "Your son sucks. And so does his wife."

"Olivia, you can't believe everything she says," Allison said. "Darrell told us she left for no reason."

Grandma waved her off. "Oh, shut the hell up. She shouldn't have married that man anyway, just like Gregory should've left your stuck-up ass in that strip club. I remember when my son married you. You strolled into my house wearing a fake Coach purse, too-tight clothing, and a nasty attitude. The only thing that's changed is your bag is genuine leather, not pleather. Now, you walk around here like you're so holier-than-thou when you're living off the money *I* gave my son. Because it certainly wasn't his dead father who supported his dreams."

"What about the estate?" my father asked. "I'm entitled to a portion of—"

"Nothing." Grandma took a sip of water. "Your father was as broke as you are."

"I don't understand," he responded. "What do you mean?"

"It's not for you to understand. The only thing you need to know is I'm not going to take kindly to you letting your wife talk to my baby like she's crazy."

"Albany is my daughter, Mother."

Grandma placed a hand on her hip. "I can't tell." My grandmother had been my biggest defender growing up, which was why she brought me to live with her in the first place. "I told you a long time ago that your wife can try to be the evil stepmother, but this girl is not Cinderella."

"So, I'm going to leave." I kissed Grandma's cheek. "Will you text me when you get home?"

"I will, Pooh."

I glanced back at Granny, who was still on her phone. "Give Granny Joyce a hug for me."

Turning on my heels, I walked out of the restaurant without giving my parents a backward glance.

"What happened with your marriage?"

I watched the scenery as Moses coasted down I-94 toward Downtown Detroit. The drive had been quiet for the first ten minutes, as I went back and forth on whether I wanted to break the silence.

"Albany"—he gripped the steering wheel, his eyes focused on the road ahead—"tell me."

"Why?"

"Because I want to know."

"He sucks."

"What did he do?" he pressed.

The details were painful and had been relayed several times. I didn't want to travel down that road again. Not today. "I don't want to talk about it, Mo. It's over."

"It's okay. You don't have to tell me. I'll ask him."

I rested my head on the seat. "Please, don't."

"What the hell did you see in him? Because I never understood."

Glancing at him, I said, "You're not going to let this go, are you?"

"I'm sayin' . . . What was it?"

"I don't know." I shrugged. "He was charming. Smart. Rich. Definitely perfect on paper."

"Except you've never been into appearances, and you've never cared what people think."

"I cared what *some* people thought," I mumbled. "For the first time in my life, I wanted their approval. I wanted Allison to be proud of me. I wanted Dad to love me."

"So you married him because they chose him?"

"No. I chose him. Now, I'm paying for it."

Silence stretched as we neared the city. Finally, he asked, "You know what I think?"

"I'm sure you're going to tell me no matter what I say."

"You jumped into that relationship, with that dude, because he wasn't Wes."

My body stiffened as his words replayed in my mind. Darrell was nothing like Wes. His demeanor, his work ethic . . . the way he talked, the way he processed things. Of course, he had good qualities, but they were surface qualities.

"I've never seen you the way you were when Wes left," he continued. "We all were worried about you. Then, you went to college, met Darrell, and finally opened up again. I didn't like his ass, but I couldn't be mad at someone who was going to help you heal."

"Is that why you never said much?"

He hunched a shoulder. "You only asked for my opinion once."

On the wedding day, before I walked down the aisle, I pulled Mo aside and asked him if he thought I was doing the right thing. True to form, he'd tossed the question back to me. I couldn't answer it then. So he told me not to marry him. I did anyway.

I blew out a heavy sigh. "I should've listened to you."

"We all make choices. Darrell made a choice, too. Since he didn't follow through with his vows, since he didn't prove us wrong, fuck him."

I cracked up. "I love you, Mo."

"I love you, too."

More silence.

"Have you talked to Wes?" he asked.

"Are we really going to talk about this? 'Cause I could ask you some questions, too."

"About what?"

"You know what." My brother and Kay had an ongoing flirtation. I couldn't be sure, but I always thought it was more than that. "She called the wedding off."

"I know."

Shifting to face him, I asked, "You talked to her?"

"Every day."

"What's going on?"

"I don't know, li'l sis." Moses veered off the exit. "You hungry?"

My stomach growled. "Yes."

"Let's eat."

"Oh"—I grinned—"what's up with the no greasy foods?"

He barked out a laugh. "Shit, I was just saying that because I didn't want to eat with them."

"Thanks for coming, Mo."

"You texted. I came."

"That was weeks ago. I didn't even know if you got my message."

"I figured when you said we needed to talk, it was about Granddad, so I just made plans to come home."

I didn't even want to ask how he found out. Mo was so much like Grandma. He moved in silence, and didn't show up unless he had to. "Wait until I tell you the story about Grandma. She never got a divorce."

"Yeah, I figured something was going on. You'll have to fill me in."

"It's crazy. But, next time, can you at least respond to my text?"

"I got you."

While he sped toward my place, I unlocked my phone and checked social media. The comment section under the latest Ms. Tea post was busy as people chimed in on Wes and the mystery woman. I took a screenshot of her face. I tried to tell myself that it was for investigative purposes, but I knew it was more than that. My initial thought hadn't changed. I hated it. That simple fact was the reason I'd left his house frazzled. We'd crossed a line, and now it was too late to course correct. At this point, I wasn't even sure I wanted to.

Mo pulled in front of Batch Place. "Order in?"

"I don't know. I guess we could . . ." I followed his line of sight and spotted Wes, Erica, and that woman as they walked into the building. Narrowing my eyes, I murmured, "Yes. Let's order in."

# Chapter 16

## *Wesley*

*Something was off.*

I noticed it.

Moses noticed it.

The only person that hadn't clocked it was Erica, who'd been talking animatedly about everything that didn't matter in this moment. Work, the gym, the last episode of *Severance*, and the latest political news . . . yeah, my sister was happily oblivious to the brewing storm.

Oh, and Whitney, because she didn't know better. My sister's childhood friend had recently moved to the city from Wellspring. Since I'd encouraged Erica to find some girlfriends, she'd invited her to lunch with us.

Erica brushed Mo's arm. "It's been a minute, Mo."

*Is she flirting with him?*

"You look good," my sister continued.

*Yeah, she's flirting.*

Moses smirked. "You do, too."

I folded my arms over my chest. "What's good with you?"

"Nothing much, man," Mo replied. "Working."

Mo didn't grow up in Detroit, but he'd often come around to spend time with Albany. He was cool. That didn't mean I wanted him to kick it with my sister. I almost said something to that effect, but I stopped myself. Because Mo could essentially say the same about me. I *did* date his sister. She fell in love with me, gave herself to me. Then, I broke her heart. And now I wanted her to trust me not to do it again, to give me a chance. To give us a chance.

The cold hard truth smacked me in the face as I turned over the reasons this would never work. Even if she'd forgiven me, how could she ever take the leap of faith required to give in to the fire burning between us? Even now, I felt it. The pull to her, the need to close the distance between us.

"What do you do?" Erica asked him.

He snickered. "A lot."

Erica smiled, her eyes sparkling with renewed interest. It was no secret she'd crushed on Mo hard. And now that she was in the market, looking for a situation . . . "When did you get back to town?" my sister asked.

"I flew in for the funeral."

My eyes met Albany's, held her gaze for a moment. "Someone died?"

Albany had the sense to look guilty. We'd spent the night together. Even before that, we'd talked almost every day in some form. And she hadn't told me her family suffered a loss. "Yes," she replied.

"Who?" I pressed.

She held her head high. "My grandfather."

"Oh, I'm sorry, Albany." Erica embraced her. "Is there anything I can do?"

Albany shook her head. "No, I'm fine. As you know, I didn't know him." I recognized the pain in her eyes before she could hide it. I wanted to reach out to her, to hold her. "I just figured I should pay my respects."

The situation between her grandparents had weighed on her heart. We'd talked about it countless times, how she'd wished her grandmother could be happy. She dreamed of meeting him one day. Not because he was a good person. He wasn't. But because he was *her* grandfather.

Erica's expression softened. "Still, he's family."

"I promise to let you know if I need anything," Albany conceded. "Thank you."

Mo eyed me curiously. "You good, bruh?"

Clearing my throat, I nodded. "I'm fine."

"Sure?"

Over the years, I'd known Mo to be very protective of Albany. Almost more than I was. He'd gone against his father, his stepmother, and even Grandma to defend her. I had no doubt he would do the same now. Knowing her the way he did, I assumed he'd already guessed that the tension was the current flowing between me and Albany. He didn't like it, and I couldn't blame him.

"Very," I replied.

One thing Mo had to know about me? I didn't back down for anybody. If he had a problem with me, he needed to tell me. While I respected him, I wasn't scared of him either.

If he wanted me to stay away from his sister? *She* had to say it.

"I'm sorry for your loss," I added, shifting my gaze between Albany and Mo.

Erica elbowed her friend. "Oh. Whit, remember the woman I was telling you about?" Erica asked. "The PI?"

Whitney nodded. "Yeah, I believe so."

"This is her. Albany." Erica grinned. "She's working for Batchelor Corp now."

Recognition dawned on Whitney. "Oh." She reached out to shake Albany's hand. "Finally, I get to put a face to a name."

Only Albany didn't reciprocate the gesture. Instead, she asked, "Are you from Detroit?"

Whitney closed her hand into a fist, then shoved it into her pocket. "No." She flashed a forced, yet polite smile. "I'm from Wellspring."

Albany glanced at me, before she turned her attention back to Whitney. "What brings you to town?"

Albany was suspicious by nature. She was always the last person to warm up to outsiders. It was one of the reasons I called her Bug. She presented with a hard shell, but it was her protection mechanism, her way of shielding herself from attacks. On the inside, though, she was delicate, gentle, harmless. Like a ladybug. When we were kids, it would often come across as mean. In eighth grade, some of the girls had campaigned to vote her Most Likely to Kick Someone's Ass. She hated the moniker because she wasn't that. While Albany tended to retreat inward when she was around people she didn't know, I'd never known her to be cold.

Whitney giggled nervously. "Um, I . . ."

"She lives here now," I answered. "Moved a couple of weeks ago."

"Hmph." Albany looked at her phone, tapped on the screen before she lifted her eyes again. "I'm sorry, what was your name again?"

Erica gasped. "Oh, I'm sorry. I thought I'd said her name when you two came over."

"You did," I murmured.

Albany glared at me. "I didn't hear her," she grumbled through clenched teeth.

"Anyway"—Erica shrugged—"Whitney was one of my first friends when we moved to Wellspring."

"That's nice." She eyed me, lifting a brow. "Is she your friend, too?"

Whitney chuckled. "I actually met Wes first. At school. I tutored him in math."

"Oh." Albany laughed. There was no humor in it, though. "I used to tutor him, too." She clapped with faux glee. "What's funny is . . . He never needed me to help him. He could solve a math problem with his eyes closed."

"Albany," Mo said.

She held a hand up. "Hold on, because I'm not done. Later— I told you this is a funny story—he told me he only did that so that he could spend more alone time with me. I fell for it." She forced a smile. "Guess that trick worked in Wellspring, too."

*Shit.* She was pissed. And I finally figured what that off feeling was. She was jealous. Which made me incredibly happy and emboldened to further my agenda of getting her back. Whit didn't deserve her wrath, though.

"It wasn't math," I corrected. "I asked her to help me with English."

Whitney snapped her fingers. "Oh, right. I think I helped Bryson with math. Sorry."

"It doesn't matter." Albany's shoulders fell. "Mo, we should probably go order our food."

"What's wrong with you?" I asked.

Meeting my waiting gaze, she shrugged. "Nothing. What's wrong with *you*?"

"You're not acting like yourself."

"Well, I am being myself, Wes. You shouldn't be surprised because I've told you time and again . . . you don't know me anymore." She walked away. "Let's go, Mo."

"Stop walking!" I blared.

Mo frowned. "Who the fuck are you talking to?"

Albany gripped his wrist when he stepped forward. "It's okay." She stomped toward me. "What?"

"Give me a minute," I commanded.

She narrowed her eyes. "No. You'll never get another minute from me."

"Give. Me. A. Minute."

Holding up one finger, she spat out, "One. You have one minute. Just until that elevator gets to my floor." She stalked toward the elevator and stepped inside.

"Hold up."

I glanced back at Mo as he approached me. "What's up?"

"I never had a problem with you, Wes," he offered. "I hope I don't have to. She's been through a lot. Don't hurt her."

"Your time starts now," Albany shouted from the elevator.

"I would never hurt her," I assured him.

"You already did." He sighed. "Look, I know there's more to the story, but it still doesn't change what you did or how you handled it."

My decision had haunted me for years. It didn't surprise me that Mo knew more than I'd ever told anyone. Made me wonder who talked to him about it because my family signed NDAs to keep everything under wraps. "Did you say something to her?"

He shrugged. "She never needed to hear it from me."

I nodded, gave him a dap. "I'll take care of it."

"Do that," he said. "Because if I have to comfort her again over you . . . it's not going to be good, bruh." He squeezed my shoulder. "Your minute's up." He peered at the elevator. "You better hurry."

Without another word, I walked toward the elevator, stepped inside and stood in front of her. Once the elevator door closed, before I could say anything, I felt the sting of her hand against my cheek. When she went to do it again, I grabbed her wrist. "What was that for?"

She wrenched her arm from my grip. "Move."

"What's wrong with you?" I prodded.

"You got me walking around here jealous as fuck and I hate it."

I smirked. "You always were a little possessive," I teased.

"Shut up." She rubbed her forehead. "That poor girl. I was mean to her for no reason."

"You were pretty shitty to her."

"Oh God. I need to apologize." She pointed at me. "It's your fault."

I grabbed her hand, kissed the tips of her fingers, then sucked her ring finger into my mouth.

She gasped.

"I'm sorry," I whispered.

"You should be." She blew out a harsh breath. "That post set me off earlier and then I saw you with her. . . . Ugh." She shoved me away. "Don't touch me."

The elevator arrived on her floor, and she barreled out of there. "Time's up."

I jogged after her. "Stop walking away from me."

She whirled around, fury in her brown eyes. "You mean like you walked away from me?"

Squeezing her wrist, I pulled her to me. "I know I hurt you, Bug. I can't change that, but I'm willing to . . ." I couldn't finish my thought because she wasn't ready to hear it. She wasn't ready to give me what I wanted.

"Willing to what?"

*If I could just . . .* I brushed my lips over her knuckles. "Let me hold you. Let me make it better." I kissed her eyes, her nose, her cheeks, then dropped to my knees. "Let me make *you* feel better."

A tear fell from her eyes, and I hated that I was once again the reason for it. "I have company," she said. "Mo is—"

Slowly, I lifted the skirt of her dress, kissing every inch of her legs as I went. "Please," I murmured against her skin.

"Wes," she breathed. "We're in the hallway."

"It doesn't matter."

She'd said the same thing to me downstairs. Seemed like that was her motto lately. And she was right. Nothing else mattered but this moment. Her. And us together.

I slid her panties down her legs and tucked them into my pocket. Seconds later, I pressed my face to her core, inhaled her sweet scent, and licked her slit from front to back.

I knew we were in the open, that anyone could round the

corner and catch us. But I didn't care. I had never felt so reckless, so consumed with another person. And I needed her to know it. I needed her to feel it.

Lifting her leg up, I slung it over my shoulder and feasted on her, slipping one finger, then two inside her sweet heat. She was so wet. So ready for more. And it didn't take her long. When I sucked her clit, she hissed my name as she climaxed.

Seconds later, her leg buckled, and she slid onto the floor.

Her eyes were wild, but she was stunning. "You can't do this."

I brushed my mouth over hers. "I can't stop."

She swallowed visibly. "I'm a liar."

"I already knew that," I whispered against her mouth, tracing her lips with my tongue, letting her taste herself.

"Since you know so much, what did I lie about?" she challenged.

"I knew we'd be here again." I traced her jawline, tucked a strand of her hair behind her ear.

Gaping at me, she bit down on my bottom lip before she kissed me fully. "Seriously, Wes. This is not good. I told myself that I couldn't do this again."

"*You* haven't done anything yet."

A whisper of a smile crossed her lips. "But I let you do something. In a public hallway."

"I wanted to."

Albany searched my eyes. "I don't think I'm strong enough to say no to you. Which is why I needed you to keep your word."

The pain in her eyes was unmistakable. I rested my forehead against hers. "I'm trying, but I can't stop wanting you."

"This is so hard."

I kissed her again, dipped my tongue in her mouth. "Yeah, but that last time . . . It was—"

"So good." She cupped my cheeks in her palms. "I *do* want

you. More than I should be admitting. But I'm getting too old to just be fucking."

Unable to help myself, I laughed.

She dissolved into a fit of giggles, too.

Reluctantly, I stood and held out my hand to her. When she placed her palm in mine, I helped her up. I stuffed her panties into her purse. "I want to keep them, but I won't," I confessed.

She brushed past me. "I thought it was possible to just have one night with you, then lock it away. Keep it in the part of my heart that wants to move forward with my life." She stopped in front of her door. "I was doing good until I saw you. With her."

"We were never together. I didn't lie to get her to tutor me. We've never been more than friends."

"Just the thought that you were with her sent me into a rage."

I leaned into her. "Is that so bad?"

"It's not good."

She unlocked her door and went inside. The fact that she didn't slam the door in my face was all I needed to follow her. Albany walked straight to the kitchen, poured herself a large glass of wine, and gulped it down.

I slid onto one of her barstools. "Your grandfather died. Why didn't you tell me?"

"Are we there yet? At the point where I tell you all my business?"

"I think we are." I reached across the countertop and grabbed her hand. "Bug, you know how I feel about you."

She lifted a questioning brow. "Do I really?"

My heart raced. I knew I finally needed to tell her everything, but it didn't feel right to say the words after what we just shared. Then again, maybe it was the perfect time. "We need to talk."

Glancing at her watch, she smirked. "Your minute is up."

Chuckling, I led her over to the couch. And she let me. "Can you sit with me?"

Instead of joining me on the sofa, she sat on one of the chairs. "What's up, Wes?"

"That night . . ." I sighed, dreading the conversation even though I knew we needed to have it. "I didn't want to leave you."

"But you did."

"After my father died, we became pawns in a world we had no idea existed. People who he worked with, who he harmed, were coming out of the woodwork demanding answers. Money. Revenge."

She frowned. "What?"

"The night we left, I wasn't supposed to be with you. Mom wanted us to disappear earlier in the day, but I disobeyed her to come to you. I couldn't imagine leaving town without seeing you again."

"But I—"

"It was a good day. Perfect. Then you kissed me and told me you were ready. We made love, and I wanted to hold on to you forever."

"Your mom called," she whispered.

"She'd been calling and texting all day. I ignored her until I couldn't. I had every intention of coming back to you that night, even if that meant I was grounded for the rest of the summer. I knew I couldn't leave without seeing you one more time. But . . . When I got home, my mother told me that someone came to the house, threatened to take what my father owed them from Erica."

She gasped. "What?"

"I had to go."

"Why didn't you just call me?" She stood, paced the room. "You could've just told me the truth. I would've been sad, but I would've understood."

"By then, it was too late. We left moments after I made it home. I couldn't say anything. It was either that or put all of us in danger. Including you."

"Me?" She shook her head. "What do you mean, me? I didn't have anything to do with your father."

"Bug, these assholes didn't care. They threatened you, too. Anybody that meant anything to me or my family."

"Did Granny know?"

I nodded. "She's the one who suggested we leave town because she couldn't trust anyone to keep us safe at the time. Since Mom was from Wellspring, Granny helped by purchasing a house there, giving us enough to live on until my mother found a job."

For the first year, we had no contact with anyone back home. Not even Granny. My father was indicted on money laundering, but he didn't do it alone. He'd built his criminal empire trafficking in drugs and military-grade weapons, and several of his key players worked for the company. It took a while, but my grandmother used her power and influence to root out all the Batchelor Corp employees involved.

"Eventually, the police traced the threats to a childhood friend of my father and John," I continued. "Ryan Baker. But the damage was already done. By then, Mom didn't want anything to do with the family, and she'd resolved to stay away. Which meant, I had to stay away, too."

Albany plopped on the chair. "So why didn't you call when everything was over?"

"Because I wasn't the same person. My father's death, and everything that came with it, broke me. I didn't care about my life. It wasn't worth much. I didn't care about waking up in the morning or falling asleep at night. All I saw was my failure, my loss. So, I couldn't . . ." I swallowed against the hard lump in my throat. "I didn't think I would survive losing the only person who meant everything to me. The one person who saw the best in me. I couldn't risk you looking at me and feeling pity. Then leaving me."

"I would've never left you, though. Not for anything."

"You say that now, but I wasn't the guy you fell in love with at that point."

"But you didn't even give me a chance to prove you wrong!" she yelled. "You just stayed away—after you walked out on me without looking back."

"I did look back," I told her. "Every day. I thought about you."

Her expression softened. "I wrote you. I sent you messages on Facebook, on IG . . . I asked Hendrix about you. When I finally got in touch with Erica, I asked her about you. Nobody would tell me anything. I worried so much. At some point, all you had to do was send three words back. *I am good.*"

"I wasn't good, Albany. I was fucked up. Drunk all the time. High. Hanging around with the wrong people. I dropped out of college. I couldn't face you."

"I see you like this, so tormented, and I want to help you. I want to make it better. You don't deserve me, but I still . . ."

I walked to her, dropped to my knees again in front of her. "You can't walk away either." I rested my forehead against her lap. "You can't leave me."

Her fingers feathered over my scalp. "This is my fault."

My eyes flashed to hers. "It's not. This is all me."

"No." She shook her head, dashed fresh tears from her cheeks. "It's me. I believe that you loved me as much as you could at the time."

"I still love you."

Her shoulders slumped forward. "But I was so engrossed in the magic we made together that I didn't see how torn you were that night. I was so naïve, and I carried that naivete into my marriage. Look where that landed me. Broke. Broken." She slipped out of my grasp and stood. "I can't lose myself in you again."

Closing my eyes, I whispered, "I'm not that same messed up, immature man, Bug." I inched closer to her. "That's not me anymore."

"I can see that." She smiled sadly. "What I don't understand is why you didn't at least tell me the truth when I came back."

"I wanted to tell you that day in the café, at the fundraiser, at your apartment. . . . It never felt like the right time. Would it have even made a difference? Does it change things for you? Now that you know my reasons, are you willing to try and make this work?"

"Honestly, I don't know. But I wish you would've said something a long time ago."

"Albany, please . . ."

"I can move past it. I can *not* hate you. I can know that things were beyond your control as a teenager, but—"

"The past is behind us," I said. "We can get this right."

"It's not, Wes. Our past is all around us." She gestured to the space. "Mostly, here." She placed a hand over her heart. "And here." She pressed her other hand against my heart.

"This"—I held her palm to my chest—"my heart is not an obstacle to overcome. It's just yours." I kissed her softly. "Bug, there's no one for me but you."

"That's not true," she insisted. "I think Ms. Tea would like a word."

"Fuck Ms. Tea," I roared. "She doesn't know anything. She doesn't know me. And she damn sure doesn't know us."

"It doesn't matter."

"You keep saying that, but I would argue that it does."

She let out a heavy sigh. "I need some time."

Tipping her chin up, I whispered, "I told you I would let you set the pace."

"Is that what you're doing?"

I held her hands in mine. "I also told you earlier that I can't walk away from you again."

"Yeah, I read that message."

"You didn't respond."

"Because I didn't know what to say."

I tilted my head to meet her gaze. "I don't believe that."

"Why can't you walk away? It's not like I'm nice to you. I don't even like you that much."

I laughed. "Maybe. But you love me."

She frowned. "I don't."

"Yeah, you do."

"Actually, I think I'm teetering toward I-can't-stand-you."

"You still love me, though."

"This is stupid. Tell me why I should believe you when you say you can't walk away from me. Because we already established that you did before."

"Walking away from you would destroy me. I meant what I said, you own my heart. Since I can't live without it, I will die."

She gasped. "Wes."

"I'm joking, but I'm serious, too. It's really that simple." I placed a tentative kiss to her lips. When she didn't pull away, I deepened it, pulling her to me. And she let me.

A soft knock broke the haze of desire simmering between us, and she jerked away from me. She didn't speak, though. Instead, she rushed over to the door and opened it.

Mo walked in, followed by Erica and Whitney.

Albany glanced back at me. "I told you your time was up."

"We figured we'd check on you." Erica eyed me curiously. "Are you two okay?"

I nodded. "Yes. I'm going home."

"Already?" Albany asked.

It was a test. One that I would pass with flying colors this time. I kissed her, not even caring that we weren't alone. "I'll be back. You said you needed time, and I made a promise to let you set the pace."

She nibbled on her bottom lip. "Okay."

I dapped Mo up, hugged Erica and Whit, then I left.

# Chapter 17

## *Albany*

I had a long day full of meetings, of research, and of uncertainty. One thing I didn't have today? A phone call or even a text from Wes. It had been three days since he'd declared his love for me, told me that he'd wait for me. And he'd stayed true to his word. The only problem is I wasn't ready for how it felt to not hear his voice, to see his face.

I'd subtly asked around about him, cornered Erica in the mailroom, rushed into the elevator to catch Hendrix. I even casually dropped hints to Granny when I met with her this afternoon. He'd seemingly gone ghost.

"Are you there, Pooh?"

I blinked. "Yes, Grandma. Fourth of July at your house. Should I bring anything?"

"No, baby," she replied. "I have money to hire chefs."

I shifted the phone to my other ear as I neared my front door. "Okay."

"Wear something nice," she ordered.

My steps faltered when I noticed that my door was ajar. Pausing, I told Grandma I'd call her back. Sighing, I gripped the piece at my hip and readied myself to draw. I pushed the door open.

I scanned the room. It was empty. Nothing seemed out of place, which was not surprising because I didn't have much. Except for my surveillance equipment, my work computers, my files . . . *Shit*. I crept toward the office. When I heard something shatter in the bathroom, I counted to ten before I kicked the door open and . . .

Bri screamed. "Albany!"

I clicked the safety and dropped my weapon. "What the hell are you doing here?"

"I stopped by after work," she exclaimed.

My friend was also my emergency contact. Bri had all of my secure information, my important passwords, a spare key, and my security codes. She was also my power of attorney. I secured my firearm. "You scared the shit out of me. I thought you were a criminal."

"This place is like Fort Knox. How would a criminal get in?"

I shrugged. "I don't know." I wiped the sweat off my brow and took a moment to gather my composure.

Bri approached me. "What the fuck is wrong with you?"

"A lot," I murmured.

Her shoulders fell. "Damn. Did you want to talk about it?"

I walked into my bedroom. "Not really."

"Good." She plopped down on my bed.

I glanced at her. "Wow."

Giggling, she peered up at the ceiling. "I'm sorry. I had a difficult day."

"Me, too." I crawled on the bed next to her. "It sucked."

"That's why I came here. I figured I'd sleep over. The apartment is so quiet now without your late-night trips to the kitchen. You walk like you have tambourines hooked to your feet."

I laughed. "I do not. You didn't hear me approaching you today."

"That's because you were in bad-ass, Albany-the-PI mode. At night, it's like you turn off that side of your brain."

"Yet, you're here."

"I miss you."

Frowning, I shot her a sidelong glance. "I just talked to you yesterday."

"Yeah, but it's not the same." She sat up. "We're both busy. At least when you stayed with me, we could catch up at the end of a day, watch a movie, or eat dinner together."

"Is that what you want to do tonight?" I slid off the bed. "I can cook dinner?"

Her eyes lit up. "Oh my God, yes! Fried chicken me, please."

I shuffled into the walk-in closet. "Are you sure?" Quickly, I undressed, tossing my clothes into a hamper. "I thought you were on a diet."

As she yapped about the lack of taste in her protein shakes and her desire for something homecooked and seasoned well, I grabbed a pair of joggers and slid them on. Then, I put on an oversized T-shirt.

When I emerged from the closet, she was standing at my dresser trying on a pair of my earrings. "Can I have these?"

"No." I took them from her and dropped them into my jewelry box. "You're still wearing the earrings you took from me last month."

She grinned. "We can switch them out."

"No, girl. These are my favorites. Grandma gave them to me for Christmas."

"Alright." She stared at me. "You look different."

I froze. Bri was like a hawk. She could smell deceit from a mile away, and I was hiding a big secret from her. Several, actually. Shifting my weight from one foot to the other, I asked, "What do you mean?"

She circled me, assessing me in the way only she could. "I don't know. I can't put my finger on it. Not yet anyway."

"I slept with Wes," I confessed with a heavy sigh. "I was going to tell you, but I didn't."

"Shut up. I knew it."

Folding my arms over my chest, I said, "No, you didn't." I walked into the kitchen to start dinner. She was on my heels, asking all kinds of questions.

Where were we?

How were we?

When were we?

I pulled the chicken out of the refrigerator. "Wait a minute, how did you know I even had chicken to fry?" I asked.

"I've been here for a while. I looked around. You know I'm nosy."

For the first time since I got home, I noticed the suitcase near the front door. "Is that your suitcase?"

"I had to pack some clothes," she said. "Pass me that bag of chips. I'm so hungry. Do you have dip?"

"How long are you staying?" I handed her the family-size bag of Better Made chips and grabbed the tub of French onion dip from the fridge. It was then that I noticed she had on my slippers. "And why are you wearing my Uggs?"

Hunching a shoulder, she said, "I forgot mine at home. Oh, and can we play my visit by ear?"

"Whatever you need." I surveyed her. "What happened, Bri? Is it Hendrix?"

"No, actually, it's me." She nibbled on her bottom lip. "I'm pregnant."

I rounded the counter. "What?"

"Yeah. It's official."

"Oh my . . . What are you going to do?"

Bri was a driven professional. She had a detailed life plan that didn't involve children before the age of thirty-five. Being a single mother was definitely not a bullet point on her list of goals either.

"I don't know."

"Did you tell Hen?"

"What makes you think he's the father?"

I hopped onto one of the barstools. "I know you."

"I haven't said anything." She buried her face in her hands. "I don't even know how to break the news to him. He doesn't want kids."

"Now?"

"Never," she said. "It's a thing with him. 'Cause of his parents."

The thing about parents was . . . sometimes they fucked their kids up. And Hendrix lost the lottery. Both of his parents were terrible people. We'd bonded over that many times. From the outside, it looked like he had everything he wanted. Yet, all the money in the world didn't change the trauma that he'd endured.

I cupped her cheek. "Oh, honey. I'm sorry."

A tear spilled down her cheek. "It's okay. I'll figure it out. I always do."

"Well, you're not alone. I'm here for you. Whatever you decide." I hugged her. "I love you."

"Love you, too," she murmured, her voice shaky. "Thank you."

We held on to each other for a moment before I pulled away. "I say we skip the fried chicken and order all of your favorites."

Bri flashed a watery smile. "Sushi? And ice cream."

"Coming right up."

An hour later, we were on the couch watching *Real Housewives of Atlanta* reruns. Porsha had just admitted Phaedra lied on Kandi. That episode was still good.

"Man, I still can't believe she lied like that," Bri said. "I would've whooped her ass."

"I know, right?" I popped a crab roll into my mouth. "She definitely needs a swift uppercut."

Bri picked up the remote and turned the television off.

"Okay, I tried to give you time to get your thoughts together. But it's time. I told you my secret. Now, it's your turn."

"It's not a secret. I already told you what happened."

"That's not good enough. The last time I saw you and Wes, you were arguing."

"We always argue."

"What is it? Foreplay?"

I shrugged. "I don't know. You tell me. Arguing to have hate sex is a you-and-Hen thing."

Bri gaped, tossing an edamame pod at me. "You got jokes."

"Just sayin'."

"I call foul."

Sighing, I said, "You're right. That was a bitchy thing to say, considering your current condition."

"Oh my God. I'm pregnant, not dying."

I set my plate on the coffee table and tucked my legs under my butt. "True."

"And I need to take my mind off my troubles. Your drama is much better entertainment."

"How's Kay?" I said, changing the subject again.

Since the wedding was called off, everyone had gone silent on it. Amir had immersed himself into his work and Kay had disappeared.

"She's fine," Bri explained. "Considering a move to Atlanta."

"Ah. Mo was in town."

Her eyes flickered to mine. "Really?"

I nodded. "He said they've talked."

"I don't know. Truth is, she hasn't said much to me. I'm worried about her. And you." She pointed at me. "We can talk about Kay later. I want to hear about you and Wes."

I massaged my temples. "Fine. Our night together was . . . unexpected, but not really."

"Excuse me?"

"He keeps pushing me beyond my comfort zone, all the

while acting like he's letting me set the pace. Then, he's so damn Wes."

She cracked up. "What?"

"He does these things." I shook my fist in the air. "It's so frustrating because then I want to beg him to fuck me out of my misery. And listen, as much as I want to hate him, I just can't. He told me the truth about why he left the way he did."

Over the next several minutes, I told my best friend everything that happened, starting from the night of the storm, and ending at our last conversation here. The more I talked about it, the more I realized that I was over it.

"We were kids," I said. "*He* was a kid. Yeah, he messed up, but he was also in a bad situation."

"So where does that leave you and him?"

"I don't know. He's very apologetic and committed to winning me over. But do I have to let him in again? I don't want to get involved with another man that doesn't have his shit together. Even if he's wrapped in dark chocolate and big dick energy. The one thing I've learned through all of this Darrell shit is I have to look out for my emotional health."

She nodded. "I get it."

I raised a brow. "That's it?"

"What do you want me to say?" She munched on a piece of vegetable tempura. "You sound like you've made up your mind."

"No. I don't sound like that, and you know it."

A slow smile formed on her lips. "I'm just glad *you* do." She sighed. "By the way, tomorrow I'll have steak and potatoes."

"You're really going to make me cook for you."

She patted her belly. "Absolutely. For us."

My mind drifted to Wes. Being home had been a whirlwind for me. I came here expecting to heal and I ended up entangled in a push-pull relationship with my ex-boyfriend. "It feels like we've just been away from each other for a day, not sixteen years," I mused. "He thinks we can get it right this time."

"What do you think?"

"I don't want to get hurt again."

"Sis, you said it yourself. He was a kid. So were you. Yes, he hurt you, but you both were young. Dealing with a love that was big, all-consuming. Some people never find it, and you experienced it as a teenager. Now you have the chance to feel it again. You're both here. You're both single."

I nibbled on my thumbnail. "I cried so much for him. About him. I was that girl, curled up in a fetal position afraid to move on because that would make the heartbreak real. I wasn't myself."

She flashed a sad smile. "I know. I was there, remember?"

"I never want to feel that pain again. I never want to feel so weak again."

"Albany, you're not a sixteen-year-old girl anymore. You're a strong woman."

"Who lost everything. I just got a divorce."

"From a man you didn't really love like that," she tossed back.

I fiddled with the edge of my throw. "What makes you say that?"

"Because you've never looked like you do now when talking about Darrell. That look in your eyes, the one you have now . . . Even though you're trying to convince yourself that Wes is not the guy for you, that spark is unmistakable. You still love him."

I squeezed my eyes shut as warmth spread through my body. "Sometimes I don't think I ever stopped."

"So why not give it a try. Maybe it will work out this time."

"What if it doesn't? Maybe I just need to start fresh, move out of Detroit. Away from the past."

"You can't move, Albany. What about your dreams?"

"I can run Keyes Investigations from anywhere."

"What about being happy?" she asked.

"With Wes?" I stood up and gathered our empty plates.

"Who says he can make me happy. The past between us is so wide and deep, what if we can't cross the divide?"

Bri scooted off the chaise lounge and approached me. "Either way, you can't just move around the country running from your feelings. Besides, I selfishly need you here. And you promised you'd help me with whatever I needed."

I cracked a smile and hugged my friend. "And I meant it."

"Good. Steak and potatoes tomorrow."

Shoving her playfully, I shuffled to the kitchen. "Yeah, yeah."

Clear blue skies and scorching temperatures ushered in the holiday. Grandma had thought of everything, from personal fans to Stanley cups filled with water to keep it cold. The food table was full of cultural Fourth of July fare—barbecued ribs, pulled pork, grilled and fried chicken, hamburgers, hot sausages, brats, coleslaw, potato salad, deviled eggs, baked beans, and so much dessert, I couldn't figure out where to start first.

But I ended up where I always ended up—with a slice of pound cake topped with fruit and whipped cream. *Yum.*

When Bri and I arrived earlier, she'd dipped off to relax in the air conditioning, while I made my rounds. Yet, as I walked through the sea of people in the massive backyard, I noticed something peculiar.

Grandma had invited all her friends, the women she played poker with, her old colleagues, and some family. She'd also invited Ace, who'd brought his grandson along with his family. But the rest of the guests were my age and younger. Single men and women, mingling with each other. *Odd.*

Typically, these soirees consisted of smooth R & B blaring over the speakers, dancing, cards, and food. But it seemed like there were a lot of hookups going on. Men whispering in women's ears, flirting with each other, while Grandma and her friends weaved through the crowd.

I took a bite of cake.

*Shit, this is good.*

Finishing it in two-point-two seconds, I made my way back over to the buffet table. This time, I grabbed a plateful of appetizers. As soon as I stuffed a deviled egg into my mouth, I felt a hand on my back.

"Still like to eat your dessert first?" Wes whispered against my ear.

Turning, I held my hand over my mouth as I finished chewing my food. Once I'd swallowed it, I took a few sips of lemonade. "It was so good."

His gaze dropped to my plate. "I didn't see the eggs."

"Want one of mine?"

He leaned in and I popped one into his mouth. "Damn, this is good," he muttered around the food. "I need to grab a plate."

"We can share," I suggested.

After I loaded up two plates with more delectable treats, we settled into a secluded spot near the pool. Sharing our food was something we used to do all the time. I never ate everything on my plate, so he usually ate his and mine.

Wes grabbed a beef rib. "How are you?"

"Good. You?"

"I decided to take a vacation," he admitted. "Two weeks."

"That's a long time to be out of the office."

"Right? I haven't taken time off like this since I've been at the company."

I ate some potato salad. "Then you deserve the time off."

He frowned. "Where's Bri? Hendrix said she was coming with you."

"She's inside. Air conditioning."

"Ah."

I eyed him curiously. "Can I ask you something?"

"What's up?" He finished his bone and dropped it onto the plate. "You look concerned."

"Don't you think it's weird that there are so many young people here? Do you know these people?"

He stared into the main area of the backyard. "A few of them."

"Where did they come from?"

"Grandkids or kids of their poker friends."

"Hm."

"Why?"

"It's odd," I continued. "I mean, Grandma loves the Fourth, but she typically only invites close friends and family. It feels a little awkward."

We chatted for a few minutes about an encounter I had near the buffet table with one of the older women. She'd grilled me about my job, my activities, my life. Then asked me who my grandmother was. Once I told her who I was, she'd quickly excused herself and made a beeline to the other side of the yard. As if that wasn't weird enough, I'd caught her whispering to another woman. Then they both stared at me.

"Maybe she felt bad for not knowing who you were," he suggested. "It is Grandma Liv's house. You're her only grand-daughter."

I shrugged. "I guess you could be right. It just didn't give me a good feeling."

"Are you going to be Albany Keyes of Keyes Investigations all night?"

"What?" I laughed. "Are you making fun of me?"

"No." He leaned closer. "I'd really like to *have* fun *with* you."

A blush worked its way up my neck, and I averted my gaze. "Where have you been?" I ate some macaroni salad and groaned. "Before you answer that, remind me to grab a plate to go. Or two. This food is so good."

"I got you."

"Well?" I pressed.

"You said you needed space," he answered. "I was giving it to you."

"You took that literally, huh?"

He barked out a laugh and my heart cracked open. I loved the sound of his laughter. He didn't do it much, but when he did, it was glorious. "I wanted to respect your boundaries."

"Thank you for that." I searched his eyes. "I appreciate it."

"You know I'll do anything for you."

"I believe that."

"I have to admit, though"—he took the plate off my lap and set it on the table next to him—"it was hard." He tugged my chair forward, closer to him.

Swallowing, I whispered, "Why?"

"Because I missed you."

My heart soared at his admission, and I ached to touch him. "You're good. Different, but the same."

"Is that a good thing?"

"It's not bad." I bit down on my lip. His eyes followed the movement. "We're in public."

"We are," he agreed.

"And we should probably have a talk."

"You know what else? Your mouth is so perfect, so ready to be kissed."

*Damn.* "Again, we're in public and we should discuss some things."

"Like?"

"The space and time issue."

"Okay?"

"So, I thought about it and if you're open to taking it slow, I—"

He brushed the corner of my mouth with his thumb, and I gasped. "You have a little potato salad there."

"Oh God." I wiped my mouth with a napkin. "Did I really? That's so . . . I'm mortified."

"Just kidding." He chuckled. "I just wanted an excuse to touch you."

"You don't need one," I said, my voice barely above a whisper.

"Wesley?" Granny Joyce called from behind us.

I jerked away from him, balling up my used napkin and stuffing it into the small trashcan next to my chair.

A few seconds later, she strolled over to us, a wide smile on her face. "Hi, Albany."

Standing, I gave her a hug. "Hi."

The best part of this event was seeing her so relaxed. Instead of a suit, she wore a coral sleeveless jumpsuit. She'd paired the outfit with open-toed sandals and big shades. Her curls were wild. I loved seeing her happy.

"Are you enjoying yourself?" she asked me.

I sat back down. "I am."

"Great." She glanced at Wes. "Do you have a sec? I want to introduce you to someone."

He looked at me, but I encouraged him to go with her. It would allow me time to get myself together for the discussion I knew we had to have. Also, it would give me a chance to weave through the crowds, eavesdrop on a few conversations. After all, I was still on duty.

Once they were out of earshot, I ventured over toward a group of ladies standing by the rose garden. I pretended to fiddle with my phone, but I was close enough to hear them.

"Olivia always puts on a great party," one lady said. "That chicken was divine."

*Yes, it was.*

"I love that she's happy with Ace," another woman said. "He's perfect for her."

"Perfect and fine," someone muttered. "I wish I'd met him first."

They laughed.

"Did you see your grandson talking to my granddaughter, Mavis?"

"I knew they'd hit it off."

As the women continued their conversation, the pieces started to click together. It appeared that the poker club was in the matchmaking business. All of them seemed to be on a mission to marry their grandkids off. Which made sense. According to Erica, Granny Joyce had given them an ultimatum to get married.

Scanning the backyard, I spotted Wes with Granny Joyce as she led him over to a group of women my age. She introduced him to one of them. Then, my blood ran cold.

*Is she trying to hook him up with one of those heffas?*

I closed my eyes as my mind conjured up different scenarios.

Wes trying to please Granny by dating that woman.

Wes falling in love at first sight with that woman.

Wes kissing that woman.

Wes . . .

"I just wish Joyce would go ahead and make her move," one of the older ladies said, capturing my attention again. "She's pulling all the strings in the background. I'm ready to shift our focus to other news."

"It'll be over soon enough, Margie."

"I hope so. Shirley told me she met Liv's granddaughter."

My ears perked up. *What the hell is going on here?*

A new voice chimed in. "She's a stunner. Saw her with Wesley a few minutes ago. They seemed remarkably close."

"Well, Joyce is with him now. I believe she's introducing him to Amber. I think they would make a good couple."

"You're just saying that because you want your granddaughter to be a Batchelor."

My eyes panned to Wesley. Granny was no longer with him, but he was talking to the woman I assumed to be Amber. I assessed her. She was beautiful. Gorgeous natural hair, brown skin, long legs. Seemed like his type but also seemed familiar.

The woman laughed, placed her hand on Wes's arm.

*Oh, hell no, I need to nip this in the bud right now.* Starting with that necessary conversation and ending with, hopefully, me sitting on his face.

I glanced at my phone and typed out a text: **Meet me at the carriage house. On the roof. Thirty minutes.**

# Chapter 18

## *Wesley*

**M**eet me at the carriage house. On the roof. Thirty minutes.

I stared at the message for a moment. My thoughts swirled with possibilities. I wasn't sure what had happened, but it felt like we'd turned a page in the long story of our life. Earlier, she'd signaled that she was open to me, to us. Considering our last several interactions, it could go either way.

The problem with letting her set the pace, though, was that I'd essentially given up control of the situation. Which was incredibly uncomfortable. Powerless was an emotional state I'd worked hard to avoid. After my father's death, I felt far too open, too vulnerable to be effective in anything. That feeling lasted for years.

Despite my desire to move forward with Albany, I was very aware of my precarious situation. At any given moment, I found myself simultaneously reaching for her, dreaming about her, and dreading the moment she finally walked away from me for good. Walking away from *her* wasn't an option, though.

As much as I wanted her to take the chance, if she decided the risk was too big for her to take, I had no choice but to accept it.

*I deserve it.*

Fucked-up father and family issues aside, I'd treated her horribly. Yes, I was young, but there was no one to blame but me. I'd hurt her at a time in her life when she needed me to speak life to her, to love her unconditionally. The way she'd always done for me. She'd given me a gift—freely, with no hesitation. She'd trusted me with her heart, and I squandered it.

I read her message again and made the decision to hope for the best and prepare for the worst. Ideally, it was the opening I needed to close the deal, to make her mine. *Forever.*

"This is awkward."

My gaze flickered to the woman standing next to me. I'd been so consumed with my thoughts, I completely forgot she was standing there.

"I'm sorry," I grumbled.

Imagine my surprise when the person Granny wanted me to meet was the last woman I'd had sex with, pre-Albany's return. The night before the anniversary of my father's death. And just like then, I couldn't seem to remember her name.

"Amber," she said, sensing my dilemma.

"Yeah. It's good to see you."

Albany emerged from the house, arm in arm with Bri. The two of them made a beeline for the food.

As always, she was the perfect combination of classic and sexy, sophisticated and soft. She wore a flowy, pink floral dress and high-heeled sandals. Her skin glowed under the hot sun and her hair was blown straight. I looked her up and down, taking in every inch of her body from her part in the middle of her hair to her feet.

*Beautiful.*

"Let me guess"—Amber leaned closer, her voice low—"Albany?"

Frowning, I glanced at her. "What?"

"The woman you're staring at." She pointed toward the buffet table. "Is she *the* Albany?"

*Yeah . . . I'm an asshole.* Calling another woman by my ex-girlfriend's name. There was really no excuse. I scratched the side of my face. "I'm sorry about that," I muttered.

She waved me off. "No worries. Glad to see that you are still in touch with her."

"What do you mean?"

Shrugging, she explained, "You were sharing a plate of food with her."

A smile tugged at my lips. I remembered her being feisty. It's what attracted me to her in the first place. If there was no Albany, there might've been an Amber in my life. "You saw that, huh?"

"And I see *you*. You can't stop watching her."

Amber wasn't wrong. I was completely transfixed with the woman who'd captured my heart with a book about the weather. Although our future hinged on whether she could trust me with her heart again, I always knew that I'd die imagining her face. Those eyes.

"Told you," Amber muttered, taking a sip of her iced tea.

Clearing my throat, I said, "You got me. About my grandmother . . . I assume she's trying to play matchmaker."

"All of the grandmothers are armed with their Cupid arrows today. I just wish I wanted a hookup. I actually met someone a few weeks ago. Coincidentally, the day after I spent the night at your place. My grandmother doesn't like him. So, I'm here. Counting down the minutes until I can leave and go watch the fireworks with him."

Again, my eyes drifted across the yard, locked on Albany's. She smiled and waved. I tipped my head to her before I forced my attention back to Amber. "Then you should go to him," I suggested.

Amber glanced at her watch and sighed. "In a few minutes. My Nana is talking business with a friend. I don't want to leave before I can say goodbye." She glanced at Albany. "She's pretty."

Once again, I stared at Albany. She was laughing at Hendrix now. A carefree, sincere laugh that lit up her face. My heart clenched in my chest. "She is," I whispered.

"You should probably do something about that."

Smirking, I nodded. "You just say what you're thinking, huh?"

"I know no other way to be. Got it from my grandmother."

"Seems like all the grannies are that way," I agreed.

"Well," she chirped, "I'm going leave you to your perusal. I forgot I can't stand too close to you anyway. I don't want to be the subject of the next Ms. Tea content."

I chuckled. "You got jokes."

"Have a nice evening, Wesley." She offered me her hand, and I shook it. "Good luck."

A moment later, Hendrix approached me. "Bruh, you might as well go to her."

"Shut the hell up," I murmured.

"No, seriously. She sent me over here to tell you to come now." Hen clasped my shoulders. "I don't say it much because I'm not a sentimental punk. But you deserve to be happy, bruh. After everything your father did, everything you've been through, I hope you can make it happen with Albany."

"I hope so," I admitted. "It's up to her."

"Well, it looks like you two turned a corner since the last time I saw you together. As long as you don't turn into me and Bri, you'll be alright."

I eyed my cousin curiously. "What exactly are you and Bri doing?"

"Shit." He finished his drink. "Living, arguing, and fucking. No commitments, no expectations."

A few months ago, I would've dapped him up because I wholeheartedly agreed that was the only way to live. Now that Albany was back, now that she'd agreed to consider something more, I couldn't imagine going back to that mentality. And as much as Hendrix would deny it, I knew that he felt the same way about Bri. Yet, for whatever reason, they were stuck in this cycle.

"If all goes well," he continued, "you might be the first grandson to collect your inheritance."

"I don't know about that." Marriage was a long way off, yet for the first time, the thought didn't make me want to hurl. "We'll see."

Bri strolled over to us, a plate of chicken wings in her hand. "Hey, Wes." Hendrix snatched a wing from her plate, and she popped his hand. "Don't dip your hands in my food. I don't know where they've been."

Hendrix smirked, a mischievous glint in his eyes. "Oh, you know where they've been."

Rolling her eyes, she shoved him away. "Shut up, man. Go somewhere. I need to talk to Wes."

Hendrix stole another wing. "Come find me when you're done."

Bri munched on a chicken wing, while she studied me, her eyes probing. Knowing.

"Uh-oh," I muttered. "What did she tell you?"

Albany and Bri had been attached at the hip for years. It was assumed that every secret told to Albany would be shared with Bri. To avoid confusion, they would often give a disclaimer before listening to gossip: *If you tell Albany, you're essentially telling Bri. And vice versa. Be good with that before you start talking.*

The two hadn't lived in the same city in years, so I wasn't sure how true that still was. But I knew that fierce loyalty had never waned. Neither of them would hesitate to throw hands for the other. That included men, women, old, and young.

Eyeing me warily, she said, "Wes, I swear . . . you hurt my friend, I hurt you."

I smiled. "I wouldn't expect anything less. Is that what you want to talk to me about? Are you here to tell me to leave her alone?"

"Actually, I'm here to tell you to *not* leave her alone. Don't give up on her."

Over the years, I used my proximity to Bri to stay connected to Albany. She talked about her often, shared little things about her life. And I'd hold on to any information no matter how insignificant because everything about her mattered to me. It was painful to think about her, to picture her in love with someone else, but I couldn't stop wishing for her happiness. Even if it wasn't with me.

"You're sure about that?" I asked. "I hurt her."

"You were so young, Wes. I can't even imagine dealing with the things you did at that age. I was too busy watching *Twilight* and worrying about whether Hendrix liked the way I looked in my jeans. Yes, I was angry with you. And I made you pay for it."

When I first moved back to Detroit, it took years for Bri to look at me without a scowl on her face. Every time I walked into a room, she smacked the shit out of me. Eventually, though, she'd warmed up to me and I appreciated it because I knew she was doing it for Hendrix. They just didn't realize it yet.

"But that was a long time ago," she continued. "You're both stronger now." Her shoulders fell. "You love her."

I sighed. "I never stopped."

"And I swear I'll deny this if you ever tell her what I said. You will be all kinds of assholes. But . . . she loves you, too."

The words weren't coming from Albany, but Bri was the next best thing. And I let that fuel my desire to go to her. "Did she tell you that?"

"She didn't have to." She smiled. "Listen, I want you both to be happy."

"What if I can't make her happy?"

"Wes, teenage love doesn't always survive adulting. And you know more than anybody that there are no guarantees in life. Today, you could be on cloud nine, ready to rule the world. Tomorrow, you could be drowning in a deep sea of turmoil. Time is not promised to anyone. You and Albany have a chance at something amazing. Don't assume the stars will align again."

This was the moment when all the elements combined to create the perfect storm. The potential was there for renewal, for a clean slate. It could also destroy us. Any sane person would've run away from the potential chaos, but I always wanted to run to it. The simple truth was there were many women that had come into my life after Albany. Beautiful, intelligent women. But none of them were her. And I would be a fool to let her slip through my fingers.

"Thank you," I whispered.

She hiccupped, then slapped a hand over her mouth. "Excuse me. Let me go find a hiding space. Grandma Liv has tried to introduce me to three different men."

"I'll walk you."

As we neared the patio door, she told me about the guy Grandma Liv had insisted she meet. "I mean, Wes . . . I can't date that man. His pants are too short. Plus, everyone knows Hendrix . . ." She froze. "Oh no."

Concerned, I asked, "What's wrong?"

"I need a hot dog." She stopped at the buffet table to get more food. "Anyway, he's cute and everything, but he's not him." She shrugged. "Alright, bye."

My grandmother walked over. "Did you and Amber hit it off?"

"She's nice."

"Good. I said that I get to pick a date for you. She's it." Before I could object, she said, "I'll send her information." She waved at someone, then rushed off to talk to them.

Sighing, I grabbed two glasses of champagne and made my way toward the carriage house. It had been a long time since I'd been there. Sixteen years to be exact. But as I neared the structure, I was struck by the significance of the moment. Waxing poetic wasn't my thing. Except lately. And only when it pertained to Albany. Yet, I couldn't help but appreciate the symmetry of the moment.

Knocking on the door, I stepped inside when she hollered, "Come in."

The space had always been bigger than it looked from the outside. Grandma Liv had made changes to the décor, making it feel more modern, almost like those new tiny homes. White walls had been painted gray. Instead of the brown plush carpet, she'd installed plank vinyl throughout.

"Up here!"

I climbed the stairs to the upper floor, then stepped onto the rooftop deck. "Hi."

Albany was stretched out on the built-in sectional. "Hi."

"This is different." I sat next to her and passed her a glass of champagne.

"Right? It's like a little oasis."

Instead of wood, the terrace was clad with tiles. Potted plants and trees lined the perimeter of the space. Lights hung from the awning over a small outdoor kitchen. "Is Grandma Liv hoping to rent the space out?" I asked.

She shook her head. "Not that I know of."

"Do you come up here a lot?"

Albany glanced at me. "I haven't been since . . . about sixteen years ago." She squeezed my hands. "This place was magic. We thought we were the shit. Acting like adults. Having dinner parties."

"Grandma Liv was cool as hell, letting us just be here with minimal supervision. Still scared of fireworks?"

She scoffed. "Are you crazy? That was so long ago."

One holiday, she'd been hit by a wayward bottle rocket. That night, I thought my entire world was ending. I confessed my love to her. In my head, though. I was only twelve.

"I even light them myself now," she added proudly. "Darrell's family had a summer home, and we'd go there for the holidays sometimes. I helped with the kiddie fireworks."

The cryptic talk surrounding Albany's ex had always made me wonder what the hell she'd seen in him. "How did you ever love him?"

"Mo said something to me, and it resonated. I didn't love Darrell the way I should've loved the man I married. I was with him because he wasn't you. I needed to be with someone who couldn't hurt me."

"He did, though."

"Oh yeah. In hindsight, though, it hurt more because I knew better. I knew it wasn't right, that I was doing it for all the wrong reasons, but I walked down that aisle anyway. You know I've always been harder on myself than anybody else."

My throat burned as shame rolled through me. The fact that she'd charged into a relationship with that muthafucka to escape her feelings for me made me sick. "I'm sorry."

"Please don't apologize anymore, Wes. I heard you the first hundred times."

I cracked up. "Wow."

She cupped my face. "My decisions were my own." She kissed me. "But I'm glad I'm here with you now. Full circle moment."

I traced the side of her face with a finger. "I thought the same thing."

"Some things never change."

A long time ago, she'd mused that we had the same brain because we always seemed to be thinking the same thing at the same time. "Right," I agreed.

"Wes."

"Bug."

She giggled. "You go."

"No, ladies first."

Shrugging, she peered at the setting sun. "It's beautiful up here. So peaceful. I didn't think it would feel that way coming back here."

"To the carriage house or here in general?"

"Both, I guess. I have a new appreciation for home these days." She rested her head on the back of the sectional. "I didn't realize how much I missed it—the food, the community, the culture. Even the potholes." She looked at me. "You. Remember our first fight?"

I chuckled. "I warned you not to touch my game."

"I believe your exact words were *If you touch my Game Boy, I'll smack you.*"

"Yeah," I scratched the back of my neck. "I was ten years old."

Grandma Liv had always hosted the Fourth of July, even back then. That year, my entire family came. Albany and I had grown closer after she switched schools, but I was mad at her that day for some reason. Probably because she'd let some little boy hold her hand at Cedar Point. We'd clashed immediately the moment she asked to play *NFL 2K3*, especially after my mother insisted that I share.

"Even at that age, you were full of yourself," she said. "So cocky. I wanted to throw that game into the Detroit River."

"You settled for that puddle, instead."

She cracked up, letting her head fall back as she laughed. "You deserved it." Silence stretched between us for a moment. Then, she whispered, "I knew one thing for sure that day."

Unable to help myself, I leaned forward, placed a soft kiss to her lips. "What's that?"

"That my life would never be the same if you weren't in it." She lowered her gaze. "Over the last few days when you were giving me space, I thought about you a lot. How you were with me, always taking care of me, making sure I was good all the time. You loved me more than anyone ever loved me. When you left, I panicked because I wasn't sure I'd ever feel it again."

"Have you?"

"Never. At least, not until now."

Unable to resist her any longer, I pulled her to me, pressing my lips to hers. Albany melted into my arms when I deepened the kiss, moaning slightly as we fell back against the cushion. She tugged at my shirt, lifting it up and off. I kissed her—from her mouth to her chin, down her neck, then back up to her lips. I wanted to crawl inside her and never leave.

The thought was sobering, but nonetheless true. I wanted more than sex. I wanted her time. I wanted to fall asleep in her arms. I wanted coffee dates in the morning before work. I wanted to share every dinner with her. Forever.

Breaking the kiss, I rested my forehead against hers. "Bug, we're here. I could make love to you, drown myself in you. But I need to know if this is just a tonight thing. Or a forever thing."

Albany searched my eyes, nibbling on her bottom lip. "Is that what you want?"

I brushed my thumb over her mouth, placed a kiss there. "I do. I want it more than anything."

"I'd be lying if I said I wasn't scared."

"I'm scared, too."

"Can we take it slow?"

I circled her nose with mine. "Whatever you need."

Nodding, she said, "Then, take me home."

Half an hour later, we stumbled into her condo, clinging to each other as we fumbled toward the bedroom. The world melted away, blurring everything but her—her soft skin, her low moans, her full lips. *Damn.* I couldn't get enough of her mouth. And I would never be able to stop touching her.

*But...*

Her dress was like a puzzle I wanted to master. Tomorrow. Right now, I needed it off, I needed her naked.

Open.

Only for me.

*Always* for me.

Frustrated, I lifted her up and carried her toward her bedroom door. I paused at the threshold. I promised myself that I wouldn't go inside unless she invited me. I needed to hear her say it, I needed to know that she was okay with this.

"Bug, are you sure?"

She sucked my bottom lip. "Very."

Finally, I crossed the threshold into her bedroom and set her down on her feet. I turned her around so that I could get a closer look at the back of her dress. "Shit," I murmured, tugging at the first strap. "Lay down."

Albany crawled onto the mattress, lying on her stomach. Straddling her, I unraveled the thin pieces of fabric slowly. Along the way, I kissed her bare skin, marking her, making sure she remembered who made her feel this way when she looked in the mirror tomorrow.

Her soft moans were egging me on. I loved that she was delirious with need for me, that she pleaded with me to come inside.

*Not yet...*

"Wes." Her breath hitched when I sunk my teeth into her ass. "Oh God."

Once I tugged the final strap, I flipped her over. I grazed a nipple with the back of my hand, then knelt to suck it into my mouth.

She cried out, "Please, Wes."

*Not yet...*

I ripped her panties off and buried my face in her core. She arched her back off the bed, begged me to keep going. Her scent was intoxicating, and I was addicted to her taste, the feel of her against my tongue. I dipped my tongue into her sweet heat, licked my way up to her clit, then sucked it into my mouth.

She came on a breathless sigh, her body undulating under my tongue. Once the tremors subsided, I nipped the sensitive skin of her inner thighs. Then, I kissed my way back up her body, lingering on her tight nipples before I pressed my lips against hers again.

Albany tugged at my belt, yanked it off, and threw it somewhere behind me. Something broke, but I didn't care. My focus was on her. Next, my shirt was gone, tossed toward the dresser. Then, I was inside her.

Closing my eyes, I savored the feel of her around me, the heat of her body against mine. *Shit*, I craved her. There was nothing better than this. Nothing better than us.

I rocked into her, swallowing her low moan with another kiss. "Tell me," I whispered against her mouth.

"Only you, Wes," she breathed. "I want you."

Lust snaked down my spine, wrapped around my waist and shot to my dick. I increased the pace, giving her everything I had. All my fears, all my joy. Every success, every worry. *Everything.*

"I love you," I murmured. "I've always, always loved you, Bug. Only you."

"Yes." She shuddered beneath me, letting herself go, letting herself fall.

Soon, I was with her, my orgasm cracking me open and baring my soul to her. *For her.*

I sat up straight, my eyes flitting around the dark room, slowly adjusting to my surroundings. Next to me, the bed was empty. *Where is she?*

Climbing out of the bed, I went to the bathroom. Empty. I walked out of the bedroom, peeking into the living room. Empty. The balcony door was closed and the blinds drawn, so she wasn't out there.

A soft voice drew my attention toward the office. I approached the door, pressed my cheek against it. It was Albany. She was talking to someone. *Is she on the phone?* Reaching up, I pushed the door open.

Albany was staring at a wall of pictures, mumbling something to herself. Her curls were wild, and she wore nothing but my shirt. The printer worked next to her, whirring as it completed its job. As I neared her, I recognized the faces—John, Jackson, Jeanette, Cyn, Samira, Elijah, Bishop Garland . . .

"Hey."

She jumped. "Oh shit." She placed a hand over her heart. "You scared me."

I smirked, wrapping my arms around her waist. I kissed the base of her neck. "What are you doing?"

Craning her neck to look at me, she kissed my jawline. "Working."

"This late?"

"Now is as good a time as ever."

I pushed my shirt off her, brushed my palm over her ass, then smacked it lightly. "Come back to bed," I cajoled, nipping her earlobe.

She slipped from my grasp, not bothering to put the shirt back on. "I love it. I love that you're here, that we're doing this thing. But I'm a PI, Wes. We wouldn't be here if I wasn't hired to find Ms. Tea."

Grabbing her hand, I tugged her back to me. "Can't you do that in the morning?"

*Whoosh.*

A chime went off, indicating the print job was done.

Albany searched my eyes. There was something there. Worry? Concern? Resolve? "Too late," she said.

"Does this mean . . ."

"I figured it out." She reached over and grabbed the paper from the tray. Glancing at me, she lifted one of the magnets and added two pictures on the wall.

I met her eyes. "What is this?"

"I'm ninety-nine percent sure."

"That means there's a one percent chance that you're wrong."

"I don't think so." She picked up her phone, tapped at the screen, then showed me Ms. Tea's last post. It was from today, about four hours ago. A picture of us at the barbecue, sharing our plate of food. The caption read.

Oh Lord. Are these two former friends-turned-lovers taking a stroll down memory lane? Rumor has it, the fire is still simmering. But is Albany Keyes ready for Wes's mess? I wonder . . . And as luck would have it, she is newly single, finally divorced from her philandering ex-husband. Ladies, guard your wallets cause these men out here ruining people's credit. #BeCareful #BatchelorShenanigans #SecondChanceSh!tShow

Speechless, I stared at the wall.

Albany peered up at me. "Are you okay?"

"I'm good," I lied.

I was not good, though. And Albany riding my face was not on the agenda. Because the woman I loved just put my grandmother—and hers—on the wall of suspects.

# Chapter 19

## *Albany*

I finished my final report around eight o'clock this morning. I worked through the night to compile all the relevant information—a summary of the investigation, evidence documentation, subject info, detailed findings.

Typically, I would offer recommendations and provide my client specific, actionable steps to address any issues I found within the investigation. In some cases, I would notify the police. Most of the time, though, I presented my report, collected my fee, and kept it moving.

In this case . . . *Damn.*

After I walked Wes through my investigative process, focusing on how I excluded certain members of his family from the list, I waited for him to say anything. When he didn't, I squeezed his arm. "I'm sorry," I whispered.

"Still doesn't explain why," he murmured.

"Trust me, I didn't want to believe it myself."

His gaze was fixed on the wall. "Why would Granny do this? Why would Grandma Liv do this?"

"I don't know," I admitted.

"When did you first suspect Granny?"

Granny Joyce's poker face rivaled some of the more nefarious criminals. She'd perfected it during her talk show era and carried it into her role at the company. But her mask slipped during one of our meetings—when she'd ranted about her grandchildren. Most people wouldn't have caught it, but . . .

I wasn't most people.

While she'd grumbled about the melee at the fundraiser, she said one thing that piqued my interest. *Jackson is next.*

I had turned over the phrasing in my head for hours afterward. It could've meant anything. After all, she'd publicly kicked Wes out of the fundraiser and let Jackson scurry out of the room as if he hadn't provoked him.

Granny could've been referring to the next meeting, the next suspension, the next marriage. But I couldn't drop the suspicion that it meant he was Ms. Tea's next target. At the time, I couldn't wrap my brain around the motive, so I shifted my attention to other potential suspects. Yet, I kept coming back to that moment. Especially after Wes revealed that Ms. Tea had held back on scathing information about Wes's "love child" in Wellspring.

Wes massaged the back of his neck. "And Grandma Liv?"

I shrugged. "There's no way Granny would meddle in *my* life without my grandmother's permission and full cooperation."

The room descended into silence, thick and suffocating under the weight of what I'd uncovered. Seconds dragged by as I watched him. He wasn't okay. I wanted to reach out, to comfort him, to tell him it would be alright. But I couldn't lie to him. The truth was . . . The entire situation was fucked up. I knew it. He knew it.

Finally, he let out a slow, uneven breath and looked at me. "I need to—" His jaw clenched. "—I need to make a call."

"Okay."

He kissed my brow and left the room. As I removed the

pictures from my wall, I thought about the ramifications of my discovery. Grandma and Granny Joyce had deliberately embarked on a mission to . . . what?

Social media was lucrative. Earnings varied depending on the type of content and number of followers. Ms. Tea had become a macro-influencer in a brief time, clocking three hundred thousand followers. That number grew every day because of her consistent posts about hot topics.

But . . .

I found it hard to believe they'd done this for the money or the clout. Neither of them needed it. Both had successful businesses that brought in millions in revenue. While some content creators earned up to thousands of dollars for each post, that money was a drop in the bucket for them.

Granny Joyce made that type of money in her sleep as the CEO of one of the biggest Black media companies in the world. Before that, she'd built a fortune as a radio personality, the host of a popular morning talk show, and even acting in a few movies. Her speaking engagements alone could support a family of five in this area.

*So . . . why?*

When I started my investigation, I assumed Ms. Tea was someone with an axe to grind against Wes. An obsessed woman. A business rival. People like Samira, who wanted attention, or John, who simply disliked him. But Granny loved Wes. She'd supported him. Why would she do this?

Sighing, I texted Grandma: **Are you busy today?**

Before I walked into Batchelor Corp to present my findings, I had to talk to Grandma. It was baffling that she could be involved. I knew firsthand that she was vindictive and very protective of me. But she was Granny's best friend. She was Bri to me. Yet, she allowed sensitive information about my sealed divorce to go public.

I needed answers.

My phone vibrated. The familiar rhythm that indicated

there was a new Ms. Tea post. Opening the app, I went directly to the page, bracing myself for more mess.

**The Tea Whisperer buckles under pressure & shuts down her page. This is who y'all thought would dethrone me? #PutSomeRespeckOnMyName**

The pic accompanying the post was a screenshot of Samira's live video apologizing to the Batchelor family for everything. On second thought, Ms. Tea did good work sometimes. I still didn't understand her motive, though. But I'd find out.

A text notification appeared as I scrolled my timeline, watching silly videos of people slipping on ice.

**Grandma: I'm home. Come by anytime.** 🖤

I gathered the pictures, stuffed them into a folder and filed it. After I cleaned my desk, I shut down my computer and walked out of the office in search of Wes.

I found him on the balcony, staring out at the Canadian shoreline. Windsor, Ontario, was a short drive via bridge or tunnel. It was a quiet town with breathtaking views of the Detroit skyline and good pizza. Bri and I crossed the border quite a few times to eat and shop.

Leaning against the door, I watched him. The sculpted muscles of his broad back flexed as he bowed his head. He was so beautiful. Last night, we crossed a line that I'd once vowed to never step over again. But the sincerity in his voice, the raw need in his eyes, and the desperation behind his words when he asked me if I was sure made it impossible for me to deny him. To deny my own heart.

He told me he loved me.

Those three words had healed the part of me that I thought was dead forever. In that moment, I realized I wasn't scared anymore. I wanted to move forward with him. Which meant I needed to close the tired threads of the past, put the pain and the hurt behind me so that I could embrace the light.

"Wes?"

His body stiffened, and he glanced back at me over his shoulder. He smiled. "Hi." He stood to his full height and closed the distance between us. Searching my eyes, he caressed my face, trailed his thumb down my neck, and kissed me. It wasn't a demanding kiss, it wasn't a prelude to me bent over the couch as he made fast love to me. It was sweet, gentle—so endearing that tears filled my eyes and spilled down my cheek.

The soft touch of his fingers to my face, brushing my tears away, made me want to weep. There was a tenderness to Wes that he showed only me. And that had always made me feel special, treasured.

"You're crying," he whispered.

I nodded slowly. "Yeah, I am."

He tilted his head, searching my eyes. "Are you okay?"

Instead of answering, I held his gaze. "I should be asking *you* that."

He flashed a lopsided smirk. "I'm not the one crying."

I reached up, running my fingers along the sharp line of his jaw. "I just . . . never thought we'd end up here again."

"Any regrets?" he asked, his voice low.

I shook my head. "None."

Then, his hands were on me, like balm over dry skin. Everywhere. Brushing across my neck, over my shoulders, down my back. On my ass. He hooked his hands under my knees and lifted me into his arms, pinning me against the window.

"I need something," he murmured against my mouth.

"What?"

I felt him, hard against my core through his boxer briefs. He rubbed his thick erection against me, stealing my breath as my nerve endings sparked to life. The fabric against my sensitive skin provided a delicious friction. He moved slowly, fucking me but not actually fucking me. But it was so hot, so intense, so . . . *Oh God.*

Wes raked his finger through my hair and licked my face as he pressed into me. His low rumble vibrated against my breasts, and I almost begged him to take his shirt off of me so that I could feel him against me, skin to skin. But I didn't have to, because seconds later, his shirt was open and hanging off my shoulders. And his mouth . . .

*Shit.*

He sucked a nipple into his mouth, teasing me, winding me up as he continued his lazy movements. An orgasm started low in my belly, building into a crescendo that threatened to shatter my mind, my heart. It felt good. He felt good.

Warmth bloomed through me, spread out to every inch of my body. I was close. So close. "Right there," I whispered.

"That's right. Let go." He kissed me. Still soft. Still sweet. "Remember who makes you feel this way."

I groaned. "You."

"Only me."

Then I felt the pad of his thumb against my clit, and I was gone, climaxing so long, so hard that I nearly blacked out.

Seconds later, my body still trembled from that orgasm. And it still wasn't enough. I wanted him inside me for real, but then he set me down and pulled the shirt up.

Slowly, he buttoned me up, his knuckles grazing my nipples. "Wes," I breathed, peering up at him through hooded eyes. "What are you doing?"

A soft smile formed on his lips. "Covering you up."

"Why?"

He chuckled. "Because we have things to do today. Jeanette mentioned Granny has some free time on her schedule in about an hour. And I know you want to talk to Grandma Liv."

*Shit, he's right.* Folding my arms over my chest, I muttered, "Fine."

"We can finish this later"—he kissed my brow—"when I have more time." He smacked my butt. "Get dressed. I'll make some breakfast."

"Eggs?"

"Scrambled soft with American cheese."

Years had passed, but Wes still knew me better than anyone. Despite what I'd told him. "Thank you."

Grandma was sitting at her kitchen table when I got to her house. She glanced up at me. "Hey, Pooh."

I joined her, taking the seat next to her. "Hi."

She eyed me curiously. "What's up?"

Meeting her waiting gaze, I asked, "You tell me, Ms. Tea."

Silence.

It wasn't like Grandma to hold her tongue. She'd once told me, "Closed mouths don't get fed." She'd also said, "If you're brave enough to do dirt, stand in it."

Sighing, I continued. "I guess I'm just confused because I don't understand why you would do this."

Grandma twiddled her thumbs. "It started as a joke," she explained. "At poker night, we would talk about the latest reality show drama. One of the ladies follows a few people on YouTube who spent their days yapping about people we didn't know. Then, we realized *we* knew a lot of people. So, we created the page and put out our first post."

"I . . ." I shifted to face her. "Let me just start by saying I don't think it's wrong that you're doing this. Many people make their living through social media. But you don't need the money."

"We donate it," she said. "All the money goes to nonprofit organizations in Detroit. Last month, it went to Crossroads of Michigan. This month, it's going to Detroit Impact."

"That's good."

"Pooh, we're old. We've lived our lives and sowed into our families. Sometimes it's hard to get out of the bed in the morning. Body stiff, pain in areas that you don't even want to know. A lot of us are lonely. Ms. Tea, as problematic as it was, sort of gave us purpose."

I placed my palm atop hers. "I understand that."

"I'm not an emotional person, but I've spent so many years angry. I wasted time allowing hatred to harden my heart. I can barely stand my own son. But you"—she cupped my cheek in her palm—"you are the best thing that ever happened to me. You brought new life into this house when you moved in with me. I don't want you to hurt. I just want you to be happy and healthy. I want you to know love and feel it. I realized that I haven't been a good example in that aspect, so when the ladies mentioned playing matchmaker for their grandchildren, I jumped on board. Ms. Tea gave me the perfect opportunity."

"Wes?"

The truth was right in front of my face the whole time.

The job offer.

Granny Joyce not accepting my resignation.

The apartment in Batchelor Place.

All of it was designed to bring us together, to force us into the same room. "Why not just tell me?" I asked.

"You are my granddaughter. I know you, and you wouldn't have been receptive. You and Wes had to come to this conclusion on your own."

Grandma was right. The forced proximity to Wes had cracked the door open. Our strong connection did the rest of the work. It made sense. I still didn't like it, but I couldn't be angry with her because I was on the cusp of something amazing with him.

"Pooh"—she squeezed my hand, placed a soft kiss to my palm—"I am sorry."

Tears sprang to my eyes. Grandma never apologized, not even when she was wrong as hell. "Why?"

"I knew why Wes left." A tear fell from her own eyes. Jarring, because she also never cried. "I couldn't tell you because of the danger surrounding the family at the time. I watched you sink further into that depression, and I knew how it felt because I'd been there. But my job was to protect you, even if that meant letting you suffer that heartbreak."

Back then, Grandma had simply told me that life happens. Yes, she was there for me. Yes, she'd hugged me while I cried my eyes out. But she'd never indicated that there was more going on. In hindsight, I couldn't blame her. If I'd known the truth, I wouldn't have stopped until I found him. I would've chased him to Wellspring, potentially causing more trouble. For myself and for Wes's family.

"We knew that Wes would make the first move."

I smirked. "He did."

"Told you."

"What if it didn't work?"

"*Did* it work?" she asked, lifting a questioning brow. "I saw you two at the barbecue, sharing a plate of food like you did when you were teenagers. Then we watched you disappear last night, before the fireworks."

I eyed her. "But then Ms. Tea posted that information about me." The only people that knew about my poor credit were Kay, Bri, and Grandma. Since I'd ruled out Kay and Bri in the very beginning . . . "I wasn't sure you were involved until that moment."

"You suspected Joyce all along?"

"Pretty early in the investigation. I just couldn't figure out why."

"I'll let her explain her reasons, but they're not that different from mine. She loves Wes so much and wants the best for him." She brushed her thumb over my cheek. "And that's you."

"Being here, spending time with him . . . As much as it frightened me, it also cemented the importance of our long-standing friendship. I missed my friend. And once I realized that, all the pieces fell into place."

"Does this mean you're going to try again?"

Last night, we'd promised to try, to take things slow. But I didn't need to try. I was already there. "I don't need to try to love him. I already do. I never stopped."

Grandma embraced me. "That's what I wanted to hear." She shuffled to the stove and put on a pot of water. "It doesn't happen all the time, but sometimes you really can find true love at an early age. You and Wes were circling each other before you knew his penis could fit in your—"

"Don't finish that sentence." I cracked up.

"Too much?"

"Always."

"I can only be me." Her shoulders fell. "I have something to tell you."

Concerned, I walked over to her. "What's wrong? Is it your hip?"

"Girl, I'm fine. I'm going to marry Ace."

I gaped at her. "What?"

"Yeah, he's pretty traditional. And I'm not. But I actually wouldn't mind being his wife."

"Wow. I'm shocked."

"Me, too." She beamed. "I knew he was the one when *he* brought the prenup over for me to review. He doesn't want my money. He just wants me."

It warmed my heart to see my grandmother so happy and in love. "I love that for you."

The teakettle whistled, and she poured the hot water into two mugs. "Green tea with honey and ginger, or Earl Grey?"

"Honey ginger," I replied.

We settled at the table again, sipping our tea as we made small talk about the barbecue. Apparently, two of the grandmothers got into a fight over Hendrix. It was so bad they almost went to blows on the lawn. Until someone's nana breezed over and pushed one of them into the pool.

Grandma laughed. "I couldn't believe it. And believe me, Hendrix didn't want either one of those homely thangs."

I snorted. "Grandma! That's not nice."

"When have I ever been nice?"

"What did Granny Joyce say?" I asked.

"Joyce told both of them heffas off, then kicked them out of the group." She snickered. "About time. They were messy anyway. The only reason they were there was because someone else invited them."

Curious, I asked, "Is Ms. Tea just you and Granny Joyce?"

"No. There are four of us."

"I have to hand it to you . . . you all did an excellent job of hiding your identities. Unlike Samira."

"That was all Joyce. She couldn't take the chance that someone would connect the dots, so she hired a computer whiz to handle all the content."

"Smart."

"The young lady is a gifted hacker."

"Figures," I muttered, still a little salty that none of my tricks worked. "I need to meet her one day."

"Maybe." She slid a folder out from under her newspaper. "There's something else you need to know."

I braced myself. "What is it?"

She handed it to me. "Here."

Eyeing her warily, I opened the folder and pulled out the documents. It was a deed. "You're giving me your house?"

Grandma sighed sadly. "Ace and I want to move into something that's ours, something new, and something a lot smaller."

"I can't take your house, Grandma. Why not just sell it?"

"Because it's yours. It's a done deal." She pointed at me. "Don't you argue with me. Now . . . there's more."

Turning my attention back to the documents in my hand, I read through everything. Most of it pertained to the property. It was mine free and clear. I could choose to live there or rent it to a single family. "I'm just . . . I don't know what to say."

"Keep going," she pressed.

I flipped the pages, until I came across a check. From Liberty Life. My eyes bugged out of my head at the dollar amount. "What?"

"My marriage was an albatross on my life. But one thing that I did right was take out that life insurance policy on your grandfather once I found out about his first side chick. I never needed the money. So, I made you and Moses the beneficiaries."

"This is a lot. What about Dad?"

"Your father will be fine. I gave him a little something— even though he doesn't deserve it."

With shaky hands, I read the note attached.

*Pooh,*

*You will never have to worry about money again. Never. Do good.*

*Love always,*

*Grandma*

I fell into her arms, holding on for dear life. "Thank you so much," I whispered. "I promise I'll do good."

She kissed the top of my head. "I know you will."

The similarities that me and Grandma shared were almost uncanny. We'd both been burned by love and now we would have the last laugh. Everyone who doubted us—Granddad, Allison, Darrell, my father . . . They didn't factor into the grand scheme of our lives.

After years of heartache and pain, trauma and abandonment, we'd both been healed by love. Her, by someone new. Me, by someone old. And, for the first time in a long time, I couldn't wait for tomorrow. I couldn't wait for forever. With Wes.

# Chapter 20

## *Wesley*

"Can you grab that folder off the top shelf, Wesley?"

My morning was spent putting out fires, answering emails, and drafting my letter of resignation.

The knowledge that Granny had been playing puppet master behind the scenes, dragging me on the internet, revealing private shit to anonymous keyboard warriors pissed me off. Even more than that . . .

*That shit hurt.*

Life hadn't been easy for me. Even before my father died, I'd struggled to feel like I belonged. That I was a Batchelor in more than just name only. I busted my ass for her every day. She'd given me the keys, but it was up to me to walk through the door. I'd done the work. And she'd embarked on this smear campaign to embarrass me, to make me the laughingstock in a family that had never really accepted me.

The anger that coursed through me after Albany revealed her findings hadn't dissipated completely, even after I'd driven her to her first orgasm of the day. I'd spent the rest of the morning turning everything over in my mind and I still couldn't figure out what I'd done to deserve this, what I'd done to make Granny want to hurt me.

"Wesley?" Granny called.

I stared at her for a moment, before I handed her the folder she'd asked for.

"Sit down," she ordered. "Did you get the report about that property near Belleville? I'm considering developing the land into a studio. Not as big as Tyler Perry's but comparable. There's nothing like it in this area, and the tax dollars it could bring . . . Hm. Let's talk about it in our next one-on-one."

"Why did you do it?"

She froze, her fingers hovering over the keyboard. Her gaze flickered up to mine. As always, her face was unreadable. She dropped her hands into her lap. "Excuse me?"

"Why *would* you do it?"

Granny sighed, leaned back in her chair, and crossed her legs. "What would that be, grandson? If you have something to say, please just say it."

"Albany kept telling me that Ms. Tea was someone close to me. I shrugged it off, because I'd never really given anyone access to me. Aside from my mother, Hendrix, and Erica—and you—I try to fly under the radar. It made sense to me that John would try to destroy me. He wants me out of the company. It even made sense that Jackson or Samira or even Elijah would try to sabotage me."

"Elijah?" she asked.

"Of course. He spent years in prison because of my father. He could've bided his time, waited to make his move, to make Cedric's son pay."

"That's ridiculous," she grumbled.

"It doesn't matter because none of them tried to hurt me. You did."

Seconds passed before Granny pressed the intercom on her phone. "Please hold my calls and cancel my afternoon meetings." She stood and walked around the desk. Leaning against it, she sighed. "I've done a lot of things to change the trajectory of people's lives. Some I'm proud of, some I'm not. Ms. Tea was never meant to hurt you."

"Why did you do it?" I repeated.

"I felt guilty," she explained.

Frowning, I stood and paced the floor. "Guilty? For what?"

"Your life wasn't easy, Wesley. You did everything you could to destroy yourself."

"That was a long time ago. Things are different now."

"They weren't so different, Wesley. I could see that you were drowning. Yes, you're productive. You show up every day. You do an impeccable job. But you also drink a lot. You were hanging out in bars, taking random skanks to bed. . . . You isolate from the family. I didn't want to watch you go down that hard road again. Not when you've worked so hard to come out of it."

Closing my eyes, I blew out a slow breath. She was right. As much as I'd tried to deny it, I wasn't where I needed to be. While I wasn't doing those things every night, I could've easily fallen back into a pattern of numbing myself with liquor and women.

I'd realized that after the fundraiser. Since then, I'd taken steps to avoid my triggers. I avoided certain parts of the city that reminded me of my father, stayed away from Wellspring, and kept my ass in the gym or at the crib. Or with Albany. I'd stopped drinking liquor and limited myself to one beer at a time. And only for certain occasions. Even when I was tempted to drink the cognac in my cabinet, the night I made love to Albany, I'd settled for apple juice.

I was good.

"Why do you feel guilty, though?" I asked.

"I started this," she confessed softly. "When we found out what your father had done, I was shattered. I was also determined to save our family's legacy, the company that your grandfather and I built together from the ground up. But then, Cedric's seedy connections put the family in danger."

I studied her face, noted the tears standing in them. Which was jarring because I could count on one hand the number of times I'd seen her cry.

She peered up at the ceiling as a single tear slipped down her cheek. She wiped it away with her finger, then glanced at me again. "I'd already lost him," she whispered. "I'd lost your father, *my* son . . . I couldn't lose anyone else. I panicked. Then, I sent you away. Told you not to tell anyone. Not Hendrix. Not Albany. And you suffered for it. I didn't stop to think about how such a hurried departure would affect you. I kept telling myself I was protecting you, doing the right thing. But when I saw you again, after the move . . . I knew I'd fucked up."

"It was my fault. I own my choices, Granny."

"True, but sometimes circumstance can push you to a point where you feel like you have nothing to lose."

"I wasn't suicidal."

"But you were reckless. What if you would've jumped behind the wheel, killed someone or yourself because you thought you could handle it? Your mother and your sister would've been devastated. It would've broken my heart."

I lowered my head. "Why not just say something? Why go to all the trouble to create an online persona and blast me like that?"

"Believe it or not, I didn't create Ms. Tea to air out your business. It started as a fun thing to do with my friends. A little mess. A little shade. Nothing too harmful."

"What changed?"

"I felt like I did something wrong in life. My kids . . . they're entitled assholes. And I could see that my grandchildren were following in their parents' footsteps. Even you."

Rage simmered in my gut. "I will never be like him."

"I hope not. I loved my son, but he wasn't a good person. It took me years to not blame myself for his transgressions."

Granny was one of the strongest people I knew. I couldn't even fathom her placing blame on herself for what my father did. "It's not your fault," I said unnecessarily. "He was just a fucked-up individual."

"Thank God you had your mother."

I smiled. "Yeah, she's amazing."

"Neither of my sons deserved her."

Silence stretched between us for a moment. Finally, I glanced at her. "What was the end game? With Ms. Tea?"

"Good old-fashioned matchmaking. Ms. Tea was already operating when I found out Albany was divorcing her husband and moving back to Detroit."

Realization dawned on me as I let her words settle in my heart. "You hired her—for me."

"Sure did," she admitted. "And I'm not going to apologize for it."

"Don't."

"Albany gave me the flux, quitting every two minutes. But I'm not a quitter. I figured the best way to get you two to see each other, to hear each other, was forced proximity."

"Giving her that apartment was genius," I agreed. "We were already teetering on something, but that was a good move."

"I knew it was only a matter of time before you made your declaration. I'm assuming that happened last night?"

Scratching the back of my neck, I grumbled, "Something like that."

"Then it was worth it." Granny gripped my chin in her hand, turned me to meet her gaze. "*You* are worth it. You're so worthy of love, Wes."

"I don't want to hurt her again."

"Then don't."

"I'm not perfect," I mumbled.

She let out a heavy sigh. "I've seen a lot in my old age. One thing I've learned is it's never too late. It's never too late to be a better person. It's never too late to tell the truth. It's never too late to apologize. It's never too late to take a risk. And love *is* worth the risk."

"I do love her," I whispered. "So much."

"I know. That's why me and Liv were running around here doing crazy shit to get you two together."

"You still could've just talked to me."

"It was fun seeing you squirm though." She grinned. "It was also fun taking that Samira Jackson down. Never could stand her mother."

"That's when *I* couldn't deny that Ms. Tea was someone close to me. Because you helped me out with the Wellspring baby thing."

"Boy, I almost went in on her for that. Then I found that lyin' girl in Wellspring and sicced my lawyers after her so fast . . . she's still apologizing to me. Every day, all in my DMs."

I cracked up. "You're funny."

"About Elijah . . ." She sighed. "Somehow, he discovered my secret."

I thought about my conversation with Unc, the knowing look in his eyes. "I'm not surprised."

"Shoot, I was. I'd done everything to conceal our identities. I think one of the women spilled because she wanted to be about that Cougar Life. Spilling the tea for some di—"

"Whoa." I held up my hands. "Alright, Granny."

"Anyway, I offered to pay him off, but he told me he didn't want my money. Said he was rooting for me to succeed."

"That makes sense too."

"I'm sorry, Wesley. I realize I could've done things differently. Even back then, I should've let you contact her. My need to be in control caused a lot of pain and sorrow for both of you."

"Thanks for that."

She frowned and snatched the envelope I'd brought off the desk. "What's this?" She opened it. Seconds later, she balled it up and tossed it into the recycle bin. "Resignation not accepted. Did you really think you could come in here and quit? You have work to do, deals to close."

"I was really going to leave, though."

"And I was really going to bop you upside your head," she tossed back.

I barked out a laugh. "Fine."

She opened her arms, and I walked into her embrace. She kissed my cheek. "I love you. Remember . . . I'm always rooting for you."

"I appreciate that. Love you, too."

"Good." She clapped her hands together and stood, making her way back to her chair. "Your first order of business . . . sign this NDA acknowledging that everything we talked about in this room will never be discussed again. And take your Black ass over to Albany's and make it official. Tell her you love her. Tell her you *always* loved her. Tell her you *will* always love her."

I nodded. "She knows."

"Alright, then. You're on vacation, aren't you? Get out of here."

Albany paused as she stepped onto my private terrace. She smiled as she took in the space. "This is beautiful."

My sister had come through in a pinch, handling all the details from the gourmet dinner to the décor. There were flowers everywhere, hanging from the awning, cascading down the building. Petals covered the wood floor. Candles flickered in the dark and the soft music played into the night air, giving the area a romantic vibe.

"I can't believe you did this."

"Yeah, I'm not that guy."

She giggled. "Yes, you are. You're the guy who hired someone to do this." She stood on the tips of her toes and kissed me. "Thank you."

The song faded, and soon Duke Ellington's "In a Sentimental Mood" played through the speakers.

I reached out to her. "Dance with me."

Beaming, she walked into my arms. We swayed to the music, letting it take us back to a time when the world moved slow and there was nobody else in the room but us. She rested her head on my chest. "I love this."

"I wanted to show you how much you mean to me, how much *this* means to me."

Leaning her head back, she smiled up at me. "You mean a lot to me, too."

"I don't want to take this for granted. I don't want to stand still. I want us to have nights like this all the time. I want to spoil you, take you on dates. I want to feel free to love you. Openly, without hesitation or reservation."

Her chin trembled. "If you make me cry after I spent all this time on my makeup, I'll kick you."

I brushed her cheek, placed a kiss there. "I'll never make you cry again."

"Good, because I'm a lot stronger now. I can knock you out."

Chuckling, I rested my forehead against hers. "I believe it. Bug, I know we've decided to look forward and not behind us. I don't want to assume that you've completely forgiven me for hurting you, but I—"

She placed her hand on my mouth, then her lips. "Stop. You don't need my forgiveness. I forgave you the moment your lips touched mine. Maybe even before that."

"You mean it?"

"Of course, I do. I just didn't want to accept it because I

thought it made me weak, and I was tired of feeling that way. I didn't want to be that woman anymore."

"You're not."

"And as you've told me many times, you're not that boy either. What we had back then was sweet, pure, the product of two people who grew up together, shared an attraction and explored it." She kissed me. "But I love the man you are now. Just as much if not more than I did then."

My eyes flashed to hers.

"You're imperfect, sometimes reckless, always cocky, moody, loyal, driven, sweet, and kind. I don't want to run away. I want to stay close. I want date nights, too. I want hot sex on every available surface. I just want you."

I buried my face in her neck, letting her words wash over me, healing me from the inside out. "You don't know how much I needed to hear you say that. I'll always hate that I hurt you the way I did."

"We were kids, and you were put in an impossible situation. When I think back on that night now, I don't think about you leaving. I'm reminded of what we shared that day, how you made it nice for me, how you've always taken care of me. Yes, you hurt me, but you've also restored me. You encourage me. You make me laugh. You make me forget everything not good in the world. And I want that forever."

I pressed my mouth against hers, deepening the kiss. "I love you, Bug. I've always loved you. I *will* always love you. I promise you, I'll do everything I can to make your life better."

She caressed my face, feathered her fingers down my cheek, over my jawline. The love shining back at me through her eyes made my heart tighten in my chest. "You already have."

Sweeping my hand under her ass, I lifted her in my arms.

"I thought we were going to eat?" she asked.

"Later." I sucked her lip into my mouth. "Right now, I need something . . ."

A slow smirk spread across her face. "Whatever you need."

Nothing else needed to be said. For the first time in a long time, I felt peace—the calm after the rain, the sun peeking out from the clouds. I had no doubt that the promises we made tonight would sustain us through space and time, through the storms of life. And no one—*not even Ms. Tea*—would stop me from loving her. For the rest of our lives.

# Epilogue

## *Wesley*

I was nervous.

So nervous that I couldn't focus on what I'd planned to do.

"What's wrong with you?" Albany asked, her soft voice filtering through my thoughts.

I blinked. "Huh?"

Eyeing me skeptically, she placed a quick kiss to my chin. "You're distracted." She settled between my legs on the outdoor chaise I'd ordered for the rooftop deck above the carriage house. It was the first housewarming gift I'd purchased for her, and we'd christened it the day we'd arrived. "You've been this way all night."

Thunder rumbled in the sky far to the east. The severe thunderstorm I was expecting had fizzled to a light sprinkle followed by a clear night sky, but it looked like it was building momentum now that it had passed Detroit.

The forecast had cemented my plan for tonight, but the actual weather conditions ruined the moment. Instead of lightning and torrential downfall, instead of the perfect storm, instead of making love in the rain, I was forced to improvise.

Albany was still naked, pressed against me, though. Which was right where I wanted her to be. Where I *always* wanted her to be.

"I'm good"—I kissed the top of her head—"just thinking about everything that happened today."

The summer had been busy with big moves and a surprise wedding. I moved into a new promotion and a corner office on the executive floor at Batchelor Corp. Albany moved out shortly after Grandma Liv handed her the deed to the house. The office of Keyes Investigations was now located in Albany's old apartment.

This morning, Grandma Liv invited us to breakfast at her new house. Instead of pancakes and eggs, we were treated to a full buffet along with a side of nuptials. Because Grandma Liv and Ace had a quick wedding right before the pastor blessed the food. There were less than twenty people in attendance.

"I know," she said. "But I'm happy for Grandma. It was perfect, though. Early wedding and good food. Lots of laughter. Everything she wanted."

"On her terms," I added.

"Exactly." She kissed the top of my hand. "Granny Joyce wants to meet with me next week."

Frowning, I asked, "Did she tell you why?"

Albany shook her head. "No, just that she had an important job for me."

"That's good."

"Yeah. I love the work. But I feel like I could do more, ya know?"

I nibbled her earlobe, brushed her nipple with my thumb. "Like open that gym?"

She giggled. "You read my mind."

A couple of weeks ago, Albany had admitted that she wanted to open a fitness center for women and children, specializing in Krav Maga and self-defense training.

"You have the money to invest in it now," I said. "Go for it."

She tipped her head to peer at me. "You'll help me?"

I kissed her nose. "You know I will."

She smiled. "Thank you."

I always knew that I'd do anything for her, but the last few months had cemented that notion. I would walk through fire for her, give my life for her. The feeling was simultaneously frightening and freeing. For the first time since my father died, I felt like a whole man. Not just pieces held together with thin threads and tape. It had everything to do with her.

"Bug, I . . ." The question I wanted to ask her seemed lodged in my throat.

Last week, we drove to Wellspring to visit my mother. I rented a private space in the Little Red Winery and Vineyard, had everything I wanted to say in mind . . . but one phone call had derailed everything.

Every day since then, there was always something. A call, a text, an emergency . . . The perfect moments were never quite perfect enough. Which was why I decided to take us back to the beginning. The carriage house held sad memories, but being here had healed our hearts and breathed new life into our relationship.

"Baby," she called. "You're doing it again."

I chuckled. "I'm sorry."

"Are you going to tell me what's on your mind?"

"Marry me."

She froze.

The silence stretched from seconds to a minute. Then, another minute. Finally, I said, "In case you were wondering . . . I don't want to marry you at breakfast tomorrow, but I—"

She laughed.

Then I laughed.

Albany shifted to face me, linking her fingers with mine. "It's so funny you said that because I immediately thought about marrying you at breakfast tomorrow."

I trailed a finger down her cheek. "Did you?"

She searched my eyes. "I told myself I never wanted to get married again."

"I know. We had that discussion, remember?"

"Right."

I lifted her palm to my mouth, brushed her knuckles with my lips. "We've spent too much time apart. I don't want to spend another night away from you."

A smirk formed on her lips. "Why not just ask to move in?"

Chuckling, I whispered, "That's not enough. I want more. I want everything."

"Don't you think it's too fast?"

"It feels like a long time coming."

"So"—she shifted again, wrapping her legs around my waist—"I don't hate the idea."

"But?"

"Shit"—she gasped when I pressed my growing erection against her—"you're not playing fair."

"I play to win."

"Before we go there, and we will, I just feel like we need to kind of get to know each other a little more."

"I already know who you are."

Tears filled her eyes. "I have a lot of baggage, Wes."

"And I don't care." I kissed her cheek where a lone tear fell. "I just want you with me."

"I *am* with you."

"Officially."

She closed her eyes, counted to ten softly. "You're definitely not playing fair," she repeated, finally meeting my waiting gaze again. "No secrets. I want the truth. All the time."

"I promise."

"Promise me that we will love each other through everything. The bad times, the good times, the quiet times, the loud times. Even when we get on each other's nerves. Even when we want to walk away, we have to stay and fight for us."

"Bug, I love you. And I promise to always love you."

Her chin trembled. "Always," she whispered.

"You never have to ask," I assured her. "And I couldn't walk away from you again."

She kissed me. "Never again," she murmured against my mouth.

"Never again," I promised.

"Long engagement," she added. "No dates. Not yet."

"As long as you promise me it won't be another sixteen years."

A whisper of a smile formed on her lips. "I promise."

"Well?"

"Then, yes. I'll marry you."

I pressed my mouth to hers as I slowly inched inside her. We made love slowly, leisurely, under the stars. And I knew that I would always want this, that I would always want *her*.

The little girl with fire in her eyes had become the love of my life, my reason why. This was where I was supposed to be. With her. I couldn't wait to celebrate the small and big things life brought us. I couldn't wait to see her pregnant with my child. I couldn't wait to make her Mrs. Batchelor.

She chose me.

And I would always choose her.

# Acknowledgments

Writing *The Ex Dilemma* was an exercise in patience and a cathartic release of built-up emotions. If you know me, then you know that Second Chance at Love is the hardest trope for me to write. Yet, Wesley and Albany's journey became personal to me. I'm so glad I took the journey. I hope you love them as much as I do.

I have to give thanks to a few people, but first . . .

God, I thank You. This past year has been difficult, but You've never left me. Thank You for hearing my cry.

To my forever bae, Jason, I can't imagine doing this thing called life without you.

To my big kids, I love you. Thank you for inspiring me.

To my family and friends, thank you for your unconditional love and support. I love that you're all #TeamElle!

To my lit sistas (and you know who you are), I can't begin to thank you for telling it like it is, holding me accountable, and letting me cry when I needed to. You're the best!

To Midnight, I can't thank you enough for everything. You're amazing!

And thank you to my readers! Nothing would be possible without you.

Love,
Elle

Visit our website at
**KensingtonBooks.com**
to sign up for our newsletters, read
more from your favorite authors, see
books by series, view reading group
guides, and more!

Become a Part of Our
**Between the Chapters Book Club**
Community and Join the Conversation

Submit your book review for a chance to win exclusive
Between the Chapters swag you can't get anywhere else!
https://www.kensingtonbooks.com/pages/review/